NEW YORK REVIEW BOOKS
CLASSICS

DURING THE REIGN OF
THE QUEEN OF PERSIA

JOAN CHASE was born and raised in Ohio. She graduated from the University of Maryland with a degree in philosophy and history and later enrolled in the Writing Workshop of the University of Vermont. After being turned down by several publishers, *During the Reign of the Queen of Persia* was released by Harper & Row in 1983 and went on to win numerous prizes, including the PEN/Hemingway Foundation Award for first fiction by an American writer. Chase is also the author of the novel *The Evening Wolves* (1990) and the story collection *Bonneville Blue* (1991). She lives in Massachusetts.

MEGHAN O'ROURKE, a former editor at *The New Yorker* and *Slate*, is the author of the poetry collections *Once* and *Halflife* and a memoir, *The Long Goodbye*. Her poetry and essays have appeared in *The New York Times*, *The New Republic*, *The New York Review of Books*, and elsewhere. She is the recipient of the inaugural May Sarton Poetry Prize, and teaches at NYU and Princeton.

DURING THE REIGN OF THE QUEEN OF PERSIA

JOAN CHASE

Introduction by
MEGHAN O'ROURKE

NEW YORK REVIEW BOOKS

New York

THIS IS A NEW YORK REVIEW BOOK
PUBLISHED BY THE NEW YORK REVIEW OF BOOKS
435 Hudson Street, New York, NY 10014
www.nyrb.com

Library of Congress Cataloging-in-Publication Data
Chase, Joan.
 During the reign of the Queen of Persia / by Joan Chase ; introduction by
Meghan O'Rourke.
    pages ; cm. — (New York Review Books classics)
 ISBN 978-1-59017-715-0 (alk. paper)
 1. Domestic fiction. I. Title.
 PS3553.H3346D87 2014
 813'.54—dc23

                    2013044733

ISBN 978-1-59017-715-0
Available as an electronic book; ISBN 978-1-59017-739-6

Printed in the United States of America on acid-free paper.
10 9 8 7 6 5 4 3 2 1

CONTENTS

INTRODUCTION

JOAN CHASE is a musical writer, and in a sense her luminous, stark, and startling novel *During the Reign of the Queen of Persia*, first published in 1983, is a kind of pagan Middle American chorale—a song of childhood, a song of innocence turned (very quickly) to experience. The four girl cousins at its heart grow up playing "in the sun-shot darkness" of a barn that abuts a charnel field where their grandfather allows dead farm animals to rot. They run wild, jumping from hay pile to hay pile in the barn, studying the marriages of their aunts and their gram, playing strip poker; they visit their uncle's butcher shop, where the "floor was scummy from the tatters of fat"; they do unnamed things with their older (male) cousin Rossie in the night; they eat ice cream and egg foo young laboriously cooked by their aunt Grace; they chew on oat grass the way the men around them do. A great deal happens, and not very much happens. The sun-shot barn standing upon the charnel yard is a kind of central image for the novel, emblematic of Chase's interest in the collision of the vatic and the grossly embodied.

One of the most remarkable things about this novel is its idiosyncratic form. It is narrated by a collective "we," in this case the four cousins, who chronicle the summers they spend together on the Ohio farm of their unsentimental, hard-nosed grandmother Lil Krauss (née Bradley), the title's "Queen of Persia," in the 1950s. The cousins are two sets of sisters ("all of us born within two years of each other") whose collective narration can't be resolved into any single perspective. The five aunts come and go—pragmatist Libby, ethereal Grace, cosmopolitan Elinor, Rachel, and May—as do the women's various husbands, but the girls are together so much that "sometimes we thought we were the same—same blood, same rights of inheritance." The four girls are barely differentiated, though we are given some identifying details: there is the redheaded beauty Celia, her sister Jenny, and their cousins Anne and Katie, whose mother, Grace, is terminally ill for much of the book. (Anne is "the biggest and fastest with the toughest feet," and Katie is sometimes "bad" for the sake of it, like her grandfather.) The collective first-person narration could easily feel mannered, but here it is essential, a device that allows the book to move forward and backward in time fluidly, in an almost Faulknerian manner, foregrounding sensual perception over the rational armature of recollection, and underscoring the novel's preoccupation with memory. The book has a dreamlike quality of immersion, as if time were not a river but a pool. Though the novel is divided into five parts, each of which ostensibly focuses on a different character or pair of characters, the divisions feel a bit arbitrary; what is important here is the communal. The adults are the medium in which the children move, the walls they bounce off in their search for understanding the world. One remembers this feeling from childhood.

Indeed, it's girlhood that is Chase's most powerful subject. Until relatively recently the literature of American girlhood consisted most famously of children's books, such as Laura Ingalls Wilder's

Little House on the Prairie series and (if we expand our category to North American literature) L.M. Montgomery's *Anne of Green Gables* series. *During the Reign of the Queen of Persia* animates the violent eros of girlhood, capturing the way it is by turns visionary, antic, sensual, and cruel. The novel is a reminder that innocence and experience are always entwined. From the start, childhood, in this novel's depiction, is inflected by insinuations, cravings, and rude awakenings. The girls fight and claw; the aunts, provoked, competitive, call one another "bitch" before making up and cooking dinner, leaving the girls to run outside in "the tutelage of the wild and natural world," while Gram presides. (In her distanced resignation she is more like an old and remote household god than an apple-cheeked template of female warmth.)

In particular, Chase has a delicate feel for the way that girls—especially those on the cusp of adolescence—are attuned to the lives of the women around them. The girls are close observers of the ways their aunts talk about men, including their uncles Neil and Dan, a butcher who gave up his dreams of living in California to support his family, and of course Grandad, a drinker who seems most at home with cows—the kind of man, we're told, who might easily enough have killed someone. Menace hangs over the book: There is nothing of the cozy domestic about its multigenerational story. In a review in *The New York Times*, Margaret Atwood called the novel a "Norman Rockwell painting gone bad," an apt description, though one suspects "gone bad" is a phrase Chase might take issue with. One of the strengths of the novel is the way it holds up the family's complexities almost without judgment; if the women are victims of their time, an era when feeding and clothing the family took much more hard labor than it takes today, so too, in their way, are the men.

Of course, in this sense *During the Reign of the Queen of Persia* is also a novel of place—specifically, of the ways that place shapes character and fates. The book tells the broader story of the changing demographics of rural America in the 1950s, and does so with an authority that grows organically out of Chase's own life. She was born in Wooster, Ohio, which appears to be the model for the town described here; her father was out of work during the Great Depression and the family moved around in Ohio while she was a girl. *During the Reign of the Queen of Persia* lightly evokes a world where "lopsided buckboards vied with flying Oldmobiles for the right-of-way" and one still saw "the black-canopied buggies of the plain people, whose faces reflected the timeless, ordered certainty of their innocence." (The novel quickly leaves any such certainty and innocence behind.)

Chase did not begin writing in earnest until after she married and had children; living in Vermont with her husband, she joined the Writers Workshop at the University of Vermont, and in the 1970s began working on what became *During the Reign of the Queen of Persia* while her children were at school, writing in a large closet she'd made over into a study. (Her husband, the writer Alec Solomita, notes that the closet was, if not "a room of her own," a practical choice: "In the cold Vermont house, it was the place she could work in and stay warm with the help of a space heater.") And in such ways novels are made. Of her three books, Chase is probably best known for *During the Reign of the Queen of Persia*, for which she received a PEN/Hemingway Award. She also published *The Evening Wolves* (1991), a novel concerning a family whose mother has died, and *Bonneville Blue*, a story collection. Neither achieved the commercial or critical success of *During the Reign of the Queen of Persia*. In both novels, one detects the influence of Faulkner, a writer she read deeply for years before she began writing.

After the success of *During the Reign of the Queen of Persia*, Chase struggled to find a subject for her second novel. It would seem that she regarded herself as an intuitive rather than "professional" writer; as she said in an interview, "I did not approach writing as a career. It came along as a way of expressing myself, the first way I'd found suggestive enough, private and leisurely enough, to be worth the effort of approaching the complexities of living and giving voice to the situation. I never thought of writing as a way to earn a living but as a way of exhausting myself, engaging with my material, using everything I could find, inside and out."

During the Reign of the Queen of Persia feels like precisely such a novel: less a plotted story than a deeply felt and powerfully inhabited symphony. Such a novel needs something to ground it, and here, unsurprisingly, it is the large opposing forces of sex and death. The novel opens after the death of Grace, as the girls, now teenagers, find themselves irresistibly drawn to sex. Celia, the eldest of the four, has suddenly become irresistible to men, though she floats through her own life almost tremulously, with all the indifference and unself-consciousness of a nymphette. Boys tumble in and out of the house, to the chagrin and fascination of the girls and Celia's own mother, Libby. One of the themes here is the danger romance poses: As Libby repeatedly warns the cousins, all too often a boy abandons a girl once he's had his way. And even if he doesn't, as Gram warns them, what happens next isn't any good either. A girl who falls in love is likely to become a wife and a hardworking mother who forgoes her "promise," a word that Gram—more given to cussing and gambling than to heart-to-hearts—uses with great gravity.

And so sex in this novel is the real truth of love. Sex is the charge that turns love, all too often, into hardship and conflict for both men and women. Lil plays Bingo every night, ignoring her husband, skittering away from home even on the night that her daughter Grace finds out she is dying of cancer. Lil likes to tell the girls she exited childhood at the age of eleven, when her mother sent her to help out a woman who was dying of tuberculosis. A sudden gift of money from a rich uncle changed her fate, allowed her to buy a farm and educate her children (rather than force them to work); her husband, one presumes, is allowed to stay on to milk the cows and keep things running. But the spouses are never reconciled, and till the end Grandad is a violent, unpredictable, malevolent force. One of the novel's finest aspects is its depiction of the way the girls take this for granted, and both follow him around in fascination and avoid him with the delicate, self-preserving instincts of wise children.

But Chase is a melancholic in spirit—which is to say that she is alive, as an artist, to the intertwined nature of beauty and grief. After its long opening set piece about Celia's suitors, the novel folds back in time to detail Grace's terminal illness. It is here for me that the world Chase explores comes most alive, that its paradoxes and tensions are heightened, and that her poetic sensibility comes into focus, bringing a kind of high mythical shimmer to the fields and farmhouse and lives it describes.

Grace's slow diminishment seems to make every piece of sun more beautiful and every shadow more threatening. Certainly it lends gravity to the girls' impressionistic narration, one that might otherwise seem more incidental. The novel doesn't shy away from portraying the violent ugliness of *dying*, a process that seems slower and more difficult than it should rightfully be, though it also leads Grace to an internal clarity everyone around her is half in awe of. "I have come to know that living and dying are a single event when considered by the mind of God," she says, at one point—and it's the work of this powerful novel to make you understand something of what she means.

—MEGHAN O'ROURKE

DURING THE REIGN OF THE QUEEN OF PERSIA

To Chris and Melissa

I want to express my thanks to the Yaddo Corporation and the Ragdale Foundation for the time they gave me, and to the Vermont Council on the Arts and the Illinois Arts Council for project grants. To Hayden Carruth and Ted Solotaroff—inexpressible gratitude.

PART ONE: CELIA

In northern Ohio there is a county of some hundred thousand arable acres which breaks with the lake region flatland and begins to roll and climb, and to change into rural settings: roadside clusters of houses, small settlements that repose on the edge of nowhere, single lane bridges, backwater country stores with a single rusting gas pump, barns advertising Mail Pouch in frayed and faded postings. These traces of human habitation recede, balanced by the luxuriant curving hills, cliffs like lounging flanks, water shoots that rapidly lose themselves in gladed ravines. Fields of wheat or oats surrounded by dark trees seem to unreel as part of a native flair. Occasionally, gloomy forgotten farmsteads loom. There are a few proud spreads, fastidiously tended enclaves of the Amish and the Mennonites.

Deep into the country originates the hump of railroad lines circling the market town that is the county seat; a small denominational college distinguishes it as the center of culture as well. The downtown square is a brisk trading area, its broad avenue resolving into a central square which, framed by three-story buildings, seems as though it is entirely walled. Within the sandstone blocks, stripped off the hillsides and mined from mountains to the south, glistens still the jewel dust of crushed quartz. All the streets are brick-paved. A dark earthen red, they bear the imprint of their manufacture—Metropolitan, Canton, 1905 Cleveland Block, Egyptian, Sciotoville.

On Saturdays in the 1950s, there was a policeman to direct traffic; the sidewalks were crowded with country people, lopsided buckboards vied with flying Oldsmobiles for the right-of-way, the clip-clop of horses sounding on the brick, drawing the wagons and the black-canopied buggies of the plain people, whose faces reflected the timeless, ordered certainty of their innocence. Stone-hewn, stone-blind Samsons of bulging strength ornamented the county courthouse, adding to the general impression of stability and sanctioned self-interest. When we lived there, on the farm which was right on the edge of the city limits, we thought it the very center of the world, and the green and golden land and wooded hollows which began two blocks over from the railroad loop and then rolled off to obscurity formed a natural barrier to the rest of existence, which we dismissed as the outer darkness.

Our Uncle Dan had his butcher shop on that town square. It was on the backside, beside the newsstand, beyond which the city buses loaded. When we went inside after the picture show or from shopping at Fitchberg's Dry Goods, we'd finger pennies out of the cup he kept on the shelf and have a round pop of colored gum from the machine while we waited for Aunt Libby to drive from our farm to pick us up. If Uncle Dan was busy with a customer he wouldn't say a word to us, wouldn't seem even to recognize us, going on with his practical and patient advice to any of his familiar clientele; he knew them all—their eating habits, the states of their gallbladders, pocketbooks and marriages.

There were the four of us then, two his own daughters, two his nieces, all of us born within two years of each other. Uncle Dan treated the four of us the very same and sometimes we thought we were the same—same blood, same rights of inheritance. Some part of each year, mostly summers, all four of us lived with Uncle Dan, or rather with Gram, for he lived with her too. Gram was the queen bee—that was what Uncle Dan called her. That, or the Queen of Persia, the Empress herself. Or just Queenie for short. Our pony was Queenie too. Uncle Dan said they had a lot in common, and although he didn't say exactly what, we knew Queenie was nearly impossible to catch, had thrown every one of us, racing for the barn. We knew she had what was called a high head.

At last, after Uncle Dan had satisfied Mrs. Wheeler or Mrs. Smucker and they had left the shop, he would look over the rim of the porcelain display case and say, "And now what can I do for you busybodies today?" His hat was perched at a jaunty slant over his lacquered, vein-domed head. "Today's specials: pickled pigs' feet and blood pudding."

"We have to wait," Jenny would say, sounding like her mother, Aunt Libby, ignoring her father except for the fractures of light in her black and almond-slanted eyes.

"Can we see the meat?" we'd ask.

"Vultures," he'd say, and then go before us into the back room and open the heavy door to the walk-in cooler. From that small room issued the cold and bloody reek of a consuming rawness. We'd breathe one enormous breath, perhaps our last, and step inside to confront the stiff, hanging carcasses. The air congealed, prickly cold on our bare summer arms. Under our sandals the floor was scummy from the tatters of fat and bristles of hair rolled in the sawdust. We'd shiver going out, and look sideways at Uncle Dan. He would latch the door, standing before us, shorter even than we were, yet fearless—in his blood-smeared apron and his sailor hat, dressed for anything.

During the war Uncle Dan had been a Marine. Although he'd lived on a ship, he had never left the port of San Francisco. He sent for his wife and two small children across all that distance from Ohio, causing them to sit on suitcases in the aisles of packed train cars and Aunt Libby to have adventures—too many, she said, her smooth face registering the folly of camp following. Once she'd had to assist at the birth of a baby during one of the endless waits at some nameless siding, so no one was able to decide which state the baby had been born in. They had pictures from that time, of themselves swimming in the Pacific in brilliant winter sunlight, Uncle Dan in his sailor hat, Aunt Libby, dark-tanned, her fine hair windblown, sweet-smiling in a one-piece swimming suit. When they were free to return to Ohio, Uncle Dan joined his father at the store, just until he'd got his feet on the ground, his same reason for moving his family into the big house with Gram and the various members of the family who regularly came and went. But both places yielded their convenience and they stayed on—Uncle Dan counting the years, planning that one day he would take another job, would move, that his life would begin.

Uncle Dan would talk to us about this sometimes while he was feeding his lustrous Irish setter, which lived a high-strung life of his own tied to the doghouse at the edge of the lawn. Uncle Dan always said it was a mystery to him how a man with a redheaded daughter could end up with a red-haired nervous wreck of a dog. He fed "the beast" when he got home at night, serving him a broth-warmed mash in a tin pan, assuring us as he mixed and brewed that the dog ate better than the rest of us, though at first sniff he'd turned up his nose, and Uncle Dan had confessed that it was probably not exactly what the dog had had in mind. He spoke as though he knew his dog inside and out. But gradually the setter would eat faster, going into the pan with increasingly desperate gulps. When he'd finished, Uncle Dan let him free for a time, his long red streamered plumes racing over the shine of evening grass in spumes of flight, circling, leaping. Until with murmured affection and resignation, Uncle Dan secured him again with the links of steel chain that seemed strong enough to hold a gorilla.

But when Uncle Dan talked to us about his job, his life, as though he too were secured with a chain, which, though invisible, bound as securely, we never worried: he was forever joking, complaining—"thrashing at the bit," he called it. Nevertheless, when he was at home we would hear him whistling up from the cellar, where he worked on his projects, and over the years he turned out an assortment of goods, one enthusiasm finding its way into another—cowhide wallets succeeded by chair caning, hand-crafted furniture, poured candles, eventually oil painting. And he knew the meat-cutting business through and through. We could see that in the patient way he could slice off chops or hook up a side of beef—as though it were all as natural and disheartening as his brown hairs sliding off on the comb.

We went into the alley behind the market to wait for Aunt Libby to come for us and we felt these lonesome things about Uncle Dan. Finally the car would come easing through the shaft, taking up nearly the entire path against the garbage cans, Aunt Libby with one bare arm resting on the open window, already, even in early summer, darkly tanned, her other arm back over the seat. Only a slight drift of a smile would acknowledge us waiting there. With the motor left running she'd seem just to pause, idly, her glance fixed off to where the sunlight chinked through at odd intervals between the brick buildings. We might scatter for a moment then, to get candy at the newsstand or look at the magazines. And Uncle Dan might slip out for a quick second to lean on the car door with his arms folded, flirting with her every chance he got. His nudges for her attention seemed to distract her only fractionally from the dark and dappled path of the alley. Then abruptly she would decide she had had enough, it was time to leave, and she would blow the horn with a sharp fret of irritation, the way Gram always did, and we'd dive out of the newsstand and jump in the car just as she started to move off. Behind us Uncle Dan would vanish as we turned into the square and then onto Main Street, one of the two parallel roads going north, the ruddy road underneath us seeming to spread out before us like a royal carpet; one which was rolled up as quickly from behind, so that we were the only ones who knew about it

—another secret part of our knowing that where we were going no others could follow.

All the car windows were down, the sweetness of mowed grass and flowering lawn beds blowing through while we were in the town, and then richer meadow clovers and the cool wooded hummocks scented with needles and vine, an interval of two miles or so that separated us from the business district of the town, a distance never calculated exactly, because it wasn't a matter of space or time but one of difference. A lane of white oaks bordered our lawn. Those oaks, perhaps fifteen of them, standing out against the open fields as far as we could see on either side, fixed for us the entrance to our farm, and even after there was a gas station built on the north corner and a restaurant beyond the hedge, those trees still loomed like a massive gate.

When almost into the house, Aunt Libby would often stop short and look at us, baffled and almost accusing. "Damn it, girls. Do you know? I was right there and forgot entirely about supper. And I suppose we do have to eat"—spoken as though it mystified her, this matter of appetite. "Well, Dan will just have to bring something home with him."

Gram, it seemed to us, watched out for Uncle Dan more than Aunt Libby did. She made us pipe down when he was home, spoke up for the privileges of a man after a day's work. We watched her sideways, suspecting her motives, her sincerity. What did she know? There were times when Uncle Dan was the only male in a household of ten or more. It was Gram's house, had been so even when Grandad was alive, for she had bought it with her own money, as we had often enough heard her say. And any of her five children was welcome to move in with her at any time, displacing one another, squeezing in as best they could, using any of the three floors and the fourteen rooms. At different times one or the other or all of her five daughters might choose to come back home: some had married and came with children, some had had husbands but lost them; Aunt Elinor married late. So, often it was one or another assortment of us females living there, and Uncle Dan when he came home from the market.

His arrival was around six-thirty in the evening. Those years two of us, Uncle Dan's nieces, daughters of Gram's dead daughter, Grace, ate an early dinner with Gram, who would be already bathed and dressed to go off for her evening's entertainment: bingo parties, horse racing, roulette at a private club—anything exciting. She cooked us a dinner before she left, something that she didn't have to think about, something she had fixed for sixty years or more. She only did it, she said, for our mother who had died, for she herself was plain fed up with cooking. She told us that nearly every day. Fed up with cooking, with work—had worked for sixty years, cooking for more damn unappreciative men, thrashers, hired hands, in addition to squalling brats, starting from age eleven, when she had been sent across two miles of meadow to help a neighbor woman with her nine children. So now she just put food out on the table: fried-down salt pork, chops or ground meat, boiled potatoes and cabbage. She ate scarcely any of it herself, preferring to have a slab of her Dutch bakery bread, dipped into coffee blanched pale with cream. She didn't care if we wanted what she'd fixed or even if we ate it; it was just put on the table at five o'clock.

Uncle Dan's two daughters, Celia and Jenny, waited for him to come home and when they were all at the table they made a romantic picture of a family, the three of them around the big farm kitchen table with a surviving male figure. We weren't supposed to interrupt them since it was Uncle Dan who put meat on the table, their table, and Gram thought he deserved that much real family life. We liked to sit there in the dark stairwell while they ate, our own mouths dark, running as if with a juice, as we watched them cut into the thick soft sirloin and lift pieces of it on the red-handled forks. Uncle Dan brought home the best cuts and gave himself up to a wholehearted appreciation of his appetite, belching out loud whenever he felt like it, talking with his mouth full, stabbing his fork across the table for extras. After they were finished we went in to help our cousins clear the table and we would pop yellow scraps of fat into our mouths, spitting it out only if it had gone cold and lardy.

During the evening Uncle Dan sat in his recliner and made his remarks over the paper—he was famous for that. Often it seemed to us that we talked or perhaps lived to inspire his comments—repetitive yet always new, his tone conveying a total although good-natured abdication, a comical weariness.

Aunt Libby would ask what they might have for supper the next evening. Feeding other people was for Aunt Libby a constant preoccupation, though, like Gram, she had little interest in food for herself. Uncle Dan would consider aloud the little difference the menu would make, since one thing burned or neglected tasted pretty nearly as bad as another.

"I've had my disappointments," he would say with a pointed melancholy, so that we would all know he was thinking again of Hedy Lamarr and her falsies. And the house brimful of females —he had really hoped for sons when Celia and then Jenny were born. And Aunt Libby did have a boy later, and another, but they were stillborn and after that she couldn't have another child, something Uncle Dan never mentioned. Every evening he entertained us, making it like a party, because later he would go out to the kitchen and make popcorn and serve Cokes to all of us, or some special concoction he was promoting at the market—for a while we had homemade root beer made from a syrup and a seltzer bottle. Then he would go off to bed, hours before the rest of us, since he had to leave at six in the morning to open up the store.

But sometimes he would bring out his trombone, the one thing left from his year at the local college, when he'd played in a jazz combo. He would get Celia to play the piano and they would try for a while to bring their two instruments and interpretations into harmony, finally breaking down into solos, each one playing for the other. Uncle Dan listened to Celia attentively, helped her with the dotted notes and syncopation. "You should have kept up your lessons," he lamented, and played for her what he still recalled of "Lady Be Good." While they worked over the music he had that same intense absorption he had when he played his Peggy Lee records. He said she was the very best. "You've got it in you to be good," we'd hear him say to Celia when they'd finished and she'd folded down the cover on the piano and spread out her polished nails to admire against the dark mahogany. She'd smile and lithely dip her head, pleased and flattered. And then she would go to her room to be alone. Uncle Dan would finish the session by himself with one of Peggy Lee's records. He would listen with his trombone laid over his knees, transfixed, his thoughts far away from us.

One early spring evening when Celia was fourteen and the rest of us girls thirteen or nearly so, Uncle Dan came home, carrying the sack of groceries Aunt Libby had ordered over the phone, and saw a troop of boys sprawled around on the porch or hanging from the railings and balustrades. He stopped and asked them if there was some problem, had their mothers forgotten something at the market. They slunk off sideways and kicked the porch steps. But when Celia walked through the front door they came alive and in a fevered sprint backed away, running and hollering, to the far road, their speeding eyes in retreat still fastened on Celia, who smiled vaguely with a certain regal privilege. For a moment Uncle Dan's face was strange to us, unshielded by his bright mocking ironies. Then he recovered. Knew what was what. He appraised her long bare legs, asked if she had taken to going about half naked because of internal or external heat. She huffed, "Oh, Daddy! Don't be so old-fashioned," her face golden-lighted in the sun's reflection off her apricot hair, and she went inside tossing that mane, her legs slightly rigid at the knee, like a leggy colt. Uncle Dan flicked his gray, dust-colored eyes over the rest of us, who were dark-haired, with sallow complexions, or altogether too high-colored; he smiled outright, also an expression rare for him, and he seemed newly primed for the changed direction life was taking.

And after that we knew too that there was something different in Celia. It wasn't just that she was older. It was a confidence that came upon her, suddenly and entirely, so that it didn't matter that summer after summer her hair had swung out with more sun-riffled gleam or that her body had swelled here and tightened there into a figure that was at the same time voluptuous and lissome. Effortlessly she appealed to boys, boys who ever after seemed to wander our place with the innocent milling confusion of lambs for the slaughter. That was what Aunt Libby called them, gazing out. "Those poor souls. They don't know what's hit them." She shook her head and sometimes found fault with Celia as if she were too provocative. "Just look at that butt": she'd frown out toward where Celia was talking fifty miles an hour to some boy, leaning on a car window, her body swiveling, her hair swooping in dips, her smiles tossed like fanciful flowers. We couldn't tell for certain whether Aunt Libby was angry or proud.

Celia's change separated her from the rest of us. She seemed indifferent, didn't need us anymore. We fell back, a little in awe. Where she was bold we were unsure, wondering what Aunt Libby would say. Anxiously we tried for Celia's attention, wanted fiercely to be included. But it was no use, that desire; we could not reach her, or be content without her. So we watched her life ravenously while waiting for her to make some slip.

But increasingly from afar, as though we were only strangers from the town. Outsiders. Even a horseback ride with Celia, something we'd done all our lives together, would take an unexpected turn, would become an excuse for an entirely different purpose—a forbidden rendezvous. We would find ourselves following Celia down an unknown back street of the town, where the factory people lived—where we remembered our family had once lived. Then, swarming from out of nowhere, came the dark-eyed foreign boys, drawn by the hooves clipping the brick and by some invisible vibration Celia set up in which the air quivered as if with a snare, or bridle bells. Ambling over to us from their slumped grimy houses, the boys would slouch against a post or picket in lazy wonder, lifting their gaze to Celia like an offering. Only the uneasy shifting of her horse, its prance, suggested any nerve or breaking through of impulse. We, her followers, subjects, were openly disheartened, far from home, uneasy about disobeying Uncle Dan, who had warned us to visit the blacksmith before we rode on pavement, to stick to known territory. It seemed Celia had forgotten Uncle Dan for good, had left everyone behind.

Still the day came when we had to face him. A customer at the market mentioned she'd seen his girls riding on South Belmont Street. He eyed us, angry and cold. Celia searched her nails for imperfections in the polish, then excused herself and left the table. Going under the door lintel, she appeared to be framed in the varnished oak. But the rest of us were still his little girls, the three of us stricken and despairing that all his goodness to us, the freedom we had, had been treated as nothing. After that we tried to avoid Celia—who didn't care and always did exactly as she wished, all her energy and her allegiance straining away toward a destiny we did not share or even understand. It was as though she trained obsessively for an event, a challenge we had heard of only distantly without comprehending any of our own desire. But when we dreamed, it was as though we too, like her, had been transformed.

Everything was changed. At the swimming pool Celia no longer entered the water unless she was thrown in by some boisterous youths, and then she let them, as eagerly, assist her in getting out, their hands now lingering and gentle on her. We peered out onto the front porch, the pack of boys more distant, even as we desired them more. It was seeing the way they waited, with a patient wistfulness for any attention Celia might chance to offer, boys who before had not wanted anything from a girl, that defeated us finally: Celia, in impartial imperious command, standing among them, her hands fixed like delicate fan clasps upon her jutting hips, her mouth small and yet full and piquant, like two sections of an orange. It seemed then that we were the intruders on our front porch, that everything belonged to Celia.

We went into town, leaving her the porch while we sneaked into the swimming pool at night, or waited at the "Y" for the arrival of a few boys so that then we could walk the two miles home with our girl friends, shadowed by the boys, who circled round us, calling out of the dark, fresh whoops coming nearer then moving further into the dark. Sometimes when we got home we'd stand behind the parlor drapes, up against the climbing roses of the wallpaper, and peek out onto the porch to watch Celia. Then we didn't laugh even to ourselves and there would be the run of saliva inside us, as though we were watching her eating steak.

Around us and behind us, Aunt Libby and Uncle Dan lived their married lives. There in Gram's big old house it seemed they had no relationship between themselves that wasn't ours as well, no function beyond their making up part of the life of the house. Uncle Dan usually came home from the market for lunch, still in his apron and hat, Aunt Libby parading around half dressed or not dressed at all, calling up through the attic stairwell— calling us girls to get up.

It was summertime and we girls talked most of every night (except Celia, who had begun to sleep alone in the room by the back stairs which had been Grandad's before he died), and it would be very late, nearly dawn, when we fell asleep. Then we slept on and on, through the mornings into the noon hours, while the increasing heat stifled us into a further resistance to waking. Off and on Aunt Libby would rouse herself to call us. Then she would sleep again too. We felt Aunt Libby could have slept forever. And perhaps Uncle Dan suspected as much, because usually he came home with something from the store for lunch. Aunt Libby would call out sharply that this time she meant business. We were already talking even as we lay waking, the two iron-frame double beds arranged side by side in the attic room, and then we would go down and Aunt Libby would be dressing herself as though her body belonged to all of us.

Aunt Libby left the bathroom door open; she talked to us while we sat on the tub or stood in the doorway; sometimes we would see a Kotex dangling between her legs. We felt sickened by the sight of it. Then she stood and arranged a fresh pad to ride amidst her prickly black hairs, between her olive stretch-marked cheeks. She dropped her used pads in the trash unwrapped; she said being female was a dirty business, no use trying to hide it. She pouted disdainfully, none of it her fault. Uncle Dan said that somehow none of this fit his particular notion of a child of nature; but he was never really offended, it seemed, although his own personal habits were discreet and modest. Perhaps to a butcher— stuffing entrails, grinding meat—such things were common enough.

But while she dressed, Aunt Libby reminded us of some swarthy half-wild gypsy woman, her face, partly obscured by her morning tumble of hair, conveying a mysterious charm as she stood by the closet door with her bra dangling from her hand, her smooth olive skin glowing around the pointed wrinkled berries of her nipples. Standing half in and half out of the closet, with no trace of self-consciousness, she appeared almost to reflect the flickering shadows of woods, while from the edge of a clearing all of us watched. Uncle Dan breezed in and out, whistling and razzing, and then he went down to the kitchen to make the meat sandwiches, talking to Gram, that old farm woman who hadn't been up that long herself but was already tapping her foot, impatient for the passing of time until she could bathe herself and put on her silken-jersey dress and go to the matinee at the Coronet or off to the races in Franksville.

Infrequent and bitter, Aunt Libby's and Uncle Dan's fights astonished us. A stifled row, overheard from the kitchen, a door slamming into its frame—then Aunt Libby shouting "goddamn" and "shit" and "turd," and Uncle Dan thundering down the stairs and out the side door, spitting gravel back at us as he disappeared up the drive in his delivery truck. Soon Aunt Libby would come down and tear into the sack he'd left on the counter and slam down the meat and pickles, the soft white bread. Gram, if she was there, her bottom lip out a mile, would take up for Uncle Dan, as if she knew all about it. We always heard her say that he was all right for a man, the best of the lot, and that Libby was too much of a damn fool to know when she was well off. Aunt Libby ignored her. Beneath the smoothness of her skin, more often sallow than golden, an undercurrent of turbulence ran now and it lit her eyes with a passion she seldom allowed to show, with a delight in the battle which had just belonged to her.

Their making up was in secret too, perhaps accomplished over the phone when Aunt Libby called the store to order the steak; usually by the time Uncle Dan drove in at evening it was as if nothing had happened. But sometimes we would hear Aunt Libby talking to her sisters while they canned peaches or boiled jam, or just drank coffee; saying that it was Dan's fault she had become so droopy-chested, a consequence of his ardent making up. It pleasured her, though, to be so desirable, fully mature and tempting, with even her brown eyes gold-shot at times like the ripe skins of the pears simmering, spiced dark with cinnamon and cloves.

There was one memorable fight; it lasted two days. Uncle Dan came home with groceries and a flowered lounge for the yard or porch and Aunt Libby hit the roof the second she saw him unloading it, yelling from the window, "We can't afford that kind of thing. You have no business. What would we do anyway with a piece like that?" Going on to tell Uncle Dan that he was forever needing some new trinket for amusement. When would he ever grow up? And when had he ever had a spare minute to lay in the sun?

"In California," he said, as he worked to adjust the mattress, "they're set up for this kind of thing. They don't mind a little fun. A fellow works all his life. What's the harm?" His face looked as though it had rained all his summers, his eyes gray from clouds that had passed over his heart.

Aunt Libby's voice spurted anger and something of alarm

too. "You! You have a sudden uncontrollable notion to lay in the sun. What are you, a beach boy? Use a blanket. A towel, for God's sake. I don't live at home with my mother, scrimping and saving, to look out the window and see you snoozing on a bed of roses—orange roses at that. That thing reminds me of an orgy, just looking at it."

"That thing reminds me of everything I'll never have," Uncle Dan said.

"Then why didn't you stay the hell in California? You liked it so well."

Uncle Dan was silent, looking up at her from the yard at the bottom of the porch.

"Then don't complain. A bargain's a bargain." Aunt Libby went back inside, letting the door slam hard, as hard as her set face.

But Uncle Dan did keep it; it rested on the lawn through sun and storm until the cushions erupted soggy cotton swabs that we kids threw at each other. We used it in various ways until the frame finally cracked clear through and it wouldn't stay upright. Then we dragged it over into the high weeds by the doghouse and no one ever mentioned it again.

Just once we saw Uncle Dan make use of it: the first Wednesday afternoon after he had bought it, the afternoon when all the stores in Sherwood regularly closed. He came home from the market, changed into a black knitted bathing suit which was a little tight, the front buckle digging into his stomach. It was the one he'd had in California. He wore a pair of dark glasses we didn't know he had and he took out a bottle of baby oil, pink with iodine, and a towel. He set the chaise precisely near the shadow of one of the spruce trees, which were taller than the house, right at the edge of the pool of darkness it made on the grass at noontime, and he turned on his portable radio, opened a beer and lay down. We wandered over near him and sat in a semicircle on the grass to watch him take his sunbath. He took a long drink from the bottle. His eyes were obscured behind the smoked glass. Perhaps they were closed. After a while, when he didn't move again or talk to us, we asked right out was he really going to tie one on. He raised up his glasses and peered at the four of us and his eyes were nearly lidless slits of slivered light. "Now that's some kind of talk. Whatever gave you that idea?" Then, his voice weary: "No, don't tell me." And we didn't want to say any more of the things Aunt Libby had muttered while she was crying and shoving the carpet sweeper over the floor. The air was stifling under the trees, drenched with resin and sap, Uncle Dan glistening with oils and sweat; for a moment we too seemed rooted together, captured in the presence of the dense trees, while beyond the swags of branch the blackbirds skimmed the field. Soon afterward he picked up all the things he'd carried out and went back inside the dark house. We sat on, transfixed before the flowered canvas mattress, until the advancing shadows covered us. Uncle Dan didn't come back to his lounge, although he left it sitting there, in plain sight, a reminder of California, of another life.

An accomplished seamstress, Aunt Libby spent much of her time in a little upstairs room, the room so littered with snips of thread, pins, scraps, it seemed she sat in an intricate nest of her own design. There was a green couch, old and sagging, a chintz-covered chair and the sewing machine console, a good one, modern and dependable. A silent, diffident, ill-at-ease woman outside the family group, with us she was absolutely herself, hardly capable of restraint. We girls flopped all over the furniture or the floor while Aunt Libby, a brace of pins in her teeth, embroidered her tales of disillusionment as with tiny needle tacks she tied off her threads. She whacked away at her own remnants of romanticism as if she could still be caught off guard and swallowed whole.

We might have passed Rosalie Morgan on the street that morning. Now she told us that Rosalie was "getting it." For shame, Rosalie Morgan. There was a thrill in it, no mistaking

Aunt Libby's tone; but the peril of it was absolutely certain and without remedy. There rose in us a longing commensurate with our deprivation and fear. We blamed Aunt Libby. Wise and embittered herself, she would deny us even our early innocence so that, just as she intended, we would never learn for ourselves the full fascination and implication of her knowledge.

We accused her. "How do you know a thing about it? You don't even know Rosalie Morgan."

"I can smell it," she said. "Besides, I've known her mother since before you were born. Just take a good look at her eyes." Rosalie had larkspur eyes sunk in the bluish-brown circlets of their own thrown shadow. Those were the shadows of despair, Aunt Libby said. "For where can it lead, girls? Either Sammy will waltz off with the next one he spies, free and clear, or he'll hang around until he ends up having to marry her. And which is worse, I ask you?" She'd seen more than enough of that particular misery —wedlock forced on a resentful man who would never let you forget it.

There was never any hiding from Aunt Libby, sniffing and patrolling, everything figured out. Other people talked, around her, of weather or shopping. Aunt Libby half listened, preoccupied with her own divinations and prophecies. There was no arguing with her. So we didn't try—better silence and subterfuge. Someday we would escape. In the meantime we would lie low, guarding secrets and longings even from ourselves or we would have nothing left when she was done with us.

"You girls make me sick. Mooning around here. Swallowing all that crap." The machine whirred under her touch with the murmurous precision of a loom.

We reminded her of Aunt Rachel, who had remarried the summer before. That was love and she was blissful on account of it. Aunt Libby had to admit that. Right then, without her makeup, her mouth pinched, yellow-skinned, sepia-splotched, her tucked chin reminding us of Gram's fallen face, she was ugly to us—a woman spurned and rejected. Poisoned, she would poison us. She raised her eyebrows; we could see the stubble stumps, unplucked, in the glare from the window. "I s'pose," she snorted, two words, her tone bleak as ditch water in November. And we knew there was something more to it, more than we would ever know or want to, Aunt Rachel self-deceived, no happier than the whole love-lost world.

"There's one true love in the world, someone for everyone." We declared things like that. Then we would stand on our heads on the back of the sofa cushions, feeling the blood rush, our bare feet slapping the wall, so we didn't have to look at Aunt Libby's face, though still we could hear her derision in the mechanical and unerring drive of the needle down a seam.

"Don't think I don't know the charms of young men," Aunt Libby said, and we knew she did; beautiful again, a trace of blood spurting from her cold heart, illuminating the texture of her skin, warming yellow to gold. And her eyes softening like a melting amber. They hardened again. We trembled to hear her. In Aunt Libby there was none of Gram's flip "You may as well fall for rich as poor." For Aunt Libby it was a matter of outrage and contest.

She spoke to us incessantly of love. Endless betrayal, maidens forsaken, drowned or turned slut, or engulfed by madness. Most chilling were the innocent babes—stabbed with scissors and stuffed into garbage cans, aborted with knitting needles. In all this, love was a blind for something else. For sex. Sex was trouble and when a girl was in trouble, sex was the trouble.

Nor would Aunt Libby allow us the miscalculation that marriage put an end to trouble. Men were only after what they could get. When they got it they didn't want it anymore. Or wanted what someone else had. The same as the cars they bought and used. It was their nature. Some got nasty about it. That she attributed mostly to liquor—which men turned to out of self-pity and petty vengeance.

These matters were serious enough so that once the lid was off she began to reveal family secrets. Long silences would punctuate her stories or comments, but we didn't harry her with questions, reminding her we were there, making her self-conscious. We waited. And finally she would continue, plainly needing to. "Dad would come in at night. When he was drunk. Fit to be tied. Get me and Rachel out of bed and beat us. For nothing."

She would begin another seam, her concentration flowing between her thoughts and the work. "He liked doing it, somehow. Like it worked through him and made him feel powerful. So then he would take on Momma afterwards."

Didn't she save you, we thought, Gram fierce as anything; we'd heard of her, straggle-haired and screeching, heading with the lye toward Grandad at the table, her daughters struggling with her for the can, rusted and half eaten through.

"He'd lock Momma out. And she'd stand beyond the door and pound and scream. After she got her money she dared him to try it again. 'Lay a hand on them kids.' But he was too smart for that. Or maybe it had all just been too much for him before. Seven of us. No money." Under the steady run of the sewing machine and her remembering, Aunt Libby seemed to open as though she were scratching old wounds. "Selma, my cousin. She told me once: her mother hid out in the barn when Uncle Del came home late from drinking. Only this time he caught her and took hold of her and forced her hand against the lantern globe until the flesh just melted. I remember seeing the mark of it when I was little." The mark of a man. Our own flesh burned.

"There's been more than one woman, I can tell you, has come to feel so degraded and hopeless she can't go on. Your father," she would begin, looking at the two of us who were her dead sister's daughters, then biting her lip. "Well. She always went back." She didn't want to say more.

"Weren't you ever in love?" we asked her.

"More than once." She smiled downward at her own admission. "Or thought I was. Those Italian boys from the old neighborhood on North Street—beautiful dark boys." She wouldn't say more about that. We imagined for her a love that had killed love. We pitied her.

"Love," she spit out. "Sex is what it was and is and will be." The way she said "sex," we knew it was something wonderfully powerful, rising with a naturalness like the deep cold suck of water at the barnyard spring on a hot day. Love, on the other hand, she told us, was something you had to learn. "Love takes time. You learn it over a long time of being with a good man." It sounded like hard work and cold potatoes.

"Marry a man who loves you more than you love him"— that summed it up. And we thought of Uncle Dan down at the market, coming out of the food locker with a slab of meat over his shoulder, his eyes fathomless, glimmering under the bare bulb, inside him a heart raw with love for Aunt Libby.

"Don't let it fool you—sweet looks and sweet talk." What were we to do, desiring desire more and more as she paraded it before us in all its allurements; even her warnings were tempting. Sometimes now, by chance, we would see, in the appraisal of a male, a vision of ourselves changing, illuminated. Playing at the brook we saw a condom, flushed down the house sewage system, floating in the slime. Sex was going on all around us, in spite of danger and disruption; in spite of love.

Aunt Libby would push harder at the machine, driving it faster and faster as if she were getting someplace; we could see sparks spray off the wheel. "Oh my God, look what I've done now," the possibilities for disaster at her fingertips—perhaps a sleeve secured to a neckline, a collar binding a trouser leg. "See what I get for not paying attention," she said meaningfully, resigning herself to the punishment of painstaking backwork. Everything she made had to be just so, otherwise she would worry it endlessly, never forgive herself. Such was the discipline required to master the upheavals of passion, constantly lurking.

As we grew older, Celia was more and more absent from our sessions with Aunt Libby. All the time, though, we were thinking of Celia and Aunt Libby was too, for it was all coming due—Celia was now attracting college men who had cars and money they had earned themselves, pumping gas or cutting hay. They took her away from the farm, the town—dancing at a lake near Cleveland, out to restaurants where there was a wine list. Celia was forbidden to touch a single drop of the stuff and furthermore to ride in a car with anyone who did. "Two dead last night over in Mullerstown. Girl fifteen. Boy seventeen. And the other will wish she'd died, five hundred pieces of glass in her face." Aunt Libby looked over at Celia as though she had counted every sliver herself, but Celia didn't seem to care much, while she ironed each tuck down the front of a blouse, evidencing the perfectionism of her mother. Her face was still so clear and abstracted it could have been made of glass. Aunt Libby increasingly made mistakes in her sewing, threw four yards of misstitched dimity into the trash, then cried. She lost the thread of her hemstitch, the thread of her conversation. Agitated and distracted, she left the iron turned on for days at a time.

"I should have locked that one in a convent," she would say. This from a woman who thought the Catholic Church primarily responsible for the suppression of women, the promulgation of all claptrap. "Ever since she was little it was always the men. Climbing on their laps, teasing their whiskers. It's a family disease, I guess." But one she would cure if it killed her.

Yet there was something else in Celia, which wasn't pure obstinacy or boldness, something Aunt Libby couldn't touch because it was natural to Celia, coming as it did from her father. That was a kindheartedness, an absence of self-regard if any creature aroused her pity. A stray cat, a toddling baby—these had her attention while the rest of us failed. She would turn down dates to baby-sit for a relative's young children and once she sat all night with an injured dog from the highway, until even Gram relented and let her bring its basket out of the cellar. When it recovered, that dog took the place of the red setter that had once lived at the back of the yard; though the dog was a mangy mongrel now dragging a leg, Celia devotedly fed and groomed it, whispered into its ear, making the rest of us seethe with jealousy so that we ignored the dog completely. It wasn't that she disliked the rest of us, or the girls at school; it was more an absentness, an inability to focus her attention. As if we didn't need her.

At school this vagueness caused the teachers to give her nearly failing grades. It shamed Celia that they called her frivolous, using her red hair against her. Miss Warren, who had once taught Aunt Libby too, kept Celia after school day after day—she would teach her to name the oceans and the continents. Celia gave it up and let them think what they would. "By God, honey, don't let it go," Uncle Dan would plead if he came in while she was idling away at the piano, working out by ear and feel some melody line with rhythmic variations, useless though it was to urge on her an ambition she couldn't feel. Perhaps in another time she would have gone off to nurse the wounded on the fields of battle, founded an orphanage. Now she comforted those she saw in need. Those she could help. And they approached her almost reverently, as if simply to be in her presence were a healing thing; and she made it so, boys so uncomplicated, their needs so apparent and her hand so easily gentling. For a while she responded to them all with the same exquisite sensitivity, no favorites, although that changed when she was sixteen and started going out with Corley, pouring her whole self out, or so Aunt Libby feared.

Though Celia stayed alone in her room, we were no less conscious of her, heard her phonograph playing, the strident riffs of Stan Kenton's saxophones and horns reaching us. We imagined Celia in there upon her bed while around her and within her everything was in motion, mounting, going toward the time of fulfillment. She had only to make herself ready. It was as though she were primed by that music and by the surrounding aromatic dark-needled trees with their depths and peaks, and then the fields and woods that slid off to become transparent at the horizon, all making for the unfolding and accomplishment of what was growing unwaveringly within her and would have her yet. Aunt Libby stitched away on tulle gowns draped with net and flounces, finely bordered with sequins, each whirl arranged to dramatize the gown's colors of limed yellow or pale melon—all of it to enhance the evanescent dangerous glory of her first daughter. Her lips pursed under her squinted eyes, intent on the meticulous needlework, and with each yank of the thread she pulled from herself knowledge of the most intimate kind.

"Don't give it away," she told us. Did she want us to be misers? She might never have heard of love, sacrifice. We said nothing, afraid to hear. But bound to stay. Aunt Libby never spoke of sin, as though she knew nothing of that and didn't need to. She warned of impulse and consequence. Flattery and humiliation. "You'll learn fast enough; once he's gotten what he wants you're finished. He'll be gone. Or worse, you'll have him for good, and something else you didn't plan on and can't get rid of."

We were fourteen and then fifteen, sixteen. Aunt Libby was still sewing and instructing us, her younger daughter, Jenny, her two nieces, Anne and Katie, the daughters of her dead sister, Grace, while Celia stayed shut away in her room, carving and buffing her nails, rearranging her snapshots to frame the mercury-splotched looking glass, laying out on the tatted runner covering the bureau the different lucky charms, menus and dance favors. As though from a faraway tower, we heard June Christie singing "Something Cool."

"Don't be a man's plaything. Make him pay a good price—that way he'll value you more." Did Celia hear?

But if you love each other? We dared only think it, but she answered as though she'd heard. "Love"—two pins held in her lips while we listened to a trombone slide in the pause—"love is what they say. What they mean is an entirely separate thing." She smiled, the pins like bared fangs, like Gram when she talked about money. Her money. Then Aunt Libby's smile failed, went slipping away as if she had unpredictably lost the grip on her own bitterness.

We asked about Uncle Dan. "You love him." We made it sound like an accusation.

"Shit," she yelped, the machine jamming. "Look at this!" She despaired over the pucker in the blue silk and for a time she strained over the mass of thread caught in the feed plate, digging with a darning needle. When it was dislodged, she went on sewing for a while, then said, "Loving isn't anything easy."

It was beginning to storm; the oak trees up by the road tossed to silver foam, fell back green again. There had been a lover once. An Italian boy with ardent glowing eyes. We imagined him for ourselves. The purple clouds were plowing in on the wind from the darker distance, weaving into garlands that hung over us like terraces as though we dwelt in Babylon. All at once, moving as one spirit, we did what we had not done for years: we dropped our clothes on the floor, on the stairs, as we ran down, and then on the porch, so that we were fully naked by the time we leapt onto the grass. The rain chilled, stung against our skin, turned to hail. Then Celia came out too, with us again after long years, flying over the grass, prancing, flowing with rain, her golden-red hair streaked dark with rain, streaming out. She was like a separate force quickening us, urging us further by her possibilities. Over the grass we ran and slid until it churned, spattered and oozed with mud; we painted ourselves, each other, immersed in the driveway ditch of foaming brown for a rinsing, before we took the mud slide again. We formed a whip, flung ourselves over the grass. Until Celia stopped and looked up the drive, sideways, hiding herself. A car passed on the highway, silent and distant as though driven by a phantom. Celia stood covered with her crossed arms and like that, suddenly, we all ran onto the porch and grabbed for towels or rags from the shelf, shivering goose-flesh like a disease.

Celia had him in the parlor. We stayed in the living room across the hall and were quiet, listening for any sounds they might make. We never heard any talking. This night Aunt Libby and Uncle

Dan had gone out and Corley had come later, so we were the only ones who saw him go into the parlor with Celia and close the door.

The hall light was out. Across the darkness we could see the slight border of light under the double panel doors and between them where they pulled together. There was no hurry. We waited.

Going out of the room, Celia left the door open so we could see Corley waiting there while she was in the kitchen. She didn't even glance at us. Corley was her new boyfriend and already she was different with him. The other boys didn't come to the house now and she saw him every night Aunt Libby would allow it, Celia arguing nonstop all afternoon, then over supper. Corley wore his wavy hair in a slick ducktail, which he was constantly combing; we watched the muscles in his arms quivering even from that little bit of movement. When he smiled, his full lips barely lifted and there was no change in the expression of his thick-lidded eyes. Aunt Libby said he was lazy as the day is long, you could tell that by looking at him, and he wouldn't ever get out of bed once he'd got Celia into one. She said he dripped sex. To us that seemed to go along with his wet-looking hair.

Still we thought he was cute and Celia was lucky. He grinned now, combing his hair. "How you all doing?" His family had come up from Kentucky and he still talked that way, with a voice mushy and thick like his lips.

"Fine." We shrugged.

"Here's some money," he said. "You want to get some ice cream?" He must have thought we were still kids. There was a Dairy Delight now on the far lot beside the gas station; Gram spoke of her fields and meadows as lots now.

Sure, we said, knowing he wanted to get rid of us, knowing too what we'd do when we got back. We took our time walking there because there were a lot of cars driving in and out of the parking lot on a Saturday night and we knew some of the guys. Walking back, we felt the connection with the rest of the world sever as we left the high lamps and passed beyond the cedar hedge onto the dark gravel, the house shadowy too now, with only one small glow of light in the front hall.

We needed no words. We moved to the grass to quiet our walking. Through the gap in the honeysuckle we sneaked and climbed over the railing and stood to one side of the window, where we could see at an angle past the half-drawn drapes. At first we could scarcely make them out where they were on the floor, bound in one shape. We licked our ice cream and carefully, silently dissolved the cones, tasting nothing as it melted away down inside us. Tasting instead Corley's mouth on ours, its burning wild lathering sweetness. In the shaft of light we saw them pressed together, rolling in each other's arms, Celia's flowery skirt pulled up around her thighs. His hand moving there. Then she pushed him away, very tenderly, went to sit back on the couch while Corley turned his back and combed his hair. He turned and started toward her, tucking his shirt in. We stared at the unsearchable smile that lifted from Celia's face like a veil and revealed another self, as she began to unbutton her blouse, undressing herself until she sat there in the half-dark, bare to the waist, bare to the moon which had come up over the trees behind us. She drew Corley to her, his face after he'd turned around never losing its calm, kissed him forever, it seemed, as long as she wanted to. Then she guided his mouth to press into first one and then the other cone-crested breast, her own face lake-calm under the moon. Then she dressed again. Our hearts plunged and thudded. At that moment we were freed from Aunt Libby. We didn't care what it was called or the price to be paid; someday we would have it.

Terrible battles began between Aunt Libby and Celia. Breaking out anywhere—in the kitchen, the hall—night or day, their screaming and slamming rocked the entire house, made Uncle Dan say he had a headache all the time just waiting for them to get started. Something had alerted Aunt Libby; she wouldn't leave the house at night in case Corley came over, and she made Celia leave the parlor doors ajar. They fussed over how wide a crack it should be, the dimensions of privacy. When Aunt Libby sniffed that she didn't hear much talking going on, Celia snapped back that they couldn't talk when they were under surveillance like prisoners by an old busybody. Old! Aunt Libby's eyes sealed, impenetrable.

Celia came into the living room one night, leaving Corley behind in the parlor. "Mom, we're driving to Abnerville." Corley's married sister lived there.

Aunt Libby wanted to say no, never. We watched her struggle. She fastened her attention on Celia's legs, long and tanned below her white shorts. "You're not going like that," she said, her voice, once found, taking the bull by the horns.

"Mother." Celia ground her teeth. The clock ticked as firmly as Aunt Libby's mind was made up. Celia went upstairs and put on a skirt. Then they fought over the time she was to be home. "Eleven," Aunt Libby insisted. "Twelve," Celia said, and banged out the door.

"Goddamn little rip," Aunt Libby said to us.

At eleven-thirty Aunt Libby was drinking hot milk in the kitchen. She kept her eyes on the table. Now and then we looked up at the clock, high over the painted wainscoting; never washed, its face was fuzzy with soot and grease. It was past midnight when the lights at last came down the drive. They lighted up the orchard as the car made the wide circle and left again. Celia came in. Aunt Libby looked pasty sick. Celia glanced at her and said, "What's the matter with you, old sourpuss?" but smiling. Her face was pale and tired, her mouth blurred at the edges from all the kisses we imagined there.

Aunt Libby got up, deliberately, and went over and slapped Celia's face. "Bitch," she hissed at her, and slapped her again, harder. "Tramp."

The slaps rushed the blood to Celia's face. It fell as fast, leaving her gray as ash dust save for her smeared orange mouth, tangled hair. "I could have, you know," she screamed, crying at the same time. "I wanted to, but I didn't. Now I wish I had. I will for that," and she ran up the stairs.

Aunt Libby was after her, her aqua cotton dress pulling up and showing her brown thighs which slapped together as she went, her face horrible in dismay, in fear of the worst, of what she'd done herself. "Well, I'll kill you first myself, if it comes to that." We could hear her, although what she said came in a low guttural moaning from the hall. "Throw yourself away, will you! Open this door, I tell you. Open it!"

We were left in the kitchen with the black sea of night awash at the screens. Fireflies like flying phosphorescent fishes sailed through the orchard. Apples fell to their ruin. We could smell them softening in their own brine.

Later Celia and Aunt Libby made up. Uncle Dan had roused himself and declared through his door, "I don't ask for a whole hell of a lot around here," and Aunt Libby quit screaming and pounding and Celia opened her door and they went in together. Once again, it was over. They seemed to us like lovers who quarrel for the sake of reconciliation.

We sat on in the kitchen until another car came creeping down the drive. We listened for the slight scratching sound of Gram coming up on the granite stoop, her step silent on the carpet, slow and halting.

"There was a fight," we told her, wanting to say more.

She snorted once, didn't ask a thing. "I'm tired. You kids turn out them lights." She'd seen a million fights.

"Did you win?" We always asked her that, although from her evasive answers there was no real telling; sly and secretive, apt to lie, we thought, to protect her little bit of magic. "Maybe," she said. "Well, I'm going up to roost. Night now." She hung her light woolen coat in the closet and treaded her way up the long curved stair toward the darkness of her room; with everybody home, we felt the fields and sky fold inward to wrap up the house for bed. Gram had survived more battles than we had dreamed of, a regular old war-horse, Uncle Dan called her. Gluey-eyed, longing for sleep, we followed her.

After Corley there was Mike. Then Bud, Roger, Hal—strange boys whose last names we never knew, only the names of the towns they came from: Oakfield, Madison, Peru. Later, for a long time, there was Jimmy, for such a long time we thought Celia would marry him—forsaking all others, finally letting Aunt Libby settle down. Aunt Libby had started to have stomach trouble; she burped so regularly that she didn't try to hide it or excuse herself, allowing the burning gas to erupt from her, the signal of her own wretchedness. She dosed herself with chalky liquids and chewed on saltines. She was already thin as a girl and grew thinner. When we went places out of town, people thought she was our older sister. But they saw her high-heeled, made up, brown eyes aglow. They didn't know the source of that fire; didn't watch her trembling over the kitchen sink, her body heaving dry and empty.

It was as though that first open battle with Celia had broken some reserve and refinement in Aunt Libby; we never knew after that when another fight would rage. The waiting for them and preparing for them preoccupied Aunt Libby, further sapping her strength. She left off talking to the rest of us about love and sex. She stopped fighting with Uncle Dan and he seemed to spend the late hours of every night getting in and out of bed by himself, trying to get things to quiet down so he could sleep a little before he had to open up the store in the morning. Out many nights ourselves by then, although never as regularly or extravagantly entertained as Celia, we were content to go around in groups and to get home on time.

Ordinarily we came home about the time Aunt Libby got out of bed to wait up for Celia and sometimes to fight. Our hearts would draw into silence until some exhausted tension or battered anxiety would give way and there would be peace again—Celia and Aunt Libby talking far into the night, an intimacy feeding off secrets and mysteries. To the rest of us Aunt Libby vowed she

would protect her daughter. Die trying. We went our own ways
—denied now her confidences and cautions. It was the fiery and
reckless Celia whom she braced for, boasting of it too. Had any
other daughter in the whole world ever been such a handful, so
wondrously alluring? We went riding with Aunt Rachel and
when we cantered the horses along the north pasture, sometimes
caught by dark and the rising moon, still letting them have their
heads as we raced toward the shed we used as a barn, calling back
and forth through the urgent dusk, our blood would sing, un-
voiced: "Oh, Johnny is my darling, my darling, a Union volun-
teer"—just then we felt we had everything that Celia had,
through her.

Still we hated Celia, hated what she was doing to her mother.
Once when Aunt Libby knocked the skillet to the floor and then
drove off in the car, screaming and sobbing—drove the way
Grandad used to career past when he'd been drinking what Gram
called firewater—we thought she would kill herself. We envi-
sioned her lurching over hill and dale until she sailed off the cliff
of the ravine. Frightened, divided in loyalty, we fumed at Celia
through the door of the bathroom where she'd shut herself. Told
her she was cruel and selfish, was killing her mother. When she
came out, pale and cold-eyed, she continued to prepare for the
forbidden dance, refused to answer.

"You spoil her," we accused Aunt Libby. "If we ever so
much as thought . . ." But we couldn't get Aunt Libby to pay
attention to us, other than a vague distracted smile of gratefulness
for our goodness, for sparing her.

She lived through her wild ride, lived to call and calmly tell
us she was with Aunt Rachel, who now lived in a small house
on the edge of the farm with her son Rossie and her new husband,
Tom Buck. Had we found anything to eat? It was Uncle Dan's
late night at the store, something he now had to do to compete
with the supermarkets in outlying shopping centers.

When we were home nights with Uncle Dan, it was like old

times. He popped corn by the bowlful, brought home chips and cheese spread, fixed icy Cokes and made his remarks, generally reflecting on the level of confusion around the place, which made him feel that at last, years after the war, his ship had left the port of San Francisco. He'd bought a television set just as soon as the price came down, just like a kid, Aunt Libby said, and we watched together in the dark living room with Uncle Dan serving us, doing his best to entertain us. Aunt Libby, passing by, would pause a moment in the doorway, half amused in spite of herself, and would then go on shaking her head as Uncle Dan called after her, "Honey, all of us can't continually ponder the darker side." When she didn't answer he would shrug and be thoughtful for a while—until *Broadway Open House* came on and he could watch Dagmar, whose tits he said always put things in perspective.

About eleven o'clock, Uncle Dan would carry the bowls and glasses to the kitchen and go up to bed and we would feel a little lonely, although not ready to leave ourselves, Gram and Celia yet to come home, perhaps the real drama of the evening still to happen. Our entertainment with Uncle Dan was the beginning of the night and as he was on his way up to bed, Aunt Libby was on her way down from reading in bed—passing like ships in the night, Uncle Dan called it. There in the downstairs hall Aunt Libby would position herself with her needlework and then later, when Celia would be parked out in the drive, staying in the car with whoever her current boyfriend was, she would begin to flip the porch light switch every five minutes, until Celia would fling herself in for a moment, demanding more time, pleading for it, then disappear again, finally to be forced in by the light signaling in warning across the dark like a lighthouse probe. Aunt Libby figured that Celia wasn't going to get too carried away in her own driveway with her mother announcing her presence. Sometime in there Gram would come home. Uncle Dan always said what a pity it was that an old woman like that had to work the night shift. When he couldn't sleep because of all the commotion, the comings and goings, he would appear on the stairs, decently wrapped in his bathrobe, and announce to one and all that there was more going on in his house after dark than in a whorehouse.

One night we overheard him talking to Aunt Libby, serious for once. "Let her be. Let her live her own life. You had your chance."

"Yes, and see where it got me."

We couldn't hear what he said next, but we knew his mild and quizzical expression.

"Oh, shut up, Dan," she said. "You know very well what I mean. It's just that I think Celia has a real good chance. Better than most."

"You've got two daughters," he reminded her.

"Jenny's like me. She can compromise if she has to. She's got good sense. Celia's different. It's the waste I object to. Pure waste. If I can just get her married to a good man. Before it's too late."

"Wouldn't hurt her to lose a little blood first. I've heard of worse things."

"Dan Snyder, are you crazy?"

"Probably am. Always was, about you."

We heard the familiar capitulation in her tone, a warming current touching her place of love. "Well, I always knew I got better than I deserve. I'm not easy."

Later we heard Uncle Dan whistling his way down the stairs to the cellar, where he was learning to draw. Following an open workbook, using an arc and a ruler, he was trying a vase of flowers. In the dimness beyond the aimed desk lamp, he told us, there were sometimes rats that scurried past, though there was no longer food stored there. Uncle Dan said he didn't mind sharing, made him feel he was suffering for art, and anyway they were a lot less troublesome than a pack of overheated females. All the same, we thought he might amount to something, mastering sepals and petals with mechanical precision in a dungeon.

When Celia was a senior in high school she met Phillip. He was going to study law when he was through at the college, and already he had more money to spend than anybody we knew, including Gram, and he took Celia to dinners in Mencina and Cleveland, for Swedish smorgasbord at country inns. During the summer he drove up the fifty miles from his hometown. Increasingly he spent time talking to Aunt Libby and after a while he was even stopping off at the store to pick up things she needed. Theirs were serious talks, Aunt Libby confiding her concerns about Celia, her high-strung nature, her willfulness, her sympathetic heart. It was as though Celia were a bred filly that Aunt Libby was handing over to an experienced trainer; Phillip had gained her confidence. There were fewer fights. He brought Celia home on time, soothing them both, the go-between.

Phillip would say, "We'll be a little late tonight; the dance is in Oakland," and Aunt Libby would nod, agreeable and relaxed, her legs hooked up over the side of the armchair, showing most of her thighs, the way she sat when she felt peaceful. Her stomach settled more easily now and her face had regained that glow, hint of gilt, suggesting the edges of pages in an old cherished romance.

"Is she smoking?" Aunt Libby would ask.

Phillip had the smoking in hand, allowed her only four an evening. Celia's best interests were his.

He was undeniably handsome, and his whole bearing expressed his instinct for command. Well-clothed and organized, he didn't interest us the way Corley had, or the other boys. Already he seemed as settled in as Uncle Dan. Uncle Dan said he certainly had the gift of gab; he said it as if it were nothing he had ever wanted for himself. But for Aunt Libby Phillip was a godsend, someone who understood Celia, and although there was plenty in him smoldering just beneath the surface, he was content to wait. She liked that in a man—self-control.

Phillip had his eye on the future and on his path for getting there in law, real estate, politics. Aunt Libby's gaze inched over him. She squinted, as though she were measuring him against a pattern she had in mind. She accepted his prospects as good ones;

hazy about the particulars of that future he anticipated, she put her stock in her judgment of the man. It was as though that future time need not concern her, after she had turned Celia over to him.

Those two would talk comfortably and confidentially while waiting for Celia to appear. She was always late. Then at last she would be coming down the stairs, calling ahead with her rattling excitement so we'd be expecting her, straining toward her.

She stood in the doorway, dressed in a gathered print skirt, newly made, the colors clear as fresh-cut flowers, her white blouse starched, open at the throat.

"I guess you just had to iron it a second time," Aunt Libby said. "And no stockings." We all looked with her at Celia's fine-boned ankle, circled by a mesh chain dangling a tiny locket heart. As yet no man's, she was ours, our achievement, our possibility. This wealth was ours—the hundred acres of woodland and field, Gram's fortune, Celia's bewitching charm. Her hand drooped against her skirt. Phillip reached for it. We could have stabbed him. But she went with him out the side door onto the solid cut-granite stoop and down the four steps. The car started up and left. We heard the leaves fanning against the screens. And smelled Celia's perfume lingering on the air, as though all of nature were excited too.

"That man is a blessing," Aunt Libby said.

"Too bad you can't have him for yourself," Uncle Dan answered, dead level, carrying a tray of Cokes into the room. "What our Libby needs is a honey-tongued talking mule." He winked at us.

"Oh, hush," she said, but he couldn't make her mad. She said, "If that's what I need, then I've already got it." And she went on peaceful, gazing into the evening light which filtered across the gray ferns of the wallpaper, bending them up and down.

"I'm just so thankful she didn't marry Corley," Aunt Libby said one afternoon while she did some hand stitching on a bridesmaid dress she had designed in pale rose silk, with insets of lace taken from an old gown of Gram's. "I wouldn't doubt he's partly

Italian. Dark like that." Now that Celia was preparing for her wedding, Aunt Libby was regaining some of her old style, thinking out loud to us, her fingers advancing over the fine silk, the rose ruffled against the ivory lace.

"He loved her a lot," we said, recalling his masking indolence, the half-glutted lion roaming behind the grasscover of his lashes.

"I never doubted that. And I thought I'd never stop her. Doubling all the time with that Ruthie Thompson and Rossie and heaven knows what they were up to. That winter her nerves were terrible; she was thinner and wilder every day. I just don't know."

We knew—for once, more than Aunt Libby maybe—what Rossie and Ruthie were up to. Ruthie told us that once when she was sitting on his lap he said for her to look down and she'd about died laughing after she got over the shock of it; because he'd opened up his pants and it was standing up beside her elbow, fresh as a daisy. We were so embarrassed for Rossie, our cousin, we could hardly think about it, but Ruthie got a kick out of it —always jolly and easygoing. About sixteen, she dropped out of high school, pregnant. "Right on schedule," Aunt Libby said.

"There's nothing to be done about it," Aunt Libby said now. She meant us, our family. Being female. She referred to it as if it was both a miracle and a calamity, that vein of fertility, that mother lode of passion buried within us, for joy and ruin. "None of us can no more than look at a man and we're having his baby. Look at Florence"—Aunt Libby's cousin, who still took in ironing to help support over a dozen children. And there was Gram with her soiled and faded apron and her exhausted face, marked like an old barn siding that had withstood blasts and abuse of all kinds, beyond any expression other than resignation and self-regard.

"It will be my release, the day I hand her over to Phillip," Aunt Libby said, molding a rose out of scrap velvet, to set in the bodice on a green-piped stem. We remembered Corley, his lips hot as a brand on Celia.

Then Uncle Dan came home right in the middle of a Friday afternoon. We knew something had to be wrong. He called out once, "Libby," crossed the dining room and went up the stairs to their room.

Before she followed him, Aunt Libby glanced out at the meadow dripping in the rain, beyond the thin aisle of lawn that every year Uncle Dan was making narrower, mowing less, leaving Gram's peony bushes as the border. It was as though it fortified her, that swell of meadow; already she looked resigned to the worst, something she'd half expected all along. Often she'd warned us that moments of happiness hang like pearls on the finest silken thread, certain to be snapped, the pearls scattered away. Up the stairs she went, from the back, in her shorts, looking like a girl, her face, reflecting darkly in the hall mirror, capable of any age.

And we were waiting, afraid; it might have been a long time, the pale rain rills sliding hypnotically over the glass. Then we heard water running above us, Aunt Libby in the bathroom splashing and blowing, and then she came down.

"Oh, God." She sobbed away, hugging her tumultuous stomach. "How will I ever tell her? And I trusted him. Fool." Our wise conspiratorial Libby thrown. Still we were giddy with excitement, deliciously free to mourn openly with her over her wounded pride and bitter disillusionment, although we didn't know exactly what the trouble was. Which caused Uncle Dan to examine us for an instant as he strode over to the high shelf where the unused milk crocks were lined up and brought down the whiskey bottle hidden there, and drank off in front of Aunt Libby one gulp which went on so long and seemed so agreeable to him that right then we understood something of her vigilance, knew we'd be just like her. His eyes darkened, then, taking on that same bordering indigo of the crocks, subject to his grim drinking mood. He drank again. Then capped the bottle. "I'm going now, Libby," he said, and so we imagined his departure for war, before they knew he would be in California for the duration.

Gradually, Aunt Libby calmed. Told us what a woman from Millersburg, Phillip's aunt by marriage, had come to town to tell Uncle Dan that afternoon. She could not stand across the counter and ask for a pound of hamburger and not tell Uncle Dan that Phillip Masterson was the uncontested father-to-be of Louanne Price's child, which was no longer anybody's little secret. At one time Phillip had gone steady with Louanne. But this pregnancy had happened recently, since his engagement to Celia. Everybody was counting. Aunt Libby said that Uncle Dan was so fired up she didn't know what he might do, and we all remembered Grandad's rabbit gun still leaning against the back of the pantry closet.

Gram came in from the matinee while we sat at the kitchen table. We could smell the rusty screening at the windows and the stale stained cloth as she pulled her apron off the hook. She reached into the potato bin and started a curl of peeling toward the drain.

"Well," she said as she plopped the first one in a pan of cold water and began a second. "I already heard. Reckon scandal borrows wings."

In the presence of her mother Aunt Libby was nearly herself again, restored to the stability of hard knocks and no nonsense. "I guess we've been fooled."

"Some fool easier than others. But sooner's better than later, I'd say. Don't ask me why she's in such an all-fired hurry to get hitched anyways. Lasts too long as it is." Gram turned the fire sky-high under the pork chops and they began to smoke and scorch right off. She couldn't wait to get them on the table. Under the potatoes she raised a great flame, setting the pan on the burner with a bang as though she still cooked on an iron stove. "Have fun while you're young, I say—not much you can do when you're old and ugly."

"You're beautiful to us," Aunt Libby said, and indeed the

afternoon sun turned Gram's coiled iron-gray curls to a crinkly crimson when she stood just so in the light. But only an instant; she was in a great hurry, dropping plates on the table, dealing tableware like cards.

"You're not going out tonight—not tonight?"

"Am too."

"But, Momma. Celia's going to take it hard."

"Phooey. She's well rid of him. Ain't nothing I can do anyways. Maybe she'd like to come along with me," she added, offering a real prize, her own one reliable pleasure.

"The roads are terrible. Twenty's closed on account of water."

"Don't matter to me. It's clear to the west. I'll take number thirty. I've gone through worse, I suspect, and the horse was scared too." Gram was proud of what she'd survived; once she'd turned eighty she boasted of her age, couldn't tack on another year soon enough. She poured water on the chops to stop the burning and clamped on a lid, opened green beans she'd canned the last year she had a garden—they had to boil fifteen minutes and she'd wait for that. She'd known more than one family that had died, every last one, from a taste of spoiled green beans. Everything was now frying and boiling at top speed. Sow-bellied, spike-legged, there was still something about her tough management of the supper that stirred like an exuberant passion that had not been so much used up as outlived.

We tried to eat what she'd cooked, working down small bits of the hard dry pork with lots of milk. Gram ignored the meat and ate through a plate of green beans with vinegar ladled on it and then cut herself two slabs of the white Dutch loaf. Its powdery dusting of flour sprinkled the table and her front; she cut it, cradling it in her arms, sawing the iron butcher knife back and forth across the front of her sunken breasts, squeezing the bread against herself. "I swear, Momma. Someday . . ." Aunt Libby flinched and held her own two breasts in her hands. But Gram paid no attention, knew what she was doing. She saw us watching her and, for once, in a shy flash of generosity, offered each of us a thin slice. "Don't pester me for more, though, or the next time you'll get nothing." The country butter had little specks of white whey. The bread was so soft we hardly had to chew it. Maybe it was because Gram had lived so long and had so much trouble that she subsisted almost entirely on these soft white loaves. As she mouthed the bread her mouth gleamed with the fat of cows—content as a ruminant herself, forgetful. But then she startled: the pale watery veiling of sunlight over the orchard struck the hammered brass planter hanging between the two windows. That reminded her. Time to be gone. She gathered the plates in one sweeping motion while we were still chewing, rested them on the hump of her stomach and pushed what remained into a slop pail, as if she still had chickens and hogs to feed. "Now I done enough. You gals, wash them dishes. Boil that cloth. It stinks like shit." She winked her childlike pleasure in her little joke, which had made Aunt Libby frown. She added then, "In my next house I'm going to have one of them dishwashers."

Then a car came down the drive and Celia got out. We heard her ring of good cheer as she called goodbye. Since her future was settled with Phillip she had become friendlier with other girls; they weren't so afraid of her now. She was even more outgoing around the house. But when Celia came into the room she knew by looking at her mother that something had gone wrong with her life. We didn't know until then that Celia was like the rest of us, always waiting for something terrible to happen.

"Goddamn it, Libby," Gram said, "tell her"—nearly mad with impatience, Celia her favorite out of all her grandchildren. She moved toward Celia with her neck extended, taut as a goose's and using every bit of her waggle of extra chin. "You ain't going to fall to pieces because of a man's fool doings." And she told Celia, just that way, telling her what was wrong, and at the same time telling her how she was to take it. "Ain't a man born yet that's interested in more than a couple of inches of a gal anyway. So now you know it too," she ended up, red as the fires she cooked over, as if to cauterize the whole house with the rage and passion that still persisted in her.

Gram laid her old work-worn hand on Celia's arm. "You go on and cry. Cry your eyes out and then get over it!" Before she left she took four nickels from her pocketbook and put them on the sink, as though we were still little kids.

Celia sat and lit a cigarette, the first time she'd smoked in front of her mother since she had learned to do it from Corley. Although she didn't cry, her face was mottled with the sudden splotch and bruise of high feeling which redheads show. Aunt Libby whispered to the rest of us, talking of Celia's nerves so that we almost felt we could see them tracing her fragile skin, the way veins are visible on the surface of leaves held against the light. The way Aunt Libby talked, we expected Celia to blow up, smoking and sizzling, her nerves shorting out.

"I can't imagine what Dan's doing," Aunt Libby fretted. The wet orchard grass and briers gleamed like washed planking, while above, the branches held green sails to the wind. Aunt Rachel had fancied that once and we didn't forget, never let ourselves forget any of it; we knew we'd have to live our whole lives off what they'd said and done around us.

"Look," Aunt Libby said. At the edge of the field two does stood. Their ears flicked. None of us moved. Gram banged out the side door.

"Momma." Aunt Libby pointed toward the vanishing tails. "You scared them."

"Ain't nothing. Come for apples. You could see them on any morning, if you'd get out of bed before noon. Makes them sick, though. Tipsy. But they always come back for more. Like some fool man." She choked a declarative roar from the car. She felt relieved, released, we could tell—getting away from us.

Aunt Libby turned back to Celia, who smoked her cigarette with a fervent concentration. "Try to get it out, dear," she told Celia. "Cry." Then Aunt Libby released a long rumble of her own discomfort.

"Mother." Celia spoke for the first time, her nerves threatening.

"I can't help it. I should eat something."

"Then do." Celia got up and went toward the stairs. "And see if you can find Daddy, before he does something stupid."

But we just sat on at the table. For hours. Aunt Libby drank milk, which we warmed for her. "I don't know how much she can stand," she said.

There were things we could tell, wanted to tell. We closed our mouths and watched Aunt Libby clutching her stomach, which we imagined tight and cramping like her desiccated mouth. We could tell about Celia, but we had promised. With Aunt Libby we stared toward the highway, expecting Uncle Dan.

"It's just like him to disappear like this and worry me to death. Up to God-only-knows-what." She told us that Uncle Dan always had had a fresh streak in him: the night she met him he'd told her she would end up married to him. "Keep on hoping," she'd said. A little dandy, not a hair taller than she was, clowning for attention all the time. A party drinker too. But of course he'd given that up for her; one way and another he'd had his way, wormed himself into her affections. "Well, I'll walk on over to Rachel's." She put on her sweater. We stared after her as she went, slender with the last light absorbing her into its quiet grasp, walking through the orchard where the deer had stood.

Aunt Libby hadn't been gone long when what Uncle Dan called the nightly excitement began. First we thought we heard Celia talking on the upstairs phone. So when we heard the car on the gravel, we ran to the parlor window in time to see her opening the door and slipping in as the car barely paused to scoop her up and continued the circle of the drive, speeding toward the highway. We could tell from Phillip's face that he'd heard what had happened. They didn't greet or even look at each other. In the silence they left behind, we felt the trees and early stars and land pitch together. Only the brick house stood firm against it, stretching away up over us, cold and empty as though it had felt each desertion, slow death and failure that had occurred and, like someone with a stern character, had been made stronger yet numb from having suffered them. "Celia's gone," we imagined Gram saying, "and she ain't never coming back." Seeing Phillip made us feel for the first time that something had really changed, feel it more than Uncle Dan's coming home in the middle of the afternoon. Like selfish and evil stepsisters, spurned and embittered, we wanted Phillip for ourselves, lusted after his newly blemished self. Now we could tell Aunt Libby—about Corley, Jimmy, the others too whom Celia still met, sneaking and lying herself, while pretending to be so blameless and true. And now broken-hearted. False herself, she played men for fools. While we, constantly nagged by an old biddy, protected ourselves for nothing, against nothing. Although it was early, we locked all the doors that were never locked and went up to our attic room.

But there was someone else on the drive. This time it was Jimmy, lurching toward the house on foot, muttering, "I'll kill him. Fucking son-of-a-bitch. Kill him." The lights from the dairy across the road glinted on the rifle he was carrying, the bottle he drank from. "Celia," he yelled. Then, "Celia," wavering to aim the gun toward the house as if he didn't know whom or what he was going to shoot. We didn't call down. He stumbled around and we could hear him crying and muttering her name and then we heard him farther away again, his voice trailing back to us from the lane leading toward the woods. Sometime later we woke up. Because we heard someone with a key scratching on the side door, trying to unlock it. Uncle Dan was talking then in the front hall. In the dark we edged, half sliding down the banister so the stairs wouldn't creak, to the landing on the second floor. Down below, through the railing, we saw Uncle Dan's bald spot under the globe and his elbows stabbing out as he made a strange girl comfortable, helping her remove her sweater, fixing a cushion for her back. Sure as anything, we knew it was Louanne Price. On her face were the inescapable purple shadows of despair and poor judgment. We couldn't see her stomach.

"Want a Coke or something while we wait?" Uncle Dan asked.

She closed her eyes. "No, thank you."

They seemed to know already that Celia had gone out with Phillip.

"Don't mind if I do," he said, and went into the kitchen. Below us Louanne's face rested so deeply she looked like a child in a dreamless sleep. When Uncle Dan returned she didn't open her eyes and he sat at the other end of the sofa, drinking calmly, his mouth holding the warming liquid; he could have been almost contented. Once he looked up toward where we were in the dark. Then at Louanne. "It won't be long, I guess," he assured her.

The leaves outside the landing window began to rustle without a perceptible rise in the wind, without force, just marking the later hour, the shifting balance, cooler air coming in. Everything seemed more peaceful as we waited.

We heard another car on the drive. We didn't move to look —leaving everything to Celia, the way we always had. She came in with Phillip, holding his hand; solemn and spent-looking, they seemed about to announce some momentous decision to their grave and startled audience. Until Celia saw Louanne. Then she stepped away from Phillip, while Louanne rubbed her eyes with her fists like a newly awakened child. Uncle Dan watched everything, a curious onlooker, relatively unconnected with a complicated affair. Phillip looked as before, stern and hopeless. He left abruptly, telling Celia that he would call her tomorrow, saying something about not being railroaded. Louanne began to shed the tears of a child. And softhearted Celia, devoted to dogs and small children, all needful things, a nurse in wartime, a camp follower for ravaged men, took Louanne in her arms and told her everything would be all right. "He still cares for you. He told me so tonight," she murmured in ballad-like cadence. Celia's clear voice rose out of the column of her throat in unfaltering renunciation of whatever was trivial and low. Only her skin, blanched white as a substratum of exposed bone, showed the strain of her feelings.

"But he seems to hate me," Louanne got out. "He was so angry when I told. I just had to tell somebody, you know. I was so afraid that he might try to kill me, like that girl in the movies. And he says he won't ever marry me."

"Of course he will." Celia stroked her hair. "He has to." She had learned some things from Aunt Libby. She was still comforting Louanne when Aunt Libby came in. With one glance she knew everything—"it" written all over Louanne, while we were thinking that if that was how "it" made you look, then who would ever want it. Uncle Dan gazed straight up at us then and said, "You might as well get in on the act." So we went down. Jimmy had wandered back into the yard and we could hear him muttering and cursing. Uncle Dan said some people had the damnedest notions of being useful; then he said he might as well take Louanne on home, and when they left, Celia gave her a final hug and promised to call her the next day. Louanne was slumped into a tiny little nobody of shame and grief, a lesson to all. We could sense Aunt Libby thinking that, after she'd shut the door behind them. But Celia said nothing and went straight upstairs; from her room we soon heard the wail of a saxophone.

Aunt Rachel came in then and we went with them to Aunt Libby's bedroom, where the two sisters flopped on the bed to talk. Aunt Rachel lay across the bed that had been hers for so long before she had married Tom Buck and moved to the other side of the farm. Now Aunt Libby was saying that Dan had been right after all. Celia would have to live her own life. Sometimes it took a real shock to make you see things.

And Aunt Rachel said, "There isn't any shock greater than a baby coming."

"Celia still sees the other guys," we broke in, at last saying it out loud, telling on her. "Not only Phillip! Corley, Jimmy and Roger." Aunt Libby gave us a scorching look.

"And I'd like to know why she wouldn't," Aunt Rachel said. "A young girl like that tying herself down. That's the silliest thing I ever heard of." Aunt Rachel had been married herself for a short miserable spell at eighteen. That was when she'd had Rossie. She asked then, "You ever noticed how that water stain on the ceiling looks like a big tit?" Changing the subject, something droll like that popping out of her like a surprise butter rum drop. She reached over and tickled Aunt Libby under the arms. "Smile, you old sourpuss."

"You're as bad as Dan," Aunt Libby said, twisting around, and then she did laugh. "Only one thing on your mind."

"Lucky you," Aunt Rachel said, and gave her the sideways slanted look from her tilted green eyes which made us think of jade pagodas and gold-threaded cloth.

"I'll have to put that bottle away where he can't find it." Aunt Libby didn't seem worried now but only resigned. "Maybe I worry so much about her because she was sick for so long and I got into the habit." Long ago Celia had had asthma and had nearly died more than once.

"It's that new baby I'm worrying about," Aunt Rachel said. Uncle Dan agreed with her as he came into the room that was full of females.

"You look awfully pleased with yourself," Aunt Libby said while he stood in the doorway, her arms propping up her head while she eyed him from the bed. But it was as though through her elongated, half-closed almond eyes she was openly envying him something he had that she didn't, only usually she didn't think about it. Then she got up and started to take off her clothes. Aunt Rachel said, "Well, excuse me!" Anyway, she ought to be going on home and Uncle Dan said he didn't know why— certainly Libby didn't mind who stayed. He said that he for one was glad he didn't have to leave the house for a strip show and Aunt Libby said she hadn't ever asked anybody to watch. Which made Uncle Dan call back from the hall that he was hardly able to take his eyes off her for even a second. And we saw a little private smile float in her eyes before she slipped her gown over her head.

Aunt Rachel walked off alone into the darkness toward

home. She refused any company, saying that nobody was ever going to catch her on her own land. She would probably run just for fun, the way she let her horse stretch out over the fields night and day. There was always that something in Aunt Rachel that we felt drove and bedeviled her. We let her go. Aunt Libby was saying to Uncle Dan when we passed their room, "Sometimes I want him horsewhipped and then I feel there probably wasn't a thing he could do about it. Poor fool."

Phillip didn't marry Louanne. Nothing could make him do it. Celia gave him back his ring and wouldn't see him or talk on the phone, and one day when he stepped out in front of her downtown, she let him have it right there. He got a flash flood of her temper—the temper, Uncle Dan said, that was not so much the fault of red hair as of all the extra attention that went with it. Anyway, her tirade shocked Phillip and soon after that he left the college and then the state. He kept staunchly to his word and never married Louanne, though he never failed to send her money for the baby, no matter where he was, Alaska or Europe. Gram said right there was the sum difference between a father and a mother.

"The son-of-a-bitch," Uncle Dan always called him after that, with something like admiration along with just plain amazement in his voice. Phillip wrote Celia once but she tore up the letter without looking at it and we never heard directly from him again. She said she didn't think she'd ever really known him, could scarcely remember what he'd looked like.

From the first Celia considered herself kind of a godmother to Louanne's baby. Aunt Libby taught her to knit, skillfully managing the gauge, and Celia knitted a pair of booties and then other garments in delicate pastels, attempting more complicated patterns as she got better.

Once in a while she still shut herself into her room with the mournful jazz she'd loved, but more often she sat with the rest of us, her fingers flying faster and faster with the needles and her tongue loosened, trying to catch up on everything she had missed, as if she'd come out of a daze or dementia. Even stories we told her of times she'd been with us fascinated her, because she didn't clearly remember. She questioned Gram too, patient with Gram's rambling and disjointed tales, got excited over old recipes, and watched Gram cook as though she might imitate the same rapid-fire style. She even got Gram to talk a little about the time when Aunt Grace lay dying.

Aunt Libby still fretted over Celia, a set habit, focusing now on her health, for rather quickly the bloom of Celia's face and figure was gone. She looked wilted by her misfortune. Aunt Libby hid her cigarettes but Celia accepted the intrusion as love-inspired, and just bought some more. Celia had developed a persistent allergy to pollens and grasses and her blue eyes seemed to have lost a portion of sight, were streaked with irritated vessels that accentuated the paleness of her skin, the prominence of her thin nose. It didn't help her sneezing that she smoked so continually. Aunt Libby coaxed her to eat.

Jimmy began to come around the house again. To us Celia was almost like another aunt, her life settling into a foreseeable pattern; she could have been the one having a baby with the father thousands of miles away. She seemed to allow Jimmy to take her out because he wanted to so much, doing it for him rather than for herself.

Sometimes Celia would go out gambling with Gram in the evenings. Then, one day, Gram said, "I'm thinking of taking me a little trip before I die," which was partly a taunt to Aunt Libby, who never wanted to think it was possible for Gram to die, who said Gram would outlast the whole bunch of us. Gram took Celia along to Hawaii. They brought home a coconut and snapshots of the two of them wearing leis around their necks, with the other people on the tour, older men in flowered shirts and their wives, who watched the hula girls with careful smiles on their faces. Celia's smile was much the same.

Jimmy, pitifully missing her, not eating, almost as distraught as when she had been engaged to Phillip, took leave from his job and flew out to Los Angeles to meet her. And when they came back they were engaged. Kindhearted Celia, no longer beautiful, devoted to needy creatures, blew her nose continually; all the flowering tropical plants had been wretched for her condition. Again she suffered asthmatic attacks. Jimmy displayed the patience and devotion of a saint, qualities she said she expected would make for a fine father. Celia's obsession with motherhood, which she got from Louanne's pregnancy, remained her lone passion and she had questioned Gram almost nonstop about the rearing of children. Gram was reluctant and gruff, because she was done with that business, thought children pretty much raised themselves if you had plenty of them. Good riddance—one compensation for being old and ugly.

Afterwards Gram referred to the trip as Celia's wedding present. Uncle Dan said it was just like her to think up a wedding gift that left out the husband entirely, but then again he couldn't think of a more appropriate introduction to the family. Jimmy was just grateful that Celia at last was his. He must have noticed, as we did, that she was not the same girl he had first loved; we talked of her bygone beauty and charm in legendary terms, as if it might have been something we made up. Their wedding was quiet, in front of the fireplace, beside the dried-up coconut, and right away they left for Beaumont, Texas, where Jimmy had been transferred by his company.

After they drove away we went up to Celia's room and lay on the bed, still in our good clothes. The call of the mourning doves across the fields went back and forth; we wondered whether we were the only ones to hear it. Jenny got up and turned on Celia's phonograph. She dropped the needle and then all we heard was Dave Brubeck.

PART TWO: GRANDAD

For as long as we could remember we had been together in the house which established the center of the known world. When we were younger we woke in the mornings while it was still dark. Grandad would be clumping out of his back room and down the hall to the bathroom, phantom-like in his long underwear. He wore it because he was a farmer, which was why he got up before first light to do the chores. In the two iron beds in the attic room there were the four of us—Celia and Jenny, who were sisters, Anne and Katie, sisters too, like our mothers, who were sisters. Sometimes we watched each other, knew differences. But most of the time it was as though the four of us were one and we lived in days that gathered into one stream of time, undifferentiated and communal.

Beyond the window glass the spruce trees were black and the sky ran silver around their silhouettes. The day smelled like clear water coming in through the open window which our mothers said must be raised at night for health and inspiration. Our mothers believed in nature, its curative and restorative power, trusted its beneficent guardianship. We were given fresh-squeezed juice with breakfast, two vegetables with every dinner, and were put to bed early. Other than that, we were left alone. They spoke among themselves in whispers, they who had their own mysteries, concerns; they left us to the tutelage of the wild and natural world. The doors of the house were always open to the drive, which turned at the lilac and rose hedges, and led to the barn at the head of the ravine and woods, the barn there like an outpost, mysterious and alluring.

One thing was forbidden. Any fighting among ourselves was punished consistently and severely—no listening to "She did this," or that. We were to protect each other, they seemed to say, for who else would? So we bit and scratched each other at night in bed under the covers, hiding the marks from our mothers.

When we heard Grandad again, the stairs creaking, we slipped out of bed, snatching our jeans and cotton shirts off the floor, nothing more to dressing than that. We were mixed up as sisters, Jenny and Katie with dark skin and eyes and Anne and Celia redheads; but we were alike in other ways, tall for our ages with long legs and large hands, like our Grandad. Passing along through the second-floor hall we saw bad-tempered Rossie asleep in his bed. If we woke him, later in the day one or all of us would pay for it. We tiptoed by; Rossie's head was a silky brown fluff on the pillow, snuggled like a little creature out of the woods. Katie thumbed her nose. Anne grabbed her as though she'd made a noise.

Next to Rossie was Aunt Rachel's door, closed; all the doors would be closed until late morning if no one disturbed the sleepers: Aunt Libby, Celia and Jenny's mother, asleep in another room, soon to be alone because Uncle Dan would leave for the store. Gram in her room, alone, because she and Grandad had two separate rooms at opposite ends of the hall. And then Aunt Grace, Anne and Katie's mother, alone too because her husband, Neil, was at their home in Illinois. She had come back to the farm for some reason we didn't know. All the sleeping around us: we were aware of the peacefulness like a transforming mist, the waiting house rapt.

Down the drive we hurried after Grandad, still fastening our pants, pulling on a sweater. We could see him in his black barn boots taking great strides, which Katie mocked. When we moved alongside him he didn't say anything and we didn't either. Grandad did not talk to girls or women. Unless he was fighting with Gram—then he yelled. That was one of the reasons we weren't allowed to fight. "We've seen too much of that," our mothers said.

Grandad picked up his hickory stick from the lean-to shed and opened the wide-boarded gate, letting it swing for us to come through, showing us that he knew we were there. We fastened it with the tied sock. He was watching for that. Once we'd forgotten and the pigs got loose; for a long time after, Grandad wouldn't let us near the barn. "Damned little hellions," he'd snarl at us. Now we went behind him into the pasture although we couldn't keep up and he never waited. We heard his voice calling out, "Sucky, sucky," suppliant on the morning's silence, seeming to originate from the wooded hollow; but already the waiting cows heard him and were coming toward us out of the faint dawn light, answering back to Grandad's call, coming like his love-tamed creatures out of the mist. Other times we were afraid of the cows and ran from them, climbed high up into trees, shivering at their wild rolling eyes, but with Grandad we stayed close, letting them come all around us, and then we turned with him and started up the incline of pasture, going back to the barn that was still dark, with the lighter sky banking it.

"Ho now," Grandad would say every little bit, talking easy so as not to disturb them. His breath lifted into the air with the cows' steamy breath, with ours, veils drawing from the earth, its sleeping solitude removed. "Blow away the morning dew," we could remember Aunt Elinor singing.

"Sweet Sal, Daisy, Belle, Matty," they were Grandad's gals; we could hear it as he urged them along, although they were going forward, as anxious as he. Golden brown or spotted black and white, they all looked pretty much alike to us. Gradually, as it lightened up, he said more to them and it was peculiar at first, always hard for us to know he was the same man who was otherwise so silent—sitting in his window corner up at the big house, listening to the radio and playing endless rounds of solitaire.

"Git on over there," he snarled to the heifers in the barnyard, who hadn't learned yet; sometimes he'd strike them across their foolish gentle-looking faces and they'd leap up and scatter out of his way. "Now you just stand still here," he'd murmur to the cow he was fixing to milk, and he'd draw up the old backless chair to sit on and settle the pail into the straw. "You always got to fight me," he'd say, and soothe the beast with his huge knowing hands before drawing downward for the milk to come. "Now, now . . . you want old Jake to help ya, don't ya? Ya little cross-eyed daughter of a whore," his hands and voice stroking. Then we would hear the milk spraying, making the zinc pail sound. By then it was almost bright day outside the windows. Where the glass was broken we could see clearly through the broken webs and feel the cool fresh morning. Around us we could hear the exultation of waking creatures, so distant from the house full of sleeping women. "Stingy dried-down bitch," Grandad cooed. When the calico cat slinked past he squirted milk right into her expectant mouth.

Now Grandad was really talking. He had forgotten we were there. He talked to himself. Up at the house our mothers laughed about it, not for him to hear. To us it came natural enough from him, seemed another of the low brute voices, more felt or sensed than heard—the animals nudging their boxes, chewing, mouthing the grain Grandad handed around. "Yepee," he said. "Snavely won't git this one here. Not for free. He'll have to pay the piper, all righty. Ninety myself, oughta bring at least double that, maybe he'll take to your looks, though—string-bean yeller gal." He'd slap the cow on her flank for emphasis and she glanced around as if she was ready to skedaddle. But Grandad was already her familiar and she only hitched her feet around on the straw and flicked her tail. Grandad was bigger than the cows, it seemed, bigger than all the other men we'saw who came around the farm, except maybe Tom Buck, who'd played tackle in college. It was a bigness of bone, as though he were solid calcium with only skin stretched over him. Sitting on the manger ledge across from him, we half listened. "Now, Miss Betsy, I'm going to braid up this here nothing of a tail with a silky piece of ribbon and put ye on the block. I reckon the day will come when you'll wish yourself back with ol' Jake." More than the milking business, Grandad was in speculation: buying and selling cattle for profit, wheeling and dealing. We'd seen him at an auction, taller, darker than anyone else, gypsy dark and silent, a man to be reckoned with. Until he got to drinking. Then, Gram told us, he'd lock in on some notion and outbid for pure stubbornness, more than once ending up in terrible fights. Or coming home with the most dearly bought, driest cow in the county.

After a while of watching the milk foam to the top of the pails, Katie would lean over to Anne, pointing to the soft pink teat with Grandad's hand on it, and say, "Someday somebody's going to do that to you." Anne was eleven, developing breasts already and ashamed of it, hiding when she dressed, so that Aunt Rachel would tease, "What do you think you've got there that we haven't seen a million of?" Anne with her red hair and most of the time her face red, because she was what Gram called a wild hyena, forever excited, talking all the time, flashing with anger. Or ashamed. Katie said those things to rile her—she knew that, we knew that. Sometimes two of us or three would watch each other, watching the differences, feeling the differences working. We could watch Anne burning. She was big like Grandad, big-boned, way bigger than she should have been at eight, nine and ten. Katie was younger and quiet but in a sly way was mean sometimes, like Grandad too in her way, bad on purpose like an outlaw, and would sometimes say anything, do anything, pull her pants down for anybody to see—she had done that once for the colored boys who lived over the hill. No one had moved or laughed, them or us, all of us shocked. She drank out of the creek where the sewage drained. Once, on a dare, she took a barn spike and whacked Jenny with it, the wound requiring five stitches. Gram said it was Anne and Katie's father, Neil, who made them act so wild.

Now Anne was steaming, holding back but poised, so that we thought one more thing and she would leap on her sister and strangle her to death. It was like watching Gram and Grandad get ready to fight.

But the moment passed without death. Anne flew up the ladder to the loft, running from her hate and shame, and we followed. From the distant rafters we heard the soft call of the doves. We forgot what had happened, running over the upper floor, making the cows edgy so that Grandad snarled out, poking with his pitchfork on the ceiling boards, "You goddamn kids. I'll hide ye," which made us go faster away from him. Into the hay. With all our scraping and scrambling we set the rafter birds into flight, wraithlike through the half dark with their sad and dreamy cries, the darkness glowing like a picture of night with the light starred through a million chinks. We lay on the hay, resting, suspended. We strained toward that deep night as if we might lift into unfathomable reaches of delight. "Hi," we heard Grandad down below, "hold up there sweet little bitch-gal," calming the beasts. Katie said, "Grandad loves Daisy," and giggled so that we all started to laugh.

We went up farther into the barn, to the top level, where the little slatted windows blazed in a luminous stillness. The sun was full up. We began flinging ourselves off into the darkness below the loft; faster and farther, spinning in the dust clouds we raised out of the hay, and then Anne began to bounce off the bales onto the second level and then to the wagon and the floor. We all did it. We would never fall. "Watch out," we cried, and left the world behind.

It was the city dummies who came to visit us sometimes who made mistakes. They'd try to outshow us, just because they were boys; we who lived there, who belonged there, knew where all the posts stood, the holes, and could have jumped out the windows into the valley of Lost Creek, far below, and never been hurt. Once a distant cousin came and Rossie sneered right off that he wouldn't be able to make the leaps, even to the first level. We all showed our style, calling out how easy it was. But the cousin was more daring than we expected and he followed everything we did. Finally he swung himself on the grappling fork rope, higher than any of us, then let go. At the second-story beam he grazed against the side of the stacked bales, lost his balance and fell all the way, lying still and white with a thread of scarlet seeping from his mouth.

"He's died," Katie said, as if we were just waiting for somebody to be dead.

For a while after that we were forbidden to play there, but the cousin recovered and as Gram said, "All's well that ends well. Damn fool younguns." Soon they forgot us again, forgot to notice where we played or what we did, as long as we were together. We went back to the haymow and learned to ride the grappling fork better than anybody.

We kept our deck of cards hidden on the rafter ledge, which we could reach only when the barn was full of hay, as sometimes it was for years, because Grandad was regularly selling off his stock and then changing his mind and starting over. Gram said she didn't care what he did as long as he left her out of it. Katie started to talk a little dirty; she said there were poo-poos on the floor. And with that we were climbing up to the level where we stashed the cards, reaching up quickly into the dark rafters where the rats clawed their swift way. The limp sour deck of cards was Grandad's and they smelled the way he did, as did the corner of the living room where he sat to play solitaire and nod off to sleep, spitting from time to time into a Maxwell House coffee tin. It was rusty and stank, Gram said, made her living room a filthy pisspot. Once when they fought over the can, Gram picked it up and headed out to the kitchen. She said she was not having it anymore; she said it was enough to put up with him. Grandad just kept sitting in the green plush chair, chewing. Then he aimed, spat directly where the can should have been. We heard the splat of it when it hit the wall and watched it dribble down onto the carpet.

Aunt Grace was crying while she scrubbed at the carpet, but she didn't make any noise; you could hear just the rag moving. Gram was still standing in the back doorway, screaming down the drive toward the barn, where Grandad had vanished as if swallowed up, his fist still raised after he'd snarled "Jezebel!" back at her. "Horse-piss, shit-face," Gram repeated until finally she choked into silence and hurled the tin can after him onto the dirt.

Our mothers wouldn't allow us to talk like Gram though they did themselves when they were mad enough. When we were alone we did it for fun. It made us feel bold and powerful. In the same way we played strip poker; it was just something that came over us, the wanting to play, the knowing we were going to, only putting it off for a little, so we could feel the excitement working in us. We were breathing hard, trembling even, when Katie threw the crumpled deck among us. Jenny might say, "Maybe we shouldn't." But there was no stopping us.

Katie started to deal the hands. Because the cards had been through so much already, it took a long time. "You're slower'n shit," Anne barked, tough as nails, grabbing the cards. Taking over. Whenever we acted movie scenes she had to be the cowgirl or the streetwalker or she wouldn't play. Now she pretended she knew how to play poker, but she didn't. None of us did. We just made up rules as we went along, proprietary and quarrelsome about them. We called the game five-card draw and used kernels of corn for chips, only we didn't know what to do about them. None of that mattered, because all we wanted to do was undress in front of each other. First our barrettes and shirts went into the center, except Anne's, for she was winning every hand. Then Celia called "Double or nothing" and Anne lost, which meant we could get dressed again, while she had to get naked in front of us.

The smartness ran out of her face. She looked at us. Nobody could help her. We didn't move even for our shirts, while the slants of light glinted off the silver hair clasps.

Anne stood up. "I know what you're thinking, about me." Even though Celia was the oldest, Anne was more developed than the rest of us, who had hardly started. When she went into the bathroom she shut the door, would have locked it if she could. Rolfe Barker, a boy from down the highway, had taken her into a back room once and put his hands on her; had made her bleed. It was wildness in her that had made her sneak off with him into that far back room. Then he'd forced her. We were thinking of that now and the rats, swollen big as cats, that swam in the grain bins, maybe blood trickling in their fur, human blood, like on the posters tacked up at the fairgrounds.

"Fraidy cat," Katie whispered. She snickered.

The blood made a splash over Anne's face then and she leaned over to unfasten her sandals, when Katie, with that ornery streak aroused, scrawny as broom straw, snatched the cards out of the center, crying, "Fifty-two pickup." They went sailing and spinning into the air, setting the birds in their restless circles overhead while the cards settled somewhere in the dark; last of all the six of spades fluttered back into the midst of us as though it bore a significant numerology. But we were having to tear Anne off Katie, who was on her back with her arms and legs flailing, blurred so that it seemed she'd grown extras, Anne holding her down with one arm and socking into her stomach. "You spoiled it," she was yelling. Anne never knew what she wanted. Katie was moaning, "Doesn't hurt, can't hurt, won't hurt." We yanked Anne's hair.

"Caught ya," Rossie said, and we nearly fell off the edge of the high platform, because we hadn't put our shirts on yet and his face was grinning up over the shelf—he was getting his eyeful. "I'll tell if you don't," his eyes were saying, coaxing us to do more; Rossie, even bigger than Anne and after us for peep shows all the time. "I'll tell," he said, knowing our fighting was forbidden. We laughed right out, the fight between Anne and Katie stopped for that time at least, although we knew it could start up again quicker than fire. We knew he'd never tell. Ha! He'd be the lucky one if *we* didn't. And right then he started to roll a cigarette as he leaned up against the bales, every little while spitting off into the hay, clear spit, white like sea foam. But if Grandad caught him smoking in the barn we knew it would be something awful; something like the time we'd heard of when he'd rammed Uncle Gabe up into the radiator and banged his head time and again against it while Aunt Elinor clawed at his back and some of the others ran to the neighbors for help. We didn't dare tell. When Rossie struck up the match the smoke was spiraling on the air. It smelled strong, streaming blue toward the high slatted window. He sat and stretched out his legs and then folded one over the other; he looked like a man himself, already taller than his mother, Aunt Rachel, and solidly built. It was scary to smell smoke in the barn. And we were afraid to tell.

"Grandad'll tan you," Katie said.

Rossie narrowed his eyes. "Fuck you." That was the most powerful thing a man could say. When Rossie said it, it was like something he'd stabbed right into the center of us. In the quiet now, listening for him, we could hear Grandad discussing matters with his cows.

"I'm telling," that renegade Katie said, the impudent gleam in her eyes that made "tattletale" no abuse at all once she got going, that made no amount of punishment too much. Katie was the youngest of us all and we were supposed to watch out for her, take care of her. But we couldn't do any more with her than we could with the weather or time.

Rossie sat and began to pull on each of his fingers so they made a popping noise. He smoked and spit. Then we heard Grandad's talking coming nearer, toward the ladder, and Rossie looked as if he was going to swallow the cigarette and we left him, went flying down the levels and across the scarred planking and leaped out over the two-foot-high doorsill, transformed by the freshness, the immaculateness, whirled into the forgetfulness of each new moment.

We went around the side of the barn. Inside, Grandad was telling himself, "By spring it'll fetch a dollar." Trying his best to outsmart the world, Gram said. She usually added that he'd never been smart enough nor had the foresight to bring in anything before it rained. Still Grandad had bought a pair of glasses at the five-and-dime store and there were evenings when he mumbled to himself over the farm journals, making notes with the stub of a pencil. Gram said it was typical of a man that now he was on easy street, where she'd put him, he figured to improve himself.

Behind the barn was Grandad's personal graveyard, boneyard really. Whatever he slaughtered or when one of the animals just fell dead, like Sally did when she got the blind staggers, still in the traces, Grandad would haul the part that was left to the back and leave it, and soon enough the buzzards and weather took care of it.

"The smell is terrible," his daughters said. "It's disgraceful." Their faces showed it, screwed up against him.

Grandad didn't answer them. Sometimes he'd sprinkle white lime over the ground and the decaying flesh. The smell was a little like what came from the eggs Rossie took out of the nests of the broody hens and smashed up against the side of the barn, so he could show us the little chicks inside and the blood they fed on. When Grandad found out, that was the only time we saw him smash anybody; he just raised his hand and Rossie went flying up against the side of the barn and then lay there.

As we walked, the calcium dust blew up white onto our feet. The bones crunched and splintered and teeth rolled loose on the ground. We could have been walking in the valley of Gehenna. Rossie had disappeared. Then Katie jumped out; she came from behind one of the spindly locust trees that grew there in a single clump. "The Philistines are coming," she yelled, jabbing a jawbone within inches of us, spiking around with a sawed-off horn.

"I'm Delilah," Celia said, and went over to couch herself where the cornfield began. The rest of us sprang at each other with spears of bone. Teeth toppled from jaws as we kicked them. Celia fanned herself with a fern frond. Anne ran into the middle. She'd taken leaves and sticks and stuck them into her wild red hair. Content for once not to squabble with Celia over who would be the great beauty, she was a mighty Samson. She'd tied her tee-shirt around her chest, uncovering one shoulder. Twirling a cow tail, she snapped it on the air. "I have slain the lion with my bare hands," she cried. "My strength is in my hair, lips that have never touched wine." Sometimes we played to the end of the story, with Samson's terrible blinding and God's revenge. But this time, when we were jabbing around, Katie rushed right into Anne on purpose and rammed her leg, which brought a quick spurt of blood. "Her tittie's showing," Katie smirked, and we looked at the unsightly lump of white flesh plopped out over the tied shirt.

"That hurt," Anne screamed, tears in her eyes, and she kicked Katie so that she fell backwards and then she shoved her down, smearing Katie's black hair into the dust. Katie kicked and flailed like an overturned bug. Anne was crying and gasping and Katie was screaming. We yanked at Anne but she was strong and kept on pounding. Then Rossie was there; he'd probably been spying the whole time. He whacked Anne's breath out of her with one powerful sock so that she fell on the ground, not moving except to double up her knees, gagging out of her mouth. Then Rossie kicked her chest, his brown boots falling like smashing rocks. "Filthy slut. Whore," he said, looking down on her.

He went away. Anne cried for a long time, the tears rilling through the pale dust film on her face, which was ordinarily so pink and warm-looking. We helped her up. Straightened out her hair, unfastening twigs which broke off some of the ends.

"I'll tell what he did," Jenny said, and she would; at times she was like a mother, protecting us when no one else would.

When Anne could speak she sobbed out, "He kicked me, kicked and kicked. I'll die. I couldn't breathe. I wanted you to help but I couldn't breathe." Sorrow for her swept over us.

"Come on, we'll wash your face," Jenny said. We trudged through the bones, down the grassy hill beside the barn and then into the barnyard where the water ran. It was from a wellspring which came through an iron pipe under the barn and ran continually into a black and rusted caldron. We splashed our faces where the animals put their tender spongy faces and sucked. Like them we laid our lips across the surface of the water. When we had enough we took turns standing in the pot and soaked our jeans through, getting all of ourselves clean and cold. We waded barefoot, sloshing in manure up to our ankles, then washed again. The swamp of manure was warm and sucked around us as if in some way it could hold us safe in that time and place.

Under the corncrib a batch of kittens drank from their mother. When we tried to reach them the mother scratched out at us. The kittens were newborn, with tiny squinched-up eyes. "We'll be back later," we told them. "We'll have to hide you." Gram didn't like so many cats hanging around; sometimes there were as many as thirty on the back porch. They were diseased, she told us. Distemper. When she couldn't stand it anymore she had Grandad put all he could fit into a gunnysack and take them to the pond. "We'll save you," we promised, going out of the entrance shed into the bright morning. Over the tin barn roof the sun gleamed so that, wet and shivering from the cold water, we were irridescent too.

"I'm starved," Anne said. We remembered—the house, mothers; up the gravel, our shoes in our hands, we raced over long morning shadows, after Anne, the biggest and fastest with the toughest feet, the most delirious, the wild hyena. She bragged all the time that she could whip any boy with one hand, sometimes doing it. She would shake out her storm of red hair, boast that she hadn't combed it in a week, in a year, would never comb it, climbed all the way to the rafters to jump. Jenny tried to calm her down, warning in black-eyed seriousness, "Sometimes things happen. Be more careful."

Before we got into the house there was the smell of coffee coming onto the porch. Grandad's straw-and-manure-crusted boots were set beside the fir-board cupboards and the shelves that overflowed with so much junk nobody could find anything. So we knew that he'd come up for his coffee and that this morning there wouldn't be a fight. It was a kind of signal that he hadn't worn the boots inside, soiling the rugs. "You got up," we cried to our mothers, Libby and Grace, who were at the table. "You got up early," we raved, finding their unexpected appearance something marvelous. They were in their bright-colored robes, drinking the lovely strong coffee, their eyes dark and shiny just out of sleep. The printed oilcloth was in the sun, the myriad surface cracks interfacing.

"High time," Gram said from the pantry, where she was peeling apples. "And you younguns ramming already. Dripping on my floor."

"Gram's baking pies," we sang as we raced up the stairs to change, with still a full day ahead, a day holding everything we could ever want. Behind us she hollered, "Goddamn it, stop that running. You, Anne." Because whenever there was noise and commotion she blamed Anne, knew without looking, she said, that Anne was in the thick of it.

"Up with the birds," Aunt Grace said to Anne when we came back. They all thought Anne was the first to wake, woke the rest of us. "It's no wonder your hair stands on end," she said, and tried to smooth it with her long-boned and frail-looking hand, graceful motion like strumming a harp. Still she was smiling along with us, as if it were of no importance, this untidiness and flightiness of her first child, not when we were all together. So they laughed at our long feet, careless spelling, dancing fits, saw us as natural wonders.

"What have you been up to?" Aunt Libby asked, halfheartedly, as if she knew we wouldn't tell.

"Just playing," we said.

"Rossie kicked Anne," Jenny said. "He kicked her over and over. Hard. For nothing." We felt the prickling of fear, revenge. The two sisters exchanged a frown. "It's not right," Aunt Grace said, "beating on girls." We were safe. We all began to accuse him.

"More'n likely she deserved it," Gram said from the pantry, as if she'd like to kick something needing it.

"She couldn't breathe," Jenny insisted. Anne sat quietly knotting her shirt over and over.

"Quit your wrangling," Gram said. "Ain't nobody hurt. Now where in hell's that Rachel. It's time she's up . . . we've got to be going."

"You get her," Aunt Grace told Anne. "You tell her what he did."

Then Anne was racing up the back stairs. We could hear her crashing, like the wild Injun Gram said she was. "Why don't she learn?" Gram asked nobody, said it like all the things she said, as though responding to a steady inner annoyance like heartburn.

It was quiet upstairs; already Aunt Rachel had lured Anne into her bed. We'd all been sent there by Gram with that same mission: Rachel was always having to be dragged out of bed in the mornings. She'd be late—for work, for church, for life. But Aunt Rachel with her siren charms adroitly seduced the one that had been sent to rouse her. And always we succumbed. In her bed it was soft and warm and she put her arms around us and snuggled up. Enclosed in her den of curves and billows, we were tempted to melt into sleep, to be absorbed into her dreams. But we were embarrassed too, too close, and we squiggled and tossed about. Then she would tickle us on the feet or under the arms, her hand moving lightly while the rest of her lay still, pretending sleep, her rosy cheek into the sheet with her dark hair in unrestrained spirals about her heart-shaped face. As we started to giggle and lurch about the bed she would begin to croon some childish song in her liquid and throaty alto. "Cat's in the cream jar, what'll I do?" tickling us out of the covers and onto the floor. It was hopeless. Anne would never get it told about Rossie; Aunt Rachel didn't want to hear it because she didn't know any more than anyone else what to do about her son.

She came into the kitchen through the back-stairway door, Anne behind her, bounding down the stairs. "Can't that youngun walk?" Gram muttered. She was scooping lard from the five-gallon pail by the stove, taking it in her hands. Aunt Grace said to Anne as she came, "Come over here and sit. I want you to calm down."

"I am calm, Mother," Anne said. We all laughed in her face. Then she sat down. On her red face was the hard crystal glitter we'd seen when she was pounding Katie.

"Anne hit me," Katie said then, trying for trouble in her own sly way. But this morning nobody listened to her. We were making toast, piece after piece, while Gram was whirling her way through four pies at once, asking Celia to light the oven, to hand her the plates. Gram liked Celia best, maybe because she was quieter than the rest of us, and didn't mind doing errands—Gram always had one of us getting her glasses from the bureau or walking for the mail, one thing or another fifty times a day.

"We oughta leave soon," Gram said to Aunt Rachel.

Aunt Rachel smiled lazily over her coffee cup, legs crossed. She lit up a cigarette, the only one of the five sisters who smoked. "And what's the point of being early and sitting around in Cleveland all day? Doctors are never on time. It's much nicer here." She had drawn around her the raspberry silken robe and we could see the creamy fullness of her bosom, bare where it strained at the fabric. All of Aunt Rachel was swelling, white and soft. "Anyway, the trip's not long when I'm driving."

"I ain't going if we're flying," Gram said.

"Of course you're going." Aunt Rachel looked around at us. "You'd go with me, wouldn't you, girls?"

We'd go with her. Anywhere. Every Sunday it was Aunt Rachel who took us to Sunday school while the others slept.

With her we were always late, eating toast in the car and helping her to zip her dress while she was driving, and laughing at the fun of it, of being nearly too late to bother going, the car rattling over the brick street, down Belden and Highland, over the iron bridge at Keeler. We'd see the speedometer go over eighty more than once on every trip. When she'd parked, the doors sprang open and we spilled onto the sidewalk, chattering and laughing at her because now she put her nose high into the air and walked stuck-up, whispering to us to be quiet and act right, because Mrs. Peabody had nominated her as president of the Ladies' Aid. "You don't want them to think I'm not fit," she said. The very idea was absurd. She belonged only to us and she could never be a lady. And neither would we. We spread our legs to wrap around the chair legs.

"I need to stop downtown first," Gram said.

"I never heard of such a thing. Can't it wait?"

"No. It can't."

"Well, I'd like to know why not," Aunt Rachel said, more seriously.

"I've got business." Business. The three women at once looked concerned.

Aunt Libby sniffed. "It's that Hank Browning. You're selling him that field."

"I am." Gram looked stubborn enough to hang herself.

"Does Dad know?" Aunt Grace asked.

"I told him. Likely he's heard one way or another by now. He don't use it anyhow. Not for anything that counts. Piddling."

"He won't like it," Aunt Grace said.

Gram stuck her neck out toward the other room, where Grandad slept in his chair, and she spoke as if to him, for him. "I'd like to know what he can do about it. It's mine. The whole place is. He can count himself lucky if I don't sell it all. One day I will too." She marched across the kitchen with the rolling pin and splashed flour on the sideboard, her stuck-out lip giving her face the spouting look of a teakettle.

Aunt Grace went over close beside her and stood with her head pressed against the cupboards, but Gram elbowed her aside, moving the rolling pin sideways, then back and forth.

"Mama," she said. "You don't need the money. Not now. And Dad is looking after the place. It's important to him."

We could hear Gram, though her voice was now low, without anger or blame, just resignation. "And who do you think's going to pay your bills, Grace? Not likely that husband of yours. Someone's got to think of that."

"Shut up, Momma," Aunt Rachel snapped. "Just shut up."

"That's not your only reason," Aunt Grace said to Gram. Tears were spilling down her face while her fingers automatically crimped the edges of the crust Gram had cut to fit the bottom of the pie tin. There was flour on both of them.

"No, it ain't. Maybe I've got about a million. And you've dug yourself into the same hole, Grady." Gram had used the name the little girls had called Aunt Grace when she was the oldest girl at home, the one taking care of them while Gram had been boiling herself into old age over a washtub and the canning baths. Just then it seemed that Gram and Aunt Grace might still be the ones taking care of all of us, seeing to the wash and meals a long time ago.

"Sometime in there I quit," Aunt Grace said. "Just lost my fight, I guess." She was looking down but not noticing what she was doing, for she was going over and over the same edge and Gram saw that and for the first time put her hand out and touched Aunt Grace. They smiled at each other. Then Aunt Grace threw back her head and her arms started flying out and she finished up another crust nearly as fast as Gram could do it. Aunt Rachel and Aunt Libby stared in pure amazement, which made Aunt Grace and Gram shrug and eyebrow each other. The respect between them was evident then, because each knew the other could be depended on, had been depended on in fact, to work from dawn until dark without a rest and without making a big to-do about it, all the while listening out for the kids and having supper on the table for a man when he came home. Gram said to Aunt Grace, smiling openly, "Them two was raised with silver spoons. What do they know?"

She whipped through the pies and put them into the oven and hung up her apron. She looked at Aunt Grace and decided to finish saying what she had on the tip of her tongue. "I seen more damned men than you would believe, drinking themselves crazy, killing each other over nothing. And their women dying with babies or something else unnecessary. But you can't tell them. I'm through trying. You can't tell a young gal nothing, nor an older one neither. Not anything she don't want to hear." First they had been talking about Grandad but now Gram was trying to talk about something more, though Aunt Grace wasn't listening and instead put her finger to her lips and frowned in toward the room where we could hear Grandad snoring. "Don't do anything to get him mad, Momma," she said.

Gram sighed as if she'd worn out suddenly. Then she was rushed again. "I need to leave early, I'm telling you. Either that or I won't go." She flared up at Aunt Grace. "And when I need your advice, young lady, I'll ask for it."

"Is May coming?" Aunt Grace asked, and went to sit down. Her eyes were sunken in, looked darker than we'd ever seen them.

"She's not sure yet that she can get away."

"She shouldn't," Aunt Grace said. "It's too much. I've got the rest of you with me. There's always somebody who doesn't show up and then May has to do either the cleaning or the laundry." Aunt May was the oldest sister. Her husband had died just after he quit his regular job to build and operate the hotel business, which now Aunt May was dependent on, the twenty rooms more than she could manage. It told on her, the muscles in her face and body often twitching, her slenderness already gaunt.

We sat and watched the horses in the orchard. Before the apples dropped, Grandad let his workhorses graze among the trees and they, in sublime goodwill, glided in and out of sight. Gram came down from dressing and put her apple and cherry pies on the sill to cool. Then she went to sit in the car. Every few minutes she would lean on the horn and yell for the others to come, getting the names all confused, the living and the dead.

Right before they were ready, Aunt Rachel still in her slip, the phone rang. It was Uncle Dan, asking to speak to Aunt Grace. We heard her saying, "I know you do. There isn't anything else to say. I guess we'll know this evening." When she hung up the phone she stared out the window of the dining room. We were watching from the stairs. Then Gram snapped her out of her thoughts by drumming on the horn.

Aunt Rachel had been staring at Aunt Grace and the horn made her furious. She raised the window as if she would tear it from the sash and screamed out, "Momma, for God's sake." Tears were suddenly running down her face. She bent over and wiped her eyes with one finger, using the hem of her slip.

Then Aunt Grace was saying goodbye to Anne and Katie. "You two be good now and no fighting. Aunt May will call later." To Anne: "Try to stop hopping up and down, and comb your hair, dear. Maybe you could read for a while. And be good to your sister. Remember, she's the youngest." Aunt Grace wore a dark blue linen dress with embroidered white silk birds flying up at the throat. Smiling tremulously, she opened the back door to the car and slid in. Aunt Rachel drove. The car started up the drive, all the sisters turning to wave their hands out the back, Gram bolt upright beside Aunt Rachel, face forward, her summer-white pocketbook upright on her lap. We ran behind the car, up the drive as fast as we could go, barefoot, running through the dust and cinders thrown up by the speeding car. The horses in the orchard began to trot toward the highway too.

"Where are they going?" Katie asked, her face tear-streaked.

"Don't be dumb," Anne said. We all knew that Aunt Grace was going to Cleveland. She'd been there before, when she had her operation. We didn't want to talk about it. We lay on the grass under the oak trees which were in a line at the edge of the highway. The grass was pale and feathery. Cars passed on the road, the ground vibrating, and it felt as though we were still connected with the car that had left us behind.

We hung around the house. Aunt May called to see how we were doing and said she'd be over later with some ice cream. She said Valerie was under the weather. Valerie was her daughter, another cousin, a little older than we were.

"Is she sick?" We wondered if Valerie had locked herself in the bathroom again.

"No, it's just her time of the month. Is Dad there?"

We'd forgotten Grandad. We wanted to go with him to the mill. He would leave us. "We have to go," we told Aunt May, and grabbed our shoes. In the hall we nearly collided with Grandad, who was padding in his stocking feet, his long underwear showing like a shirt under suspenders. He wore it all summer long.

"Quit your rammin'." He went into the kitchen and carried a few things to the table and sat down. We stopped, uneasy about being alone with him in the house. His lunch was cold cereal with half the sugar bowl emptied on top of it. "If you're going to do it why don't you stab yourself. It's quicker," Gram would snarl at him.

"Where's Rossie?" we asked. Grandad didn't answer, the question gone as though it had fallen down a well. He finished his cornflakes, then filled the bowl with Ritz crackers and dumped his coffee over them. They bloated and dissolved. Gram said he'd been feeding pigs so long he ate like one; sometimes he cooked a rank mash for them on a hot plate in the cellar.

Since no one was there to care, we made ourselves sugar sandwiches on white bread and went onto the back porch to eat. Grandad went to the sink and began to splash and snort, washing up. Gram would have had a hissy, him spitting there, using her sink for his slops the minute her back was turned. Other times she swore at him for not washing all over except a few times a year, when he changed his underwear. She made a great fuss over the event—once she held his long johns suspended from a stick to burn in the trash can. After Grandad washed, we heard him shuffle toward the living room and later he snored. Peaceable, we waited on the porch in the dappling noontime. In the Mason jars stacked up dusty and fly-specked on the side shelves, in the broken-webbed snowshoes hung there, the heap of rusty hinged traps waiting this long time to be oiled and set to catch something in the night, was the visible imprint of the past we were rooted in.

The way Gram told it was that all she had ever had in life was kids and work and useless men and what she wanted, and had earned besides, was to be left alone. Part of that was nobody accusing her or expecting anything from her. She took care of herself, did her own personal laundry, cleaned her room, cooked her own supper, and what's more, did the breakfast dishes for the whole family. Plenty. Beyond that she felt put upon, although she continually nagged her daughters and grandchildren to see to one chore or another, as if she couldn't rest easy, didn't really believe anyone else would take responsibility. At eleven she had been sent out to work on a nearby farm, to take on many of the household duties of a mother of nine children who was dying of tuberculosis. That was the end of her childhood. "My ma hated it," she told us, "but they was feeding me instead of me taking from the family. All the same my ma hated it."

We were about eleven ourselves when we first paid attention, playing all day, quarreling over our share of the supper dishes. The stories she told seemed made up to impress us, to wheedle sympathy and make us feel guilty. But we knew for certain how she'd felt about one thing, staying with a dying woman, because Aunt Grace was already sick.

Gram had been Lil Bradley then, and the two miles she walked or rode, clutching the mane of an unsaddled horse, was usually covered in the dark—going before sunrise, returning after nightfall. As soon as she got there she took up the baby, shook down the ashes in the cook stove and, the baby on her hip, prepared breakfast for the family—this only the beginning of a day that wouldn't end until the dark miles home.

In later years Gram liked to be driven the thirty miles south to Marland, where she was raised, and she would point out the fields she'd crossed then and we would wonder how she'd ever been a thin wiry girl in a cotton wash dress. She would point proudly to the house where she was born, by now refurbished with a grandness she had never known. Though her father had built it, he had been unable to give it the touches—small-paned windows, shutters and lattice detailing—which made it, when we saw it, so substantial and original-looking. Gram was possessive about it, even then, as though in some way it still belonged to her and affirmed what she had become. She would smile out of her late-model Pontiac, nod and point. Even if the present owners were in evidence, she would stare just as greedily, bold by right, so that Aunt Libby would have to get out of the car and explain our interest. Or rather hers and Gram's, because we kids were only thinking of the ice cream Gram would buy us at the dairy. We had already seen her old house a hundred times. It was not until we were much older that we wished we'd paid attention, although Gram was always more interested in how people had improved things than in what the house had been like before— rather like appreciating her connection with a friend who had risen in the world. We had to dig her past out of ourselves as much as out of her.

For the most part, Lil had grown up without her father. The 1890s were a time of speculation and fortune hunting and her father was one of the many men who couldn't stay home. Lil's uncle, her mother's brother, had gone to California in the years of building the cross-country railroads and the family heard all sorts of reports about his associations with the wealthy and famous. They didn't believe most of what they heard, but Lil's father developed a frantic anxiety that he might miss the boat— remain at home in poverty and wistfulness.

Time and time again he went out to the oilfields of the West.

Back home, out of money and chagrined, he stayed and worked the land awhile, until it seized him, the urge to try again, and then he would be gone. They might not hear from him for a year or longer. At first a little money would come for Lil's mother and her six children. Then nothing, until he was back with them once more. Until the time he was gone for so long they thought he might be dead and later heard word he was. He had been killed sinking a dry hole in east Texas.

Then Lil's mother became ill and it wasn't long before she was dead too, another victim of tuberculosis. Lil gave up working for the neighbor and went to stay with her older sister, Hat, who lived in town. It was the first Lil had lived anyplace but on an isolated farm and it was a lot more lively than any life she'd known before, different young men seeing her home from church or visiting her in the evening. It was then that the piano arrived, first evidence that her rich uncle might not be entirely a family myth. Ordered from New York, the piano was a gift for their mother. But, too late for her, it was brought down from Cleveland on a wagon bed by Hat's husband and put into her parlor, up against the plank walls, with a rag rug under the stool. Lil took in washing and ironing and with the little extra money she kept, above room and board, paid a woman to start her on the piano.

Then Hat's husband lost an arm in a farm accident and Lil was forced to take another job, to contribute what she could to Hat. By now seventeen, Lil went to live away from home again, six miles out of the town, where she cooked in a farm kitchen, peeling a peck of potatoes before noon, and boiling tubs of salt pork and greens, finally to bed down in a blanketed-off section of a barn loft, where she froze in winter and melted in summer. Once more she was excluded from the little bit of town social life, but she was too exhausted to care, certainly too tired to walk the six miles, and there was no one to take her.

Unless she favored Jacob Krauss. She didn't think much of it at first, his still wanting to see her in the evenings, now riding out from the town, but she figured if it was worth it for him to travel that distance to sit and watch the fire, there wasn't any harm in it. He never did have much talk in him, even as a young man. He was out of the plain people, maybe shunned for something, folks suspected, though no one ever knew his past for sure. But Lil was seventeen and the mystery of Jacob's past was part of what intrigued her—she liked the different way he dressed, in shirts of home-dyed indigo and suspenders, and she liked his quaint old-fashioned manners, so at odds with his rough hard look. Tall and lean, he had straight dark hair falling to frame both sides of his face, and the little habit he had of tossing his hair back showed the strong bones clearly and his slanted, long-lashed eyes; and she began to want him in the way you want something you think will occupy you until Doomsday. The wanting felt like enough. There was no mother to warn her, and the other girls she knew were thrilled with Jacob too and envied her, though there was not a father or mother who would have sanctioned his attentions to their daughter. Lil did not desire the children that would come in a marriage; already she knew their demands well enough. But neither did she fancy the endless monotony of cooking for twenty farmhands every day while guarding herself against the teasing, fresh-mouthed married ones who, sensing her loneliness, determined to break her off and make use of her. Better that she should have her own man and the life he would bring her.

She did not deny it—Jacob drew her. He would sit with no words for her, before the wood stove, watching her continually with his dark, dark eyes, and she began to feel his hunger, so that often she would get up to put more wood in the stove or busy herself at the sink, just to avoid his eyes and hide her trembling. Every night his eyes were watching, wanting her and letting her see it in him; but he wouldn't touch her, not so much as to let a hand graze hers, though when she would pass close beside him she would hear his breathing, harsh and quick. It nearly drove her wild and her mind came to dwell on him nearly every second.

Sometimes, when she lifted up the handle of the stove to stir the wood, the glutted, ashy coals crumbled at the slight touch and something inside her seemed to fragment in the same way.

Lil would plot to forget him. During the day, going about her work, she would plan how she would be gone in the evening when he came. But she never was, and again she'd open the door to him, to his silent and steady need. It got so peculiar between them that neither of them said a word to the other through whole evenings. Lil would back against the wall when he entered and feel the exact dimensions of his body, the insistent presence of his nature. He would pass close to her, nearly touching her, his eyes locking on her, where they would stay fastened through whole evenings. Eons. She forgot time.

It took Hebbard Watson coming to court to change things, or else, Lil thought, they might have jumped together off a cliff to end it, both of them stubborn beyond belief. But Hebbard tied his horse by the gate a time or two, and although Jacob didn't even come to the door, his feelings were plain enough on his face as he stood outside and glared as if he wanted to strangle the horse. Then he tore away in the direction of town without a further glance, though Lil was certain he'd known she watched from behind the parlor curtain. After a third evening of that, Lil was in the kitchen in the morning, peeling through a pail of early yellow apples, thinking about Jacob and his silent withholding, when she heard a commotion on the road. She went to the door and then out in the yard, wearing her flowered apron, her braids frayed with curl. Coming along was a wagon team of six horses driven by Jacob, who was so intent on managing things he didn't even glance up to see her, though they both knew she was there, the same as when they sat beside each other at the fire. The piano from her sister's house was strapped onto the wagon bed, swaddled with quilting and roped down to keep it steady. She watched it pass, slow and resounding, the wagon out of sight but the raised dust keeping its memory a little longer, almost like a song resonating, and Lil knew they would be married. It was the only semblance of a proposal that passed between them.

Married, they moved into rooms up over a store on the town's one street and in the secret dark Jacob touched her and moved himself in her, and though she got accustomed to it, a part of her was more aggravated by his touch than satisfied, and then it came to seem more invasion than touch, his need something he took care of, quick and by dark, by daylight no trace left, as though it had never happened between them. Lil felt resentment rising in her; his tacit denial shamed her, convinced her that he felt he stole something from her, was taking without asking. Every night, nearly, he turned to her and held her against him while, rapid and brutish, he moved in her. She began to be sick to her stomach nearly all day long. Afraid that it was a baby coming, dreading it, she lay under his heaviness, which blocked out any trace of light, and thought: Soon I'll be dead.

Then Jacob became more active in his cattle business. He left her alone, stayed away for days at a time, and Lil began going out to the church for prayer services or hymn sings, a little society one way to distract her mind from continual hating and grieving. Jacob didn't like going to church. He'd left his own religion but some of the teaching stayed with him, that fancy music mixed with religion was an abomination. Though he didn't try to stop her, a few times she'd seen him standing outside the church window staring in. Sometimes she was harmonizing with the schoolteacher and she felt it served Jacob right to see her with another man, for she had come to hate him for his neglect.

One night Lil watched him standing outside the church window for a long time. She trembled, knowing something was changing. When she got to their rooms, she felt certain of it, smelled the strong drink in the air though he stayed hidden and didn't answer when she called, "Jacob." She built up the fire because of her shivering, though that wouldn't touch the part that came from fear. She felt him watching her again. Waiting. Wanting her and still hiding it like a thief. She would give him something to want, and she began to remove her clothes, with the fire hot and dancing over the walls, shattering the shadowy places, Lil excited, knowing she was beautiful and that he had never seen her and that it would be a power over him and would cause something between them to change. The thought of it made her fumble over the layered items of winter clothing and her nipples stood erect, chafed by the fabric. It came into her mind that she would take his head in her two hands and place it against her breasts, each one in turn, press his mouth to suck on her, his tongue to lick her nipples. Wanting that all through her, she turned, fully naked, toward the doorway, where she heard his step.

By firelight all his need was finally visible in his face, what she'd longed to see. But there was such anger in it too that she tried to cover herself. When she saw the kindling hatchet raised in his hand, she thought that would be the end of it and part of her was glad, fire staining the blade red before blood. She couldn't get her breath even to scream. He brought the hatchet down then, on the piano, and twice more he struck, to leave it then, anchored in the wood, the piano vibrating as though it shrieked out and held to its voice long afterwards, as though it were her voice. Still she seemed to hear it, after he'd gripped her to bring her hard against him and then carried her to the bed. She couldn't take breath but repeated wordlessly: why didn't you, why didn't you?

The piano quieted and while Jacob strained into her, Lil's breath regained its regular and solitary pattern and, quieted, she heard in the distance the repeated howling of a dog left out in the cold. She began to count the times it sounded while Jacob finished and rolled off her. Then she went on counting. Sometime in the night she was sick, threw up everything she had eaten, and let herself think about the baby that was growing in her. Then she went on counting. It was a fearful and lonesome thing but finally she went to sleep and it was possible to imagine how its small eager mouth would fasten on her and pull at her breast. She never told Jacob a baby was coming. She let him see it for himself as if it had nothing to do with him.

Lil and Jacob went on living and sleeping together for more than twenty years and they never spoke of these things between them. For Lil there were the children they had, seven finally, although the two boys died in infancy, and they meant more to her than she had expected, kept her too busy for worry and lamenting. Looking around, who had it any better? It was the lot of women. Who among them wasn't stuck with something she couldn't abide? She, for one, determined to forget it. Sometimes she knew it hurt her children, to see her with bruises or a swollen face, or to find something in the house smashed while there was never any money to give them even the little they needed for school. But she wouldn't ever give Jacob the satisfaction of showing that she cared, that he could hurt her.

She left him only once. The children were young and he had started drinking hard and coming home staggering and falling dead asleep. This night, though, she had awakened in the night and found him gone from their bed and she'd followed him to the end of the hall where the little girls slept, hardly knowing where he was or what he was doing. Something in that scared her and she left the house as soon as she got him asleep in their bed again, and went to stay with her sister. But she couldn't stay on there indefinitely, crowding in with the four children she had then, and when word reached her that Jacob had stopped drinking, she went back to him. He was soon drinking again but he didn't wander through the house at night; in fact, he often stayed away at night, drunk, or on business. It was a relief to Lil, although the money, always short, became even more scarce. But Lil kept a large garden to feed them and she took in washing along with the Italian women in the neighborhood. Most of those women had it worse than she did.

It satisfied Lil to do so well without Jacob and for him to see it plain when he came home. Their girls were nicer than there was reason to hope for. They helped her, were bright in school, and all of them were good-looking. And they were with her, set against Jacob, ashamed of his ways and determined to better themselves. The more crude and brutal he became, the more they locked against him. None of his abuse could touch them. Spitting in the wind. About the sum total of all his whammings—save a moment's hullabaloo. She would show him. There was always the hope, too, that like her own father, he might one day go away and never return.

Of her children, Grace helped Lil the most and seemed to feel the closest to her, always hanging around and taking an extra chore. She would say to Lil, her black eyes concerned, appealing, "When I grow up I'll buy you the prettiest dress in the world and we'll wear hats and go to tea."

"Phooey," was all Lil would reply, impatient with romantic nonsense. Better put your money in the bank or buy a spread of land. You'll be needing it. As for putting Lil in a silk dress, you may as well dress up a sow and put it in the parlor: she hated the way she'd come to look so soon, all stomach and a wrinkled face.

Mostly she tried to ignore her appearance, the way she ignored whatever she couldn't mend. If Jacob would finally come home and then, for spite, spill the evening's milk over the floor, or do some other fool trick, Lil would scream at him until she choked, while beside her on the floor, cleaning up, Grace would cry, making something hurt worse inside Lil so that she'd snarl for her to get away. The child's sympathy weakened her, another female groveling at the foot of a man. The very effort of cleaning up, though, was relieving in its own way, and Lil let her flare-ups with Jacob slide out of her mind, and planned for the children. She kept them in school, sewed their clothes, raised chickens out back for the egg money that would give Eleanor (as she spelled her name then) music lessons. It was indulgent and the others resented the favoring, but Lil figured Eleanor to be the most promising, the one who might eventually get away altogether. The piano could still be played; a draped shawl concealed the disfigurement. For Lil it was a reminder that changes can come in the twinkling of an eye.

And her life did change just about that fast and that miraculously. When Lil was our Gram, this was the one story she relished telling, the one she treasured. There she was, as she saw it, living her whole life up to her elbows in a copper washtub, her face hag-lined from steam and exposure, as though it bore the punishment directly for what it had brought her, when her entire prospect changed and she, like the Goose Girl, was acknowledged as the true princess.

"It begun at the reunion," Gram started the story. "Naturally the old chap"—she meant Grandad, this tale making her more tolerant than usual—"wasn't nowheres about, off helling. But I had my children with me, even May from over yonder where she'd gone to live with her husband. And they was all looking right, clean, with here and there a touch of fashion to show they were somebody. We went over in the wagon and it was the nicest sort of a day. The girls felt it too, and when we stopped to rest on the way, Grace and Eleanor picked bunches of daisies and lace out of the fields so that when we pulled into my aunt's yard, we were singing, all of us wearing flowers, including the horse.

"I was having my first day off in a while, though I was busy enough chasing after Libby and Rachel. Of course I did my share, helping the women with the dinner too. Along in the late afternoon, when all the food was a shambles and we was sitting on the grass resting, some of the younguns asleep and nearly all of the men, who hadn't done a thing all day but stuff themselves, we heard one of them new motorcars on the road, chugging along. And then it pulled up our road and stopped in front. We was too startled to even tidy our hair, just staring. Out of this car steps a fine-dressed man, wearing a tailored suit with starched cuffs and collar, purely white. It didn't take but a second for Aunt Molly to know it was her brother Burl come back from California, New York City, the world. She was on him quick as a wink, hugging and crying over him, saying, 'Now ain't he the limit,' over and over. She took him around to visit with all of us and he made a great fuss over Hat and me especially because of our mother, who was his favorite sister. My girls was always a credit to me, pretty and sweet-natured, none of them a bit lazy. He seemed to notice they was a cut over the others and everyone knew I'd never had it easy with Jacob. I thanked him for the piano and pointed out Eleanor, who could play it—she was always the prettiest thing too, with that bright hair, like my ma's. And Grace had that dimple in her chin and was so devoted to the others; I could see how taken Uncle Burl was with watching her and Libby playing, daisies still wound through their hair. He give every one of them kids a silver dollar, and they come up to show me, big-eyed. A little shamefaced too, so I figured they'd been telling him how we lived on North Street with the Italians. But I spoke right out to them, same as always: 'You just be proud you have such a fine uncle and don't ever let being poor shame you, unless you never tried not to be.'

"Uncle Burl ate some of the dinner that was left and then looked at his gold watch and said he had to leave. Before that, he went with Molly on a tour through the house, and after coming out he stared at it awhile, the house he'd been born in, hunkering down under two maples with sunset bringing out the windows' gleam more than Aunt Molly could, and she was famous for the way she kept that house. He made all of us a sort of bow, formal and dignified. Kissed his sister. I was standing off to one side of the car, holding Rachel, who was asleep on my shoulder, and he come over to look me directly in the eye. 'I'm taking care of you, Lil,' he says. His exact words. And by the dead serious way he said it, I knew it was so. I thought to myself: I'm going to be all right. I am. And maybe I'm even going to be rich. One day. It was coming to me from a man and it was going to save me from one, just like the world was paying me a debt. Inside I felt so free, thinking: How do you like that, old mister? I wanted to see his face when he got the news."

But when she did see Jacob he seemed more pathetic than dangerous and she didn't have the energy to tell him what was what. Not just then. Until he made her furious enough to pitch him out; then she told him that she didn't have to answer to him no more, that he could leave and never come back, far as she cared. He went off for a while but was home before long, dragging his tail, no place to go, and it didn't seem worth it to rile him again. And when he came to her unsteady and flushed, impatient and harsh with her, the way he always was when he was wanting that one thing, she took a backward glance at pride and ultimatums and shut her mouth. If it hadn't killed her by then, likely it wouldn't. And she didn't figure getting maimed or having the children hurt on account of him. Not when life was finally starting to happen to her. With one of the early checks from Uncle Burl she had bought a brand-new nightdress. She lay in the dark wearing it, and Jacob never saw it or felt the difference in the material, and Lil cried some of the tears she'd stored up —the last time she would cry over that. After Jacob dropped off to sleep she removed the gown and put on the old one. It could wait until she slept alone. After that, his wanting her seemed as perverse as tales she'd heard of men desiring the dead. She felt that hard.

Once Uncle Burl was dead the money came in fast. It took the old Nick out of Jacob quicker than Lil's patience was being used up, and he began to let her alone. By the time she bought the farm and they moved into the big brick house, he went off to the back bedroom meek as a lamb and never bothered her again. Not in that way, though he was resentful to the end of his days and stood up against her for meanness and spite. Lil would ignore him and fight him by turns. Feel sorry for him. More than anything she seemed to feel he was a nuisance, getting in her way, trying to get attention like one of the kids. Partly, though, it made her feel stronger to have Jacob around. There he was, living proof of where she had been. "I felt like I'd been let out of a prison."

Eventually Gram owned, beside the farm, three houses in town, four places of business and later another couple of farms to the south, bought for speculation in gas and oil. Sundays she would drive to see the tenants there to talk about the crops and the nearby wells that were coming through. While she talked we stared away at the tiered steel rigs poking up out of the rolling pastureland, steeple-like spires that could have been proclaiming a new religion, higher than the corn and wheat. And more productive too, Gram said, when afterwards we'd drive around to see if more land was for sale. She vowed it was peculiar—her father spent his life in the West, searching for oil, when all along it was right out back under the corn crib. Now wasn't that just like a man? Like life.

We were still waiting for Grandad to go to the mill. It seemed he would never wake up. We walked down to the barn so he couldn't run out on us. From where the house sat, the land sloped at a gradual downward tilt and didn't become really level again until the far creek bottom. The barn was built into a mound of earth, with a stone foundation and then boards dried to tinder, topped off by a cupola. It belonged to Grandad and Grandad to it; it seemed in the same opposition he was to the encampment of fun-loving females who had seized the manor house and held it by superior numbers and adaptability. Just going down there made us feel adventurous. Made us feel divided. We sat on the barnyard railing and dared each other to touch the single-strand electric fence Grandad had newly installed to keep the horses in the orchard. An old hired hand had coaxed Katie to grab hold of it. He'd pointed out the birds sitting there, not feeling a thing. The trick was to put your whole hand around it and take hold. He did it, standing regularly, with a grin. So Katie did the same, clasped the wire and held on. As the current went through her, she stood as if she'd been planted in the ground. The man thought it was funny, Katie standing like that. We laughed too.

Grandad didn't call to us, just suddenly appeared, got into the cab of the ramshackle truck and started it up. We scrambled over the side rails while he was cursing to himself, bitter, unlike his casual bovine profanity at milking time. "You'll goddamn buck me, will you?" as he overshifted the gears. He had put on a striped shirt and a dark broadcloth coat that had once belonged to a suit. In the rearview mirror, we saw his eyes beneath the brim of his tweed schoolboy's cap. Abruptly we knew he was a man, braced in the iron strength of his willfulness.

At first we lay among the hunks of dung-soiled straw. We rolled into the boards when the truck lurched forward, clutching each other. Then we looked and the house was out of sight; with it receded our mothers' warning: "Don't stand up, it isn't safe. The way he drives." We did, as soon as the house wasn't watching us anymore. Grandad never told on us. We felt he didn't notice. The wind was in our hair and through the crazed glass of the window we could watch Grandad, who seemed to control the vehicle as though it were some fiercely independent creature that battled with him. His head jolted violently as we bucked over the bricks of the road until we reached the smoother blacktop. Between the floorboards we could see the road's black streaming under us; surrounded by the dung-crusted slats of the truck bed, we identified with the innumerable pigs and cattle, rams too, that had ridden in it to their final destination. The oaks that lined Summer Street dropped their branches low so that sometimes we could catch them, stinging and staining our hands with the blood of leaf veins. After we reached the back dirt roads again, we lay down to give ourselves up to the dust and thudding stones, daydreaming into the forever fleeing land.

At the mill, Grandad stomped up the ramp in his knee-length boots, a burlap sack of wheat loaded high on his squared shoulder like a young ram tied up for slaughter. We went behind him, more slowly, hesitant to enter the large frame building, dark beyond the entrance ramp, bare-looking without shutters or trim. Inside, the air glowed in a white powdery radiance that reflected off every surface. Down below, the miller stood, a ghostly figure, overseeing the grinding of the stones. We could feel their heave and shudder, on and on.

Grandad greeted the men standing in the yard and those inside with a nod of his head as he dropped the sack to the floor and kicked it right as though it had become the fit object of his contempt. Grandad had a reputation in the county for being still, even in his seventies, a strong man; and the farm was beautiful and they admired his family. We'd heard them, some of these same men, at threshing time when they ate their noontime dinner at our kitchen table, which had been opened up and boarded to sit twenty or more hired hands, Gram herself cooking, without a word to anyone, and us girls waiting on them. "Save that redheaded gal for me, Samuel," one would say with a wink. "I'll take me a black-eyed Susan anytime," another joked; but with one eye out for Grandad, for the talk was serious and respectful when he was there with the women around. Now, with his cap on, tall and lean, and his expression proud and distant, he made us all uneasy, wondering what might be in him, what he might do.

He stomped out for another sack. The men eyed us. "There's shorly a fire," one said because of Celia's and Anne's hair, and they all gave a spurt of something like laughter, though it mixed with another thing we couldn't name. But Grandad was coming back in, nodding and grinning at us, and it was as if we'd been set loose about the place. We watched the sacks of wheat or other grain descend on the conveyor and disappear below. On another belt the sacked flour ascended. Grandad handed each of us a penny for the gum machine, feeling good now, forgiving us abruptly and with as little reason as he'd had for conceiving his grudge. Or maybe his anger had never really had anything to do with us. When he went over to stand with the men, they offered him a bottle to drink from. After that we saw him drinking from it again and again.

An Amish boy stood off to one side with his father. The man's face was frizzled with an untended beard, but it seemed that underneath, his bare face would have had an innocence identical to the boy's. The boy was trying to conceal it, but we could tell he was watching us, wishing he could be with us. We felt exhilarated ourselves, with ourselves, in our blue jeans, tee-shirts, with the shiny thick hair of our family. Whenever we caught his eyes we'd smile, coaxing him.

Then his father went off a moment and Celia walked over. "Want some gum?" she asked, and held out her piece, which she had saved. The boy got red against his blue home-dyed shirt and stared blankly into the floor.

"Well, I don't want it," Celia said, and looking up at the father, who came then, she threw back her head with its lush fall of red-gold hair. He flushed too, looked as unsettled as the boy, his eyes blinking rapidly. Celia kept standing there, the gum offered, and they both stood, father and son, heads hanging before the round satiny piece of blue enamel. The wide brims of their hats cast a dark ellipse of shadow to hide their eyes. We pulled at Celia finally, to make her come away with us. "He's not allowed to have it," we whispered, reminding her, embarrassed over the fuss. The round of gum seemed unnatural, a wicked worldly thing resting on her delicate hand, and we saw—was it the first time?—that her nails were polished scarlet, long and crescent-shaped.

"All right," Celia said at last. "But I'll leave it here, in case you change your mind," and she placed it on the oak railing where, grained with sifted flour as though bleached for effect, the wood gleamed so the gum seemed precious. In our relief, released from the stricken pair, we chased after Celia, pushing and running, and raced out onto the ramp, oblivious of Homer Snavely, who was coming up with a load of grain, until we were right on top of him and he was already fighting for his balance, then he gave up half jumping and let himself roll off the ramp onto the ground. We went rolling and skidding after him. We saw his set of teeth pop out of his mouth and sail away.

Grandad was standing at the top of the ramp. We could see him from where we lay in the dust. He didn't say a word. We could scarcely breathe in the quiet that Grandad held in deliberate tension. Right then he could have come at us with a horsewhip and we would only have waited. He leaned over the railing and spouted a brilliant stream of amber into the dust near us, raised a flask and drank, then turned his head back toward the men, who must have waited too, knowing about him what everybody knew, and said sometimes even for us to hear: that he was as mean as a man could be who hadn't yet been brought in for actual murder, though men might have died because of things he'd done. We could hear then the loud, relieving guffaws at whatever he said to the men above the tireless scraping of the stones. With his stick he reached down to help Homer Snavely pull himself to standing. There on the ground were the false teeth, grinning with embarrassment, it seemed. Grandad speared them on his stick and went swaggering inside, diving left and right to balance them there. "Lookie what I catched," he said. The men were stomping with the fun of it.

But we were uneasy still and slunk around the yard, feeling that something had really just begun more than finished with Grandad, who stood apart from the rest, and superior, until he started to drink whiskey with them, and then something stirred in him that still set him apart but was what excited them. Homer Snavely disappeared inside. "I wonder you didn't swaller them," somebody cackled.

Beyond the fence the Amish boy and his father were loading their buggy with tied-up sacks, neither of them looking away from their concentration on positioning the load, as if they wore blinders, like the standing, well-groomed horse. Everything about them was intentionally dark, even the buggy's curtains, except the blue shirts—quite like the fierce blue of the boy's blue eyes when he tilted back his hat and looked at Celia once, before he pulled up beside his father and took the reins. The heavy-spoked wheels creaked through the dust and the tussocks of grass bent and sprang back. In a while we heard the clip of the horse's hooves, after they had disappeared and gone over the dirt to the paved road on the rise that led to Orsonville Flats.

"His hat was funny," Katie said, and we giggled. Celia said, "I thought his eyes were fine." And then she went inside and we got the same idea and ran after her, but taking care this time, going in at the side door. Even before we looked at the railing, we knew the gum would be gone, because we saw first, from the landing, the expression on Celia's face, her calm acknowledgment. That was the first time we saw it in her, that sureness. "Celia's sweet on a plain one," we teased, trying to bring her back to us, make her blush and deny it.

"And I'll have anyone I want," she said.

We squatted in the yard and chewed on oat grass, the way we saw the men do, chewed and spit, long-legged, bony, the daughters of our family, like Grandad, waiting for him. He came then with two sacks of grain mash loaded on his shoulders. One of the laughing men leaned out the doorway, swaggering, and called after him in a slurred voice, "My woman goes to the bank, she just better keep on a-going, she knows what's good for her." Then he ducked inside. Grandad didn't pause even, but we could see he was furious—so quickly, as though he had been astonished to have the men, loud and drunk, laugh together like that. His face was dark but he went on throwing the sacks into the back and then headed for the cab, leaving us again, and we had to spring onto the slats and scramble in, even as the engine sputtered and the truck began to lurch across the uneven dirt. His face was visible in the rearview mirror. Though the crazed glass faded him, we could see the muscle beside his mouth twitch and pop. We recalled how Gram said he'd sold his soul to perdition. And this day she had sold land.

And from the way he drove we were certain he had been taken by a power, going like something suddenly pushed over a dam, carried by a force beyond himself and mere machinery. The truck swayed and bumped. We tumbled about and stared at the road flying beneath us, sickened almost, and on into the gray opening the road made through the corn and scattered grasses and flowers that disguised the steep pitch of the roadside ditch.

We were looking back toward the retreating and lost distance when the truck settled down to a more even ride. So it was all the more startling when the truck suddenly swerved. We half tipped over and then we heard the horse, its squeals like our own screams. Beside us then, nearly under us, the Amish buggy was fighting to stay upright on the road. The horse, blinded to the sides, threw back its head, trampled into the roadside weeds, stumbled and lunged for balance, the man now pulling on the reins, heaving backwards, trying to steady and slow him. We watched then as we moved away, the horse losing its battle, overwhelmed by the earth giving way, so that he went sliding into the ditch and fell sideways, the entire buggy tipping over. Scenes we'd watched in the movies at the dime theater came to us as we gazed back, watching the two figures in black moving around the downed buggy. We couldn't tell what had happened to the horse. We could see his legs, though, thrashing as if he still intended to travel. We never heard a single word or oath from the man or boy, even as we'd passed and they were struggling with the horse, trying to avoid Grandad's truck, the unprovoked assault. Their faces weren't anything other than intent.

After they had disappeared we clung to the rails, not looking even at each other. We felt the rude shifting of the boards beneath us and sometimes our bodies hit against the slats.

It was only when we reached the final turn into the drive at home that we stood up. Again the truck picked up sudden speed. We were flung against the cab. There was a streak of fresh blood on Celia's cheek. Now Grandad was making a final lurching run toward the barn, and we spurted past the haven of home we now yearned for, followed down the drive, past the house, by the three grown women, mothers and aunts, who came first onto the porch and then on the lawn, furiously following behind us to the barn, where the truck slammed to a stop like the sudden cessation of a scream. But it was we who screamed then, crying while scrambling again over the rails. We sobbed, disconsolate, shamed before the women who reached us at last and held us in their arms, crooning. Grandad was gone somewhere into the depths of the barn, or into the woods, or off into the arms of faithless women. We'd heard Gram's disdain.

"Even today," Aunt Libby said. And then we remembered this was the day they had taken Aunt Grace to the Cleveland Clinic.

"Where's Mother?" Katie asked.

Before anyone could answer, Gram came straggling along, her gray tangle of curls damp on her hot face and the low sun shadowing through her loose hair, wrinkling her face absolutely. Breathing painfully, she stood before the empty cab. The door dragged off its hinge, desolate. She jerked her head toward the dark barn, shook her fist and yelled, "And that's only the first part, mister." From the near pasture a cow began to low, the sun setting down the wood's line. "Well, he'll not neglect them. That I know," she said, all her resignation at what she considered his myriad other neglects in her tone.

"Where's Mother?" Katie repeated, singsong, until someone would pay attention. Aunt Rachel was staring toward the darkening barn. Then she put her arm around Katie's shoulder. "She's stopped off at Aunt May's and we came on to fix supper. She'll be here soon."

Anne called down from the tiptop of the sour cherry tree. In the evening light with the sun striking there, her hair was brighter than the cherries; with the leaves twined and shadowed about her face it seemed the spirit of the tree had materialized out of the gold-spun air. The tree was swaying from Anne's being so near the top.

"Goddamn it. Git down from there," Gram yelled, the way she always yelled at Anne. "You'll tumble. Then we'll see who's the smarty pants." She was so angry it was like a curse. Anne swung down. We could see her white arms winding against the black form of the tree.

Gram started up the drive. She called back to us while we still gazed at the barn: "Don't look up a dead horse's behind," and went marching on. She had her good dress on under her apron.

"Hey, old woman," Aunt Rachel called in her loving mocking way. "Where's the fire? She's just too fast for us," she reminded us, her pride strong.

"You younguns dawdle all you like." Gram marched on. "I got things to do."

"You're not going to go!" Aunt Libby snapped in disbelief. Her eyes flashed at Aunt Rachel, who shrugged.

"I am. It's an early party and I'll be back before she will. I know what you're thinking, but I can't help it. I've got to go." She stopped by the house yard, catching her breath, eyeing her daughters straight on.

We followed up the back steps onto the porch and then into the house. Already it was dark in there, and muffled too, as if nobody was saying what they were thinking. Almost out of a dream we heard Grandad's call: "Sucky, sucky." He was going to milk.

"Work me clear to death," Gram said, her recent fury at him dissolved, absorbed into the usual unremitting discontent. "There's two gallon already standing," she muttered. Now that Grandad was old and good for nothing, as Gram told him and us, his cows gave up their milk so lavishly that Gram, curdling with resentment but country bred, still skimmed the blooms of yellowed cream from the sideboard crocks and churned butter by the back door in the late mornings; the rhythm of the paddle hitting the wooden bottom seemed to calm her for a time. When the butter came she felt it and washed it, slapping it into a crockery bowl, washed the churn and banged the whole assembly into the corner. All her hours at home were restless ones, tasks to rush through. Others would have done them for her, but too slowly to suit her, the family a relentless nuisance to be coped with, so that time would roll by and take her away.

Aunt Libby asked, "Why does Dad have to be like this? Of all times."

"I quit asking that long before. There's never any right time for it, I reckon. It's drink every time, one way or another. Should've pitched him out."

"Don't any of you kids tell Dan what happened," Aunt Libby told us. "He'd want to kill him." Uncle Dan had all the equipment for killing in the way of tools, but we couldn't imagine his doing it.

But Gram said, "Since I ain't done it already, there's none that's likely to." She said it in braggadocio, exactly the way she described Grandad as the handsomest man in Marland County when she married him. Now she maintained he couldn't be beat for his meanness either, or herself for long-suffering. "He'll sleep it off. Then maybe won't even recollect. Wisht I could sleep that good."

Aunt Rachel was on the phone, calling all over for Rossie. Nobody had seen him. She said she couldn't eat and went off to find him.

Anne and Katie ate with Gram. She put a big plate of food in the oven for Grandad. She had made fried cabbage with cream and dumped on pepper to suit her—her own tastes the ones that mattered. Katie wouldn't eat it. Anne moved hers around with her fork. Gram merely raised up her chin and ate as fast as she'd cooked, smacking her lips. *Eat it or starve,* her manner said. *That's all there'll be.* She carried her dish to the sink, swallowing off the remainder of her coffee as she went, and hung up her apron. "In my next house I'll have electric," she said, as if that would make all the difference.

Aunt Libby went toward her. "We need you," she said.

"You! Shut up! I told you I need to go." The webbing of veins on her cheeks popped red. "Probably I'll beat her home anyways." Before she left the room she told Aunt Libby, "They count on me," meaning the women she went out with at night.

"So do we," Aunt Libby said, but Gram had already turned away.

"You feel lucky?" we asked her when she was waiting by the front door, holding her lightweight coat, her neck craned up the drive, her pocketbook at the ready in her lap like a shotgun. She didn't answer, her thoughts withdrawn, owing us nothing. Sometimes she seemed as unapproachable as Grandad.

He came in the kitchen with the milk pails clattering. "You gals show him his supper," Gram said over her shoulder as she saw a car turn into the drive.

Aunt Libby went into the kitchen with us. She whispered, "Now forget it. There's to be no trouble tonight." Grandad was straining milk through the cheesecloth he kept washed and drying over the cleaned pails. Some bits of straw and a dead fly came out in the mesh. He poured himself a glass of the milk warm from the cows. The back counter was lined with crocks of milk and there was more overfilling the refrigerator. "Confounded lazy women," he muttered. "Too busy putting on paint and powder."

"There's your supper," we said.

"Where's she at?" He was still looking at the milk. Behind his spectacles, when he glanced at us, we saw his eyes. They were the brown eyes of his children, except Aunt Rachel, and they were the eyes of a real person.

We couldn't answer. Gram was just out. She always went out. Aunt Libby answered, though. "She stayed over with May. She'll be home later." Then we knew he had meant Aunt Grace. Where was she, his daughter? We'd never known before that he noticed her, or any of us, just as we'd hardly noticed him, unless he was nearly killing someone or something, as he had that day.

The supper Gram had fixed he ate with the same hungry indifference with which he ate what he fixed for himself in the morning. There was one of Gram's pies for dessert. They were her crowning achievement, the pastry tender with dissolving layers, the filling both tart and sweet. Grandad plopped his piece into his bowl of coffee and spooned it up as though it were his usual Ritz crackers.

Nearly in darkness, we played croquet beside the spruce trees.

Uncle Dan came out and sat on the back steps. The hollow sound the balls made knocking together or against the mallets was lonely, and with Uncle Dan just sitting there, not wisecracking for once how darkness improved our game, we lost interest ourselves and quarreled over whether the balls were in or out of the wickets. Grandad had gone, the kitchen light snapped off. He would sit up against the radio with the cards laid out and fall asleep. We started hide-and-seek. But we stayed in the yard this evening.

Aunt Rachel came home with Rossie. She marched him straight past us into the house. She said he had to practice his piano lesson. Right then. Before he could eat. We saw the light go on in the parlor. Their shadows streaked the driveway and Rossie's yelps and whines reached our hiding places. We quit the game and went onto the front porch to watch him get it.

"Thick-headed dunderhead." Aunt Rachel sat on the bench beside him. She held the wooden ruler, tapped out the time. And when he blundered, she rapped him, tweaked his ear. Rossie scowled into the book. His fingers were dirty and stubby against the white keys. The ruler cracked against his knuckles. "Two-four": Aunt Rachel beat the accent on her palm. She hit him again because he looked out the window. We moved further into the shadow.

Rossie shrieked and rubbed his hand. "What'd you do that for? I did it right." He was sobbing a little. We giggled. Aunt Rachel only pursued the measured beat, arching her eyebrows toward the score.

We made faces into the window and Rossie caught us once, almost as if he'd felt them land on him. He stuck out his tongue. We did it back. Aunt Rachel hit him again. "Play," she commanded. Rossie took a last glance at us and then sat up straight, collecting himself, and began "Stepping Stones." We'd all learned it.

"There now," Aunt Rachel said when she was finished with him for the night. "That wasn't so bad. Before long you'll be another José Iturbi." She brushed his fine hair out of his face, while her tilted mocking eyes lingered on him lovingly, as if she doubted herself that he'd ever amount to anything. As he left the room, Rossie shook his fist, and then he went to the kitchen for supper.

We were all waiting in the night, not thinking for what. Then a car was once again steering the turn off the highway, its lights spiraling the dark, washing over the trees. Aunt Grace was coming home. Aunt Rachel and Aunt Libby came out under the carport. We all called out together, against the silence, against the dread we felt. Aunt Rachel opened the car door and helped Aunt Grace, holding her arm and supporting her, as if she had become very ill since going away to Cleveland. We stood back a little, watching. All their faces, lit by the parlor light, seemed briefly to glow. Aunt Grace hugged us as together we went crowding into the narrow hallway. "Sh," we said. "Grandad."

But right away we heard another car on the drive, the formal lumbering swing and crawl of the sedan bringing Gram home. The hall was ghostly, lit by the replica of a lighthouse in pink-veiled marble which cast a steady beam onto the marble rocks sculpted at its base. Rossie had appeared from somewhere, and Grandad rose from his sleep, adjusting his spectacles as he came. He looked solemn and uneasy with all the family around him, and rubbed his gnarled hands together in mute supplication, as though he were sorry—for sleeping, for everything. Aunt Grace went over to him and put her arms around him. "Somebody will have to call Neil," she said. "And Elinor."

On the stone steps we heard the little scratching sounds of Gram's feet and then the opening of the screen. She stood before us, her pocketbook dragging from bone handles, her woolen coat sagging with her shoulders. In one hand she held a silver-painted candy dish which was mounted on a pedestal base.

Grandad lifted one hand toward her without any particular directive force but in appeal to her—as if in losing land he felt a part of himself was going too. Gram took offense, said, "Leave me alone, old man." Then her face softened as if she remembered why we were all waiting for her. "Phooey anyways. You'll scarcely notice any of it's gone. I can't see why all the fuss over a little scrap of meadow."

Then Anne shrieked out, "Oh, I hate it, I hate it," clutching her stomach, and we thought she meant selling the land or something else that was terrible which we didn't know yet. But then we saw a mouse dive down into the dark space under the sliding parlor doors.

"For crying out loud," Aunt Rachel said, laughing a little. We all did, relieved by Anne's well-known terror, its insignificance. "That child has the Saint Vitus' dance."

But Gram wasn't paying attention. She had her hand on Anne's arm, gentle this once. "There, there," she crooned. "There's worse than that to cry over, girl." Her hand continued to stroke Anne while everyone hushed and looked with her at Aunt Grace.

"Well, you're back," Gram said.

Aunt Grace nodded. "Yes. It's all done. I called up there from May's. The tests were ready. Not good, I'm afraid." It seemed that her hair, so black that in sunlight it shimmered blue, was folded in two glistening wings that held her face, protecting her slender throat. We saw how her chest heaved so that the embroidered birds in flight over the bodice of her dress seemed to vibrate, although underneath was the unyielding rubber cup she wore to simulate the live flesh which had been cut away in an operation three years earlier. We wondered how she could still look so alive with all that gone.

But Aunt Grace wasn't looking afraid or sorry now. She looked steadily more amused, with some mock horror showing too as she reached for the silver-painted candy dish. "I do believe, Momma, that this is very nearly the worst thing you have ever won. I guess if we have to keep it we'll think of it as a kind of trophy won in the wars and handed down to us for what we have to go through." In the light which trailed over the sculpted marble rocks, Aunt Grace's oval fingernails shone transparent, and the half-moons at their base seemed mystical and unearthly. Beyond that bit of light our eyes dilated to form one dark place. Gram kept stroking Anne's arm. The tears running from her eyes immediately filled the crevices of her ancient face the way rain first puddles clay seams.

PART THREE: GRACE AND NEIL

Our mothers and aunts were all proficient swimmers, although neither Gram nor Grandad had set foot in open water, if they could help it, since they were children. It was not a skill common to country people. Aunt May had been taught by a college student who boarded with the family one summer and she taught Aunt Elinor, who passed it on to Aunt Grace, who worked with the two younger girls. Even as grown women, they liked to go to a lake or swimming hole, just to be doing together what they had always enjoyed so much. Usually they didn't want men around, just each other. Perhaps it was that exclusiveness that had prompted Neil to follow them once when they'd gone to the pond at Taylor's farm. This was a remote place and as usual they took off their clothes and swam naked. Although we were told, over the years, only the bare bones of the story, we made up the details and fleshed it out. We seemed to imagine even the thoughts of these women. And we could see them, young, well-formed, water-licked and dazzling.

Aunt May and Aunt Elinor, the two competitors, would have challenged each other to repeated speed trials, while Aunt Grace taught Aunt Libby and Aunt Rachel dives off the limestone boulder which marked the deep end. They would all look at each other openly and appreciatively, strong in their shared beauty.

All the more reason for the shame and fury they felt when they left the pond to dress and found their clothes missing. Right away they knew that it was Neil who had spied on them. While they became hungry and chilled, waiting for the cover of evening, they plotted their revenge. As it approached dark they opened the car, hoping to find a blanket or at least a few oily rags, and found on the floor their carefully concealed clothing.

After that they had to laugh. But their plans were made. They took the back farm road and parked by the barn. Then all together, stifling their laughter, they sneaked up to where Neil's car was parked on the drive, released the handbrake, took it out of gear and pushed and steered it downhill to the barn, where they felt it was safe to start the engine. Both cars proceeded to the next county. By a creek where fishermen left their cars, they hid Neil's, after letting the air out of the tires. Back at the house, they teased and joked with Neil, who was surprised at their good humor.

The next morning he discovered his car was missing. They couldn't imagine why he was accusing them. Neil became furious. Aunt Grace wouldn't let him get her alone. When the sheriff brought the car back, his two suitcases were already set on the porch and he left without a goodbye. The women—what did they care? They had each other.

Aunt Grace had met Neil for the first time at the town lake. She had driven her mother's brand-new white Chrysler convertible on that July day during the Depression when most people in their county considered themselves lucky to have a plow horse. Neil couldn't take his eyes off her, slender, with very dark eyes and hair, and when she went home that day he was sitting up front alongside her and before long he was driving them everywhere.

Neil liked Aunt Grace. He liked the car. He visited the farm and before long he asked to live there. He paid for his board and room; Gram liked putting the empty attic rooms to good use although she didn't care much for Neil from the beginning. She sometimes laughed at him, along with her daughters, but mostly his jokes seemed silly and her girls daft, for Aunt Grace wasn't the only one who encouraged his fooling. All of them, along with their dates, seemed to end up at the house and in the evenings the kitchen was noisy with the cooking and fixing, the card games and the constant horsing around. Aunt Grace's lovely face, nearly always sad-looking when not lit up by her white teeth and sparkling eyes, astonished her mother, who even as she saw the evidence of love became increasingly short-tempered with the cause of it. She said Neil was just hanging around their place for what he could get, that all he was wanting was a good time.

"Well, I hope so!" Aunt Elinor had said. She didn't think any of them should be in a hurry to get married. She was an aspiring actress then and one of the liveliest of the crowd when she was home from New York for a visit. More seriously, she would remind Gram that Neil was in college and that he had been made captain of the baseball team and didn't that show a pretty responsible nature under all the kidding around. Aunt Elinor admired Aunt Grace and thought it appropriate that her beauty and intelligence would have attracted a man who balanced her serious side, someone who could make her laugh. Aunt Elinor was further impressed that Neil was the son of a country doctor and she thought the chances of his eventually making a successful career as a writer were good—heaven knows he had a flair for the dramatic, the gift of gab and a lot of charisma.

"Speak English," Gram told her.

"Well, I'll never marry him anyway," Aunt Grace had said. She had plans for herself, thought someday she would get a master's degree in zoology and maybe teach at a college.

And for three years she held firm, while Neil continued to hang around, sometimes in school, sometimes not, pursuing her in an offhanded way, so that no one could really be certain he wanted to marry her. Off and on he rented one or the other of the attic rooms, whichever was available, and then he might follow Aunt Grace around the place for quite a while, dallying with her, weaving garlands of daisies to hang about her until, sitting in the high meadow grass, she was nearly buried, her chin aglow with pollen. Under the apple trees she took down her hair and he lay with his head in her lap, a buckwheat stalk tickling her throat as he chewed on it and said things that made her push at him and laugh out loud. He followed her into the henhouse when she gathered the eggs, and pretended to block the door, grinning and holding on to her when she tried to leave. Then for a time he might seem indifferent; they would quarrel and he would move into town, and Aunt Grace would not speak of him. They would all feel his absence through her and be relieved when one day he would be there again.

Neil took great liberties to make Aunt Grace laugh. Once when he was renting a room still, although he and Aunt Grace were on the outs, she entertained another young man in the parlor. Neil stopped in the doorway, holding his shoes in his hand, and yawning and stretching, he said, "I'm going on up, Grace. Don't be too long." She was so embarrassed she could have killed him; but she could laugh at it too, her reputation not quite so sacred a thing now that she had a college education and her mother had come into money. It was all new to her, the large house, new clothes and new opportunities. Neil's background as the son of a doctor impressed Aunt Grace also and although he often drank too much at the parties they went to, there seemed little connection between his revelry and her father's drunken isolation. Aunt Grace and her sisters now felt increasingly pity and tolerance as both their father and the past he represented became more distant, less binding.

Sometimes Neil went too far and Aunt Grace would send him away—for good, she said. He would comfort himself any way he wanted, making a scandal of himself in the ingrown town, exaggerating and glorifying his whoring and dissipation to everyone, until there didn't seem that a word of it could be true. Anyway, Aunt Grace and her sisters would be delighted to have him around again and Neil would say he felt like he'd come back home. He always seemed brand-new; though he was never remorseful, he still could convince them that he was just sowing his wild oats and would soon grow up.

Then both Aunt Libby and Aunt Rachel, seven and nine years younger than Aunt Grace, almost her own children from her years of caring for them, were married and pregnant. Neil ruined his knee stealing home; the team star abruptly became a has-been. Aunt Grace, holding on to her teaching job by the skin of her teeth, decided life was passing her by and married him. They ran away in secret because the school board immediately fired any female who was married and gave the job to a man with a family, and they kept their secret for eight more months until school was out, living on Aunt Grace's money while Neil finished college.

When he did, they announced their marriage. Gram was furious and declared she would never contribute to that marriage. She had made no secret of her disapproval, hadn't really imagined that Grace would marry that kind of man—which partly explained why she'd let him hang around the farm in the first place. The further reason was that she didn't pay a whole lot of attention to any of her children after they were grown. But now she couldn't stop talking about how Grace would rue the day! Neil was a trifler, with women and affection, a drinker, and furthermore greedy. When this last was repeated to Neil, it made him howl. "Those pitiful pissant dollars. The woman has deluded herself." But soon after their marriage, Aunt Grace and Neil were living back at the farm with Gram and the others; Neil could not find a job and Aunt Grace had compromised hers. Neil and his mother-in-law were locked in open hostility, with Aunt Grace in the middle.

It was hell for everyone: Gram and Grandad still warring, the constant sniping between Gram and Neil, his partying in the kitchen nearly every night and then drunken episodes in which he attacked Aunt Grace. It was a relief to everyone when at last Neil landed a job as a book salesman. They moved away to Chicago and Aunt Grace got substitute teaching work with the expectation that the following year she would have a full-time position, which would allow Neil to quit his sales job and devote himself to his writing.

But before long Aunt Grace was pregnant and unable to work at all, she was so sick. When her time was near she went back to the farm so she could deliver her baby where she was truly happy, in the room where Gram slept, with its open view of fields and woods, above the fireplace mantel the picture of the Indian brave. They called Neil in plenty of time to be there. Two years later, when Katie was born, Aunt Grace's labor was faster and they couldn't contact him in time. Over the phone when finally they reached him and told him he was the father of a second healthy child, another girl, Neil retorted: "How come you bothered to call?" By now Aunt Grace was living back at the farm, on and off, for reasons other than delivering babies, sometimes for as long as a year. There was plenty to do with family always about, Aunt Rachel already divorced and home with Rossie, Aunt Libby and Dan occupying the attic. Aunt Grace couldn't make up her mind. She'd come home furious and depressed, would talk about a divorce, and then would as abruptly go off to join Neil wherever his job had placed him, and they would begin again. Then something would happen between them and Aunt Grace would show up at the farm. Gram would just say, "Well, it's you back, I see," and take her and her girls in, same as the rest. For all Gram complained about the commotion, it seemed that it was less bother to her than the alternatives of sending money or feeling guilty, as long as she had the room. Besides, she'd told her so.

We would hear the women talk as they went about their work at the farm, as they sat for hours over coffee at the kitchen table. We heard all sorts of things. Once Aunt Libby said that Neil would do anything when he got drunk, that he had stumbled into many beds where he didn't belong and in some he had stayed until morning. She snapped her eyebrows up and down, whispered. We would hear Aunt Rachel's name. Hear that Aunt Grace had left Neil again and again, that it had become a little tiresome—same old thing. Sometimes, though, Neil was a hero in the stories—he'd saved Gram and Aunt Grace from being poisoned by leaking gas and he had saved a little girl from drowning, jumping into the river current in his Sunday best. Once he had fooled Gram into changing her bet to another horse while he stayed with the winner. To us it was all romantic and fun to think about, seemed scarcely to concern us, like fairy tales or cautionary fables that are not to be taken literally or to heart.

But now the Hudson is in the drive and we know that the Neil who is real to us is back. This time he has come because Aunt Grace called him after she came back from the Cleveland Clinic. A buzzard had flapped over the house at dawn with three red-wing blackbirds diving and pecking at it, and Gram said that meant the coming of trouble and confusion. Though Gram still hates Neil, she doesn't let his coming bother her. She just goes right on plowing through whatever she has to do, the few chores that occupy her, her struggle with time and the rest of us, until she can get away. We want to be like Gram, who says whenever anyone crosses her, "I know better," her lower lip stuck out a mile. When we are grown up and have been through everything, we'll be like that. We'll order kittens drowned by the bagful. Then at night we'll dress in our silken best, pile on jewels and whiz off to parties, bring home prizes for the family. We'll bet on horses.

We all see the car. Celia says, "He's here. Neil's come." We stop and stare like the mouth-breathers Neil says we are—idiots bound for the cannery, the sweatshop, goods headed downriver. "Well, we're going in": Jenny speaks then like her mother, the expert fatalist. She and Celia go away toward the house.

The Hudson, slouched under its metal visor, the sun shifting over it, gives the impression of a wild beast in repose, the light skimming a fierce though disguised wakefulness. We hear a voice calling us; it is our mother, Grace, calling and calling. Do we only imagine she wants to come out with us and run away? We feel separate from all of them, and we will have to go in alone, stupid and tardy, exposed, the family watching. "Well, if it's not Mutt and Jeff," Neil will say, because one of us is taller and the other shorter. Other times he calls us the two sad sisters, two sad sacks, two milkmaids, two of everything, as if we are just the same, would fetch the same price. The others laugh when he says these things, but they will put their arms around us and whisper for us not to mind, to smile even, although that won't fool Neil. We know that—we know him. Better than anybody.

When we go in, Neil is sitting at the table with his drink before him. No one else is drinking, none of the women. They fear it and keep their distance. They feel that they have the same weakness the men have and must guard themselves from becoming sots. None of the women has a taste for it either. Sometimes Neil coaxes Aunt Grace to loosen up and have some fun; so she drinks and gets glittery and laughs a lot. Later she sometimes gets sick.

Neil notices us the moment we step inside but he doesn't show it to any of the others, goes on teasing Aunt Rachel about her new boyfriend, Tom Buck. Neil knows him from college, when they were on athletic teams together. Also at one time Tom Buck had wanted to marry Aunt Grace. We don't understand exactly what Neil is saying now but we know it has to do with the private, disturbing and exciting things between a man and a woman. That shows, as does the whiskey, he's drunk.

"You know you need it. If you don't I do," he's saying to Aunt Rachel, whose white skin is aglow; the color seems to float on her in blooms like water flowers. Then she isn't laughing anymore, while he raises his glass and drinks a sip with that intimate knowledge of her plain and bold on his face while he stares at her. For all to see. Aunt Grace has her back to him as she works at the sink.

He looks at us now. Before he does we know it is time, feel the connection. "Well, my own two daughters. Come give your old pappy a kiss." He wants us, asking us from deep inside. We feel it. We resist. He tightens his mouth, shrugs, shrinks backward, angry. There is a place hurt in him now. It's like when he sings, "Frankie and Johnny were lovers and oh how that couple could love." He drinks and makes us more ashamed with his high laugh. "I see nothing's changed here. Turning out like the rest of the bunch." When Gram comes into the room he nods toward her: "Here's to the Queen of Hearts," but she's already left without a glance, before he can raise his glass to his lips.

"You know you love all of us." We hear Aunt Elinor, who has also been called home to be with her sister. But still we are eroded by our shame, by the wearing force of our separateness and our attachment to him. In the pantry we stop a moment beside Aunt Grace, watching the arc formed as her long slender arms and hands move quickly and capably. She is too busy to notice us and we are in the way. Supper will be late because he is here and everyone, fascinated, can't break away and says helplessly the things they know he's wanting them to say—their eyes darting and ardent, playful, safe as long as they are together.

Or until something happens to upset them. Neil leans back in his chair and holds his cigarette like a prop in front of his face as he says to his wife, "It's a good thing that the girls' school starts next month. Any longer and I might end up so lonely I'd have to get a girl friend."

Aunt Grace takes a deep breath and says, "I thought I would stay on at the farm for a while, Neil. I have to keep going back and forth to the clinic and the girls might as well begin school here." We are all very still, but by the looks on their faces and the sound of their voices we know that it is best for them to say this to each other in front of everyone.

Neil starts to say that he guesses there aren't any other doctors in the world, then mutters, "Never mind."

Aunt Grace says, "We'll see."

"Yeah," Neil says. "I don't know what more it takes, Grace. A house. A raise." He is weary.

The women get up and find things to do. Aunt Rachel makes coffee and it smells wonderful. We even hear the bell strike from the town clock—the wind amplifies it, or the silence. Uncle Dan rattles into the drive in the delivery truck and we kids run out to greet him. It's like a reprieve, for now Neil will talk to him and be the way we've seen him sometimes, on the street, serious with an acquaintance, or at a table in a room by himself where he fills page after page with his words.

When Neil is on the farm the days begin with a grand breakfast. He says that being here puts him in mind of the summers of his boyhood, though he doesn't know why exactly, since that was a working farm, where his relatives were, not some kind of refuge for misfits or playland for the idle rich. As though it's a holiday, just because he is here to enjoy it, we all eat late, take several fried eggs from the oval ironstone platter, have extra bacon and Aunt Grace's homemade bread toasted, with jam she has boiled from fresh fruit; all except Grandad, who has had his boxed cereal hours before and is already asleep in his chair in the corner of the living room, up against the console radio. It is nearly lunchtime when Aunt Grace goes to the sink to empty the coffee grounds and says, "You go on now," to Neil. "We can't get a thing done with you around." When he rolls up his daredevil eyes at her, she adds, "Certainly nothing useful," letting her hand for a second fondle and caress the back of his neck where his blond hair curls over the pitted scars of acne. Soon afterwards, Neil lifts his straw hat off the rack and says, "I know when I'm not wanted," and strolls out the door, calling back over his shoulder to us, "See you gals in back of the barn." He gives Aunt Grace a saucy look when she says, "Now, Neil. Nothing mean."

"When have I ever?" he asks her in a bold and mocking

pretense of disbelief. Already we are thrilling with excitement, fascinated by the blue again burning in his eyes. There is no stopping us either. But Aunt Grace is by now distracted, sorting through laundry on the floor, laundry for ten people that must be bleached and blued, starched, washed and dried, sprinkled and ironed; she scarcely notices when we leave, singing under her breath, quite content. She seems well, like her old self again.

Linked in the force of our expectancy, we go to the back of the barn and sit there to wait for Neil where the cedar log is so dried and whitened with lime and calcium dust it appears to have drifted over the surging sea to rest finally on this desolate shore. Soon we are sweating under the full impact of the sun; the few locust trees scatter a skimpy shade into the quivering heat. Neil takes so long to come to us that we forget almost why we have waited here. But we wait on because he told us to, and then Celia cries out because a hickory burr has struck her head and we glance up just in time to catch Neil's head drawing back out of the eaves window of the hayloft.

"We see you. We see you." We are shrill in relief.

Neil sticks his head out again. From upside down under the brimmed hat, his face appears cloven at the chin, in shadow under the shiny petal yellow of the bleached straw and the surrounding fall of yellow hair. "If you're ready for the spelling bee," he says, talking down the hay sprig dangling from his mouth, "get yourselves lined up."

We arrange ourselves into formation after finding for Neil the stout stick that he always holds. It is an old-fashioned school, like the one he went to as a boy when, he has told us, the teacher was as mean as Silas Marner, as severe as God and as relentless as the devil. Neil commands his class with the absolute authority of his own justice. During the session we will call him Master Higgenbottom. He knows the name will make us laugh, but only for an instant. Uncannily, his abrupt transformation into the dreaded master completes for us the entire setting of his boyhood —the raised platform where the teacher's desk presides, the cen-

tral wood stove which must be fed continually although everyone is always either cold or sweltering, and the actual whip, long,
of a narrow braided leather, which is hung up in plain sight. He
has told us how fortunate we are that he as master does not insist
on the complete historical accuracy of employing the strap; although he looks quite capable of resorting to it, should it become
necessary. We tremble, waiting in line.

We have entered the school. It is a hundred years ago and
we are trapped there, by fate, by our own intention. Before us
stands the demoniac Master Higgenbottom; we even conjure for
him a tailored rusty black waistcoat. There is now no humor in
his name, none in his always unsettling yet once familiar eyes,
which now stare from the distance of an incomprehensible lost
world. We stagger, almost faint in the glare of high noon. Again,
we have not recognized him until it is too late.

"And now, my dears," he says, and addresses us especially, his
two daughters. "I have appraised the fact, made known to me
through the word of several of your more infatuated and silly
admirers, who shall remain nameless, that you, although the
erratic disarray of your clothing, your disheveled appearance in
general, would deny it"—and here he takes the tip of his stick
to flick the dragging hems of our cotton dresses—"that you," he
repeats, and curls up his top lip, "have recently entertained aspira-
tions that would forever sever you from the taint of this miserable pig wallow and thrust you into a broader, and presumably
receptive, world."

None of us responds, in part because we have to struggle with
the words he uses. He has heard that we have been listening to
the country radio broadcasts, coming out of West Virginia, that
we have in turn sung in harmony like those pairs of sisters we
have listened to, that we have talked of singing on the radio and
being famous. Good singers like good actors, he has always told
us, are a dime a dozen. If only he had a nickel for every mother's
son who wanted to be a star. It seems entirely shameful and
ludicrous to us now, this ambition which is against all that Neil

has taught us, about vanity and self-denial, humility, against all that he truly admires and has wanted us to be. We have been seduced, spoiled for him. We deserve punishment. We cannot meet his eyes.

"Therefore," the master continues, "duty impels me to uncover this betrayal or else to discover if there is a single shred of evidence that such clandestine hope should reside in the breasts of common farm girls, should be given an iota of encouragement.

"Sing," he commands us.

Our mouths hang open, like mouth-breathers', but we have no power to move them. There is a prolonged silence. "I thought as much," he says finally, himself for an instant, laughing at us. Then he slaps the stick against his open hand, causing it to resound smartly. The master again, he speaks: "I won't flog you this time. But should such vain conceit appear in the future, it would be clearly incumbent upon me to expunge this detestable and affected foolishness which would persuade you from your plain and rightful course. Unless, of course, you should ever wish to perform."

We are humiliated. He has shown again that we are his stupid, flighty, undisciplined daughters, certain to end our days in the laundry or as bar wenches. He has told us so.

"Attention," he begins. We straighten ourselves involuntarily, caught in the flow of his power.

"Was." He gives the first word to Jenny.

"W-a-s," she responds. Nobody smirks although she is by far the most able student among us—only ten months younger than Celia, she seems the older of the two, perhaps because Celia was so sick as a baby. We all know Neil asks Jenny the easiest words, always does, because he admires her sensible ways. She is safe in her role as the prize student, the role he gives her.

To Celia: "Give." Again, what we expect, a simple word which, although she is always pressed to her limits at school, struggling mightily just to pass the grades, he knows she will spell easily.

But for his daughters, the next pause is extended into an unreeling suspense. It could be anything. "Shame": he delivers the word, and we are flooded with the joy of being able to spell it out. After this the game moves easily, and with a skill we seldom manage, we spell all the words he gives us, even multisyllabic ones. Increasingly our voices reflect our assurance and confidence; our disregard of what, underneath, we know is only a temporary respite.

"Symbol," he calls to Celia.

"S-i-m-b-l-e," she tries.

"Come forward." It is very hot in the locust clump, which holds heat and casts a shallow pool of shadow into its own roots with the sun high overhead. Above Celia's pink trembling mouth we see the dewy salt. Master Higgenbottom renders her the punishment—one blow with the stick across her bare calves. Celia's tongue licks over her lips but she does not cry out. The actual blow does not hurt very much; he strikes his own hand harder.

We begin our plunge into the final predictable though unavoidable moments of the session; for in surefire and rapid order we miss each of our next words and suffer the noisy blows. Once. Then again. As we become more flustered we miss even the simple words. And with our mute failure to even attempt "conscience" and "uranium," as though we had been commanded to sing, we have received the ten strikes which end the game. The last are the hardest and we at last break down. He regards us with contempt. "You wanted to play. Nobody forced you. And now you blubber and bawl. Can't take it, can you?" He hurls the stick against the barn siding, turns his back and walks away. He kicks through the bone piles as though he is thrashing willful stupidity.

We four climb up into the haymow, up to the rafter window. We vow we will never forgive him. We swear to avenge ourselves, even if we have to pay with our lives. We tell each other how he'd feel if we died. Dry-eyed, exhausted at last, we lie in the sun-shot darkness of the barn, and the soft cries of the doves seem to be the sound of Neil's grief when he knows that he has lost us, when he views us, innocent girls, cold and still in death.

We are released then, forget again, and begin to descend the levels of the barn, down through the shafts of sunlight, and then we run off down the pasture lane into the woods, walking by the stony shallow stream until it is deeper and runs clean. We slide into the water; our dresses fill and float about us as though we have been altered into water lilies. After our dip, cool, absolved, we lie upon the bank, brushed dry by the coarse grasses, which hold a mosaic of daisies and Queen Anne's lace.

When we hear the rock chuck into the water beside us, we sit up. We don't see anything but we know he is here. Feel him. Somewhere, hiding. When the next throw comes, we are ready and pop up our heads to see a streak of bright blue among the trees, a blue bluer than the sky painted behind the trees, his shirt, and we are up, shrieking, "We see you, we see you," leaping away over the brook with our wet clinging dresses slapping against our legs, going on into the denser woods, where immediately the silence takes hold. We feel lost, stop, strain into the winding tangles of brush and vine. Has he been there? Then from nearly on top of us, from behind, comes a menacing growl. We wheel round. There it is, the leaping blue, and we race after his retreating form. And then he trips or falls somehow and we are upon him. We jump on top of him, seizing a wonderful victory. We have hold of his yellow hair. We tickle under his arms and pinch the loose skin by his belt. He puts his arms around us and rolls over the ground, going downhill toward the creek, and laughs so that we can feel his body shaking, with his hard legs wrapped around us. "Did my little girlies get mad at their daddy?" he whispers. "Did the little girlies think they would never love him again?" Sky and trees dissolve behind his enclosing shoulders.

At the bottom of the hill we lie, surrounded and quiet. We can smell his tobacco and the wild parsley and clear water. We are at peace, enthralled. Sometime in there he becomes restless and leaves. When we realize he has gone we search and call into the solemnity of the woods. Then we forget again, dreaming.

The sound of the trampling feet rouses us, provokes in us the fear which flickers always just beyond the edge of our senses and which, triggered, drives us crazy. We see them as horned, creatures with foaming mouths breaking through the branches. We dash in circles, scream, laugh and push into each other until we are able to pull ourselves up into an oak tree, to safety, twisting ourselves right out from between the teeth of the beasts that mill about on the ground near the base of the tree right beneath us. But then, laboring painfully, spent, they simply stand there, calming. Grandad would be furious if he knew someone had run his cows. All the same, we want to see them scared and running again, want them to pay. We wonder when we will ever get away—as if, shipwrecked, we're stranded in a swaying oak tree island.

Then Neil is coming down the path swinging his stick, whistling as though he has just happened along. We know better. He walks right into the midst of the cows, pushing at them, poking. With a start they amble on down the curving path along the streambed. Neil is singing about Frankie and Johnny. "Frankie drew back her kimono," he sings. His voice inclines toward us, mellow and insinuating. A certain inflection tells us he knows we are there, although he doesn't look up. It's in the way he lingers over "kimono." Then he says, "Reckon you gals are safe now. Now that I'm here. Whatever do you suspicion commenced them critters to skedaddle like that?" He's mocking Gram now, the way he does sometimes, so we'll join him in laughing at her, even though it makes us feel disloyal, bewildered. Also he wants us to know exactly what he's been doing. Although he'll say we're lying if we tell. We don't know what to think of him, but it doesn't matter and we sail out of the tree and seem nearly to waft to earth. Then with him we follow the path winding along the stream, skipping rocks, jumping the wider banks, naming aloud the meadow flowers for him, to show we remember what he has taught us. And we sing through to the end the long droning ballads of forsaken love, to which he learned all the words when he was a boy. In the shallows where the stream is divided by a sandbar, we take hands and for a while make a bridge the width of the stream, Neil in the middle. It all affects us, the deep of the woods and the songs, as though we are legendary maidens drowned in the deep salt sea.

It is only when we are going up the wooden back stairs onto the porch and then into the house that we know we have been gone longer than long. We smell onions frying. Aunt Grace is preoccupied, moving over the length of the two joined kitchen rooms, for the stove is in the larger room with the table, and the sink and refrigerator are in the smaller pantry room, the countertops here and there. Everybody is at the table. Waiting. When Neil comes in and sits down, still wearing the straw hat, it's as though they relax and tense simultaneously, preparing for him. When he passes Aunt Grace, going for a drink, he slides an ice cube down her dress front and she yelps and squirms around to dislodge it, then leaves the room to remove it. We all laugh like crazy.

Rossie calls from the yard for the four of us to come out. "Hey, I got a new shiner. I want to show you." He sounds friendly and we let him talk us in closer to him, the way we draw Queenie toward us with grain when we want to ride her. He wants us to admire the new marble he has won in a game. We don't understand his moods.

"Honest," he says. He stands across from us, holding out his hand. We stand like draft horses, shifting nervously, unwinking, even afraid of a shadow. Then he empties the whole sack of marbles and we are caught. They roll and spin, are beautiful, some clear as jewels, and in others shattered crystals resemble sugar or milky spills. We are impressed that he has so many, and the shiner is mammoth. He impresses us further by giving each of us one

—he lets us pick. We love him again and want to take care of him, this neglected and fatherless boy.

He wants to show us a new trick. He lies on the grass and raises his knees. His plan is for us to balance on the bottoms of his feet, full length, while he gives us rides up and down, back and forth. He wants Jenny to go first because she is his favorite because she is sensible. We all take turns then and we like doing it a lot so that when he offers one of us an honest-to-God flip we all want one. Celia goes first—she asks him to be careful and gives him her hands. The next thing we know, she is off on the ground some distance away, as if she has flown there. Now she is still.

"You killed her," we say, and go to her. She opens her eyes when we lean over her. "What happened?" Her voice is hollow-sounding. We think she is pretending, trying to get attention. "What do you mean, what happened? You were doing the trick." We want to hit her.

Her face is very white and she doesn't answer. "Don't be dumb," we tell her, and lie down beside her on the grass, watching the first coming of evening, lavender among the dark branches. Rossie has gone away and we wonder about him, how he can be this way and the other way we know him too, the way he is sometimes in bed at night with one of us. Those nights, it seems to us in our attic beds as though we are together and forgotten in an isolated tower. The cars out on the highway that sometimes splash the walls with their lights proceed like our thoughts, solitary and dreamlike, at a great distance. Sometimes there is a mashed and wrecked car brought into the garage down the highway, late at night, and if we wake up we get out of bed to watch the crane drop the car, watch the spinning red light. In the morning we will go across to see the car; sometimes there is blood on the seat or mixed in with the windshield glass. After the night is quiet, we feel lonely and shivery, and if Rossie is there he gets into one of the beds and waits until only one of us is awake beside him. We are so far away from the rest of the world, up in the branches of the trees, it is as if the curving stairway is a fragile mooring line on the end of which we bob and drift. Soft and warm and secret, we touch each other and in that way we are able to fall asleep. In the mornings afterwards we fight. We are ashamed because of what we can mean to each other. We want everyone to believe that we despise Rossie, that he despises us. Everybody is fooled. Except Neil maybe. He knows about boys; his lip curls up at the very mention. He says he wishes Rossie were his own boy—for about five minutes.

Now we get up and walk toward the house and Celia stumbles a little and wants to know what happened. We ignore her, looking at the lights which appear in various rooms of the house, lights that have been left on, for days maybe, a negligence that drives Gram wild with the waste and her bills. As we go in we still hear everybody laughing. We have forgotten for a moment that Neil is here.

"I don't know how Grace does it," Aunt Elinor says. "Do you know that when I'm by myself in the city I don't even boil water." That seems natural enough to us, her New York affairs far removed from the minor concerns of food and drink. We are sitting on the dining room floor, beginning to play gin rummy, but we watch Aunt Grace move back and forth and we listen to their talk.

Neil begins, says, "That never was a favorite of mine anyway," meaning Elinor's boiled water.

Aunt Libby says, "You know, it's the truth—what Momma says: If I used a barrel of butter and cream in everything I make, you'd rave over my cooking too. But I think Grace is the best cook." She says this with the impartiality of someone definitely not in the running.

"Well, I never will understand what all the fuss is about anyway," Aunt Rachel says. "Seems to me anybody that can read can cook."

"Hear, hear," Neil says. This is it, what he's wanted. "That explains it, Ellie. You can't read. And all this time you've hidden it. By golly, I wish one of you barmaids"—he turns away from the table so he can see us watching and listening to him—"would take off a little time and teach your auntie to read. She'd probably be a good study. Although, considering your spelling, I don't know. Maybe none of you can read." He gets the disgusted look that we see sometimes when he says privately to us, "I don't know how I ever got tied up with such a bunch of stupes." Still they all are laughing; it comes out of their love for each other and the keenness of its trance. Aunt Elinor laughs too, expansively and musically, the way she does everything.

Neil stops lifting his eyebrows at us and looks at her, directing the attention of all of us. "It's for certain no one ever said you couldn't *talk*. No siree! Nobody ever said that."

"Now, Neil," Aunt Grace says. "Ellie doesn't talk any more than the rest of us."

"Uh?" He plays dumb. "I declare. That's not exactly what you told me in bed last night." Aunt Grace stops moving at the sink, and we can see the stain of red rise under her dark skin. Her expression darkens too as her eyes seem to sink further back into the hollows around them. Without answering, she goes on with the knife, quick, with Gram's inbred speed, slivering celery on the diagonal, quartering green peppers and tomatoes.

But Aunt Elinor is still genial and Neil looks toward us again, and winks; he knows we are going right along with him, knows what we think. Although we give no sign.

"Now let's get on back to this cooking thing. I'd like to get a few things straight, for once get you girls to admit what you really think. Instead of always this boring wishy-washy sweetness and light. You must have an opinion, May." Neil says.

Neil has told us that Aunt May is the only one of the sisters besides Aunt Grace who showed promise—that she wasn't just an Ohio peasant putting on the dog. Now she gives a gurgle of self-effacing denial of her worth; but we think immediately that her food tastes the best, perhaps because her table is covered with a stiff ironed linen cloth and is set with polished silver and her rose-patterned china is complete with separate vegetable dishes, so spinach or broccoli floats in its own delectable butter sauce. She says only, "I guess we're all good cooks. Must get it from Momma."

"Well, if your preference is for pepper and dough," Neil says. He lets out a prolonged breath, which glides into a whistled rendition of "There's a long, long trail a-winding." It's one of the songs he's taught us, a song from the days when he used to sleep on bare ground under the stars on the lonesome prairie, when he was a vaquero, and learned to distinguish crow bait from bred stock. Sometimes on summer nights he lies beside us on the cooled grass and traces out the constellations, teaching us to find Cassiopeia and Pegasus, telling us of the endless reaches of light that separate us from the stars. We never know when the thing he tells us is true or made up. Now he stops his song for a second and says in rhythm, "Yes. Uh,uh! Guess you get your beauty from your Momma too." Then he goes on whistling until he adds, "From the knees up."

With the cessation of the melody, the silence of the room is such that we can hear the oil scatter in the skillet. Their legs are one of the things we aren't supposed to mention, like their ages. Secrets. Once we found letters to Aunt Rachel which a boyfriend had sent in 1935. She was seventeen then; we figured back and forth, came up with her age, accused her of it. "Sh," she had said, her eyes with their peregrine tilt, conspiratorial. And immediately we forgot because she wanted us to and because we thought of all of them as beyond ordinary time or distance—like movie stars.

"If only I had me a piano": Neil baits them some more. That's the way he describes the dense, heavy, although curved ankles that support their bodies. Again they are laughing, Aunt Elinor the most adventurous, risking the most, because of all the five sisters, she is the one who is somewhat plumpish, although solid-fleshed—a feature, Neil tells us secretly, which would have won her a sure reputation as a lady wrestler. This seems to us particularly funny though our snickers feel nasty, provoking an image of Aunt Elinor, squat and muscular, pinning her opponent. We must hide these jokes from her. Like the others. Aunt Libby Neil privately calls Penelope because he says he doesn't know anyone else who takes so long to get things done, says he figures she'll be there when the last die is cast. Gram is Hecuba—that's when he says he is feeling kindly toward her.

But this summer evening Gram has already flown away to pleasure herself and Grandad is down in the barn milking and Neil lets the feeling in the kitchen become peaceful; for a while he talks seriously to Aunt Elinor about the advertising world. Aunt Grace works hard over a complicated recipe for egg foo yong and we can see her enjoyment in displaying her competence. Neil says she is going through a lot of fuss for an omelet, though he looks proud too, and Aunt Elinor says it is highly regarded at the best restaurants in Chinatown, and Aunt Rachel says she'd stake money on it that we are the only people in Sherwood eating it this night. Which makes Neil say that he's glad to be in such select company. He walks to pour another drink and when he passes Aunt Grace he suddenly gooses her, which makes her startle and glare at him. But he only laughs more determinedly and she puts on a smile for us to see, even while he says to everybody that sometimes he has to go out of his way to liven up old Grace or else she would shrivel into the awfulest old prude. Aunt Grace says, without paying much attention, that she guesses that would be a fate worse than death.

We eat our dinner in stages while Aunt Grace stands at the stove and adjusts the heat under the oil, calculating exactly this final stage in the preparation of the exotic vegetable patties; she seems very pleased to be serving us, and her sisters are raving over this delicacy. When Grandad comes in with the milk, he refuses to try any, and then won't even sit at the table to eat what Gram has left for him from her meal but stands at the sink in the pantry. Aunt Grace doesn't fuss at him but pours coffee into the ironstone mug he prefers, takes it to him, and helps him scald the milk pails. He says then, padding toward the living room in his socks and grinning sheepishly, "Guess you can't teach an old dog new tricks," and she smiles as if she agrees. Still he has learned at last to leave his barn boots on the porch, except for a few times when he goes ahead and stomps his path over the carpet to his corner chair, leaving the scattered chaff and smudges of barnyard waste —which Neil says is done to show that Grandad still has something running in him that makes him feel like a man.

Neil and Grandad like each other well enough, at least we think so, because sometimes they get drunk together on the hard cider Grandad hides in the barn. Uncle Dan has joined them on occasion, but he gets so sick and desperate he prays to die, and since it is as much guilt as octane that gets him, that and Aunt Libby's disapproval, he figures to let the stuff alone and save it for the big boys. But Neil says he can't let old Jake catch all the hell there is around there, and he joins Grandad more than seldom, and then the two of them come up along the drive in the late dark, bellowing Neil's western songs, their arms draped around each other, reeling and hugging. Complaining about the women. "Acting," Aunt Grace says. "Just sheer playacting," and she fastens the locks on the doors, the only times they are all secured, and turns out all the lights so the house is dark, and then she goes to bed while they pound and sing and get mad. Once Neil had sneaked up onto the porch roof and was climbing in Gram's open window, when she, thinking someone had at last come for her pocketbook, which she kept under the mattress, threw the bedside clock at him. The clock smashed to bits and startled Neil so that he pitched backwards and was saved from sliding off the roof only by the venetian blind cords, which he had grabbed until he caught his balance. Everyone agreed that it was a wonder he hadn't broken his neck. Which, he agreed, was no doubt the case, but it had been outrage alone that had saved him—when he realized that he wasn't taking the old witch along with him. He said that if Gram had risked throwing her pocketbook at him she would have finished him for good, loaded as it must be with gold bullion, considering how closely she guarded it. "Missed your chance," he reminded her from time to time, raising his brows and narrowing his eyes simultaneously.

After we have all eaten the egg foo yong, the special hot and sour sauce, Aunt Grace is still going between the stove and the sink, stacking the dishes, wiping counters, while Neil is hand-wrestling with the rest of us, using his left arm and letting two of us at a time try to force his lean, hard-muscled arm to the tabletop. He says that none of us knows what hard work is: how many hours of a summer's day have we spent on a haywagon? He challenges Aunt May, who at least, he allows, has put out many a load of washing; after he has played around with her a few minutes he pins her arm abruptly, as though it's no more than a stick. Around her thin wrist is a crimson chafe mark and we see a slight skim of tears fill her eyes. Aunt Grace has put her own plate on the table, getting ready to eat, and says to Neil, "You ought to be ashamed," while he sweeps back his arms to shake hands with himself over his head, declaring his mock victory, and sends her plate and the egg foo yong spinning and crashing to the floor.

Aunt Grace hops up as if she's done it herself; while the rest of us stare, she kneels on the floor beside her ruined dinner, her hair hanging over her face. And then she just collapses into a heap amidst the mess and starts to heave in an odd tearless retching despair. We are still stricken. It's as though she cannot breathe and we cannot move to save her. Aunt May says, "My God in the mountain," as she hurries over to Aunt Grace, lifts her up to sit on the floor, straightens and smooths her hair, murmurs, "You must be so tired. Slaving all afternoon for us while we just sit here enjoying ourselves." By this time all the sisters have come to life and are busy, sweeping the food together and drawing water into the scrub pail. They pull Aunt Grace up and over to the table. Aunt Elinor holds her hand. But Aunt Grace draws away and lays her head down on her folded arms, breaking into sobs again. When everything is cleared away they start the kettle for tea water. Aunt May says she will fix Aunt Grace a regular omelet since the other mixture is all gone, and she starts to beat the eggs. Aunt Grace says that she is too upset to eat, but she lets them bring her a cloth to cool her face and gradually she becomes calm and nibbles on some toast Aunt Libby brings her.

"Oh, I don't know what's the matter with me," Aunt Grace says, a tentative smile oddly combining with her swollen red eyes. The dimple in her chin is like a tiny keyhole. "I don't know. It seemed so sad, the mess and everything. The waste. And after it was all so nice." She looks at Neil for the first time. He hasn't moved or spoken.

His mouth is tight and his eyes are myopic, slitted, as though constricted into a single-minded comprehension. Then he speaks: "I wish to God you could just once get through a simple accident without turning into a martyr." He is furious with her. She lays her head on the table again and we watch her shoulders shake. There is nothing we can ever do to help her. Aunt May strokes her hair and nobody is looking at Neil.

"For God's sake, Grace," he says, "get hold of yourself. If you keep this up, one of the girls here is going to have to offer up a fur coat or something." He rears back his head and drinks, looking down the pitch of his mobile thin nose, and it seems he is inwardly imitating a mirthless laughter for us to see. He glances around, ashamed of nothing, while each of us feels mortified, stripped naked before him and each other.

"Momma gave me that coat because she's giving you the down payment on your house," Aunt Rachel says to Aunt Grace. "How greedy can you get!"

"I don't care about the coat," Aunt Grace says, while her face is still covered by her disordered hair. "It's not that."

"If it isn't, you sure as hell ought to start getting your stories straight, sister. Makes me look like some kind of liar. Or jackass." Neil says that as quiet as truth.

The rivalry among us is contagious, in our blood, perhaps, as Neil says. Now he sits back to watch. The women forget all about the dishes.

Aunt Grace shakes back her hair and her eyes flash so that we feel the heat, though she speaks to Aunt Rachel. "Don't think I don't know what you're up to. The whole town knows. A married man! But when has that ever stopped you? Hot little dancing girl." Aunt Grace hates Aunt Rachel suddenly, and her voice is clogged and nasal. "Same old thing all over again. Well, you won't have to worry about me much longer. I'm sick, I tell you. Sick." Her sobbing sounds like someone throwing up.

Aunt Rachel hangs her head as though she deserves this abuse. We think of her hasty marriage. Rossie and her divorce. Ever so long ago. We do not understand. Now she teaches ballroom dancing at a local studio. What shame twists her hands in her lap?

This time Aunt Libby flies in to protect Aunt Rachel. "I won't hear it, goddamn it, I won't. You don't like the way things are, well, I won't listen to your bellyaching. You turned Tom Buck down flat after you'd strung him along. Turns out you're not so proud." She looks at Neil—when roused, his rank match in scorn. "Neither of them's worth shit, far as I can see."

Neil tips his hat to her, making a tsk-tsk sound, then slides the brim lower to enhance the wicked pleasure of getting just what he wants. He often wears a hat, playacting with it, sometimes one of Gram's with a stiff netted veil, or a visor which makes him resemble the croupier at a gaming table. He can play all the parts. Aunt Grace gets up from the table and goes to stand at the back door, looking into the dark. In the quiet we hear the crickets.

"Don't be so hard," Aunt May says. "Grace doesn't really mean that. She's tired and under a strain."

"We know that," Aunt Elinor says. "All the same, it's resentment and envy. Self-pity. You have such great blessings, Grace," and she smiles at us, thinking to make everybody grateful with a reminder.

Aunt Grace speaks then with her back turned, wistful and repentant. Sorrowful. "It's not Tom. Or you, Rachel. Nothing you've done, or even money. It's kind of a feeling of being left out and alone and sometimes it seems as if Momma's turned against me. Half the time I'm living back here, doing most of the work. I don't blame you girls; it's always been that way. As if, if I didn't work I couldn't stay. And now I wonder if I'll ever have a chance to live in that house now that we've got it, or enjoy any of the other things I've wanted." With her half smile and her arms raised with empty hands, she turns to look at her sisters, shrugs and says, "I'm awfully nervous."

Then even Aunt Libby stays quiet, though she had seemed about to interrupt when the subject of housework came up, a quarrel between her and Aunt Grace we had often heard. Neil tells us privately, from the days when he had been a time and motion analyst for a large manufacturing company, that Aunt Libby performs motions below a level yet to be measurable, sophisticated calibration notwithstanding. Aunt Grace has finished speaking and returns to the table, staring at her folded arms, so thin that the knobs of her elbows seem almost to pierce the skin; her true-black hair, skin shadowed darker by her lowered head, the taut stretched eyelids, give her the stolid look of a half-breed, as if she is in fact only partly related to the rest of them. "I'm sorry, Rachel," she says. "I didn't mean it."

"By God, sister," Neil says. "You ought to be able to do better than that. I thought that at least I'd picked the one of you that might not be altogether a sniveling momma's baby."

"You bastard." Aunt Rachel speaks for herself now. "Let her alone and shut up." She continues to glare at Neil, a look set enough to last forever, which becomes clear to him and he does not take her dare but snorts, slaps his knee and changes his mood like a wizard. "Hot dog!" he says, and goes on doing the talking then, fast and not waiting for any responses, as though he's on the stage or spinning yarns by a campfire. He says he doesn't think there is anything in the world half so invigorating, or grotesque for that matter, as the female of the species in her native habitat. He is surely glad his little daughters can be there to observe and learn, though neither of them has a snowball's chance in hell;

already the air they breathe is treacherous, contaminated with greed, self-pity and the stench of a petty vanity. Puts him in mind of a mule skinner he'd known when he was out in the West, that fellow himself part weasel and part snake. "Once a dude come up to him and asked him for the meanest, sorriest nag on the string. 'You cain't have her right now,' he said. 'She's a-washin' the dishes.'" To Neil we are all horses, skittish, apt to catch our death in a draft.

Neil goes on recounting his adventures in the West, how as a cowboy he learned early that if there was anything more disappointing than humankind it was *Equus caballus*—that on a Saturday night the stench of horseflesh was pretty much just exchanged for another, only this time you had to pay. The sisters ignore him, bustle about, circling around each other in weaving patterns, almost a formal dance figure, their loose dresses and hair like streamers as they pile the dishes and wipe the table and counters. They make Aunt Grace sit still; they say again they have been horribly thoughtless, allowing her to carry the whole burden. Aunt Rachel refills Aunt Grace's teacup, one of the fine rose china cups from the dining room buffet and Aunt Grace lays her hand, bony, with thick-corded veins, on Aunt Rachel's rounded plump one. They sit that way, the trouble between them settled.

Beyond the screen, across the drive, is the rustling orchard, the trees there bent close, entwined in the heavy scent and fester of ripening apples and furrowed earth where the horses tramp. Neil has stopped paying attention. Then he looks at Aunt Grace and takes one of the curls that hang by her throat and cones it over his finger, where it makes a netted veiling. With that touch she trembles and returns his look, her eyes sad. His are humorous, gentle even, as he asks her has she taken to dosing herself with belladonna—her pupils dilated like that. And that word and some love showing in his eyes affects her. Her face loses its despairing drained look and she smiles back a little, saying that there is poison enough as it is in the air we breathe. Then she sends us away, only now really aware that we have been there and seen and heard them—out into the yard, where, she says, in the fresh evening air we will be happy and can wish on stars. Although we are running down the porch steps, released, we can still hear Neil's voice: "God forbid they should ever have to face things just the way they are." Then his embittered laugh. " 'What is truth?' " he asks. "You see, Ellie, you aren't the only one who reads the Bible." After that their voices fall low, soft and intimate, and only sometimes does something of their laughter reach us, penetrating the obliviousness which we find in the fantastic dark.

We hear something move in the weeds at the back of the yard. At first we are scared but when we edge closer we see that it is Rossie leading Queenie. He hardly ever rides her, is considered too heavy, but still he is bossy because she came as a gift from his father. Queenie is the only material evidence we have of that man's existence, other than Rossie, although Gram remembers him and has told us that his friends called him "Dopey." Sometimes we are afraid Rossie will hurt Queenie and we try to protect her, and tell on him. But this night we are too amazed and excited that he would have her here with him in the dark.

"We want a turn," we yelp when we see the two of them clearly.

"Shut up," he says. "Who's there?"

"Us."

"Okay. Today I showed you a trick. Now I'm going to do one. Like they do in the rodeo. And you can watch. Go turn on the light." Celia says she doesn't remember a trick, but the rest of us remember how she flew across the yard.

After that we make a little audience for him between the cornfield and the lawn, where he mounts Queenie. He carries a willow switch. Usually it is the most we can do to get her to move at all, either that or she runs away with us to the barn.

The porch light comes over the lawn and seems like a spotlight for a stage. Rossie draws Queenie up tight on the reins. Then he kicks her and lashes her with the switch. She is so startled she bucks, going straight up, so that Rossie nearly slides off. Even in the faint light we can see his face and something in us cringes. We know that look which comes over his face when things don't go his way, comes on him when he sits on our stomachs and pounds our chests. He slams Queenie again. And, as if recognizing fully her situation, she explodes into motion in the direction of the barn. Rossie is so tall his feet would touch the ground if he didn't hold them up. The empty stirrups slap. The saddle creaks and shifts. We have never seen Queenie go so fast. She races as if Rossie has become too much for her, the way he is too much for his mother and for us.

Then Rossie begins to lift himself to his knees and then, nearing the clothesline post, he is standing in the saddle. Bravo! For an instant. For then he has vanished in the dark as though taken by the hand of God, while Queenie disappears at the corner of the drive. From the orchard comes the pounding of the work-horses as they run beside her, nickering softly.

We stand over Rossie. Beside him on the ground an end of the clothesline still dances. We are scared and sorry we have laughed.

"Leave me alone," he sputters, struggling to sit, brushing tears away with the back of his hand. He lies down again.

"He's dead," Katie says, and we laugh again.

Rossie sits up. "Shut up, dummies." He coughs and it sounds feeble. We laugh some more, skipping back so he can't hit us. When he lurches to his feet we run toward the house. "Mad dog. Mad dog." We can't wait to tell about Rossie's fall. We know that Neil will be secretly glad.

But we don't tell. They are playing a game and have forgotten us. We wonder what Neil knows about Aunt Grace. He seems the same. Now everything has been cleared away from the dinner and all the women sit with Neil at the wide boarded table playing hearts. Grandad is asleep and Uncle Dan is late at the store. Neil tricks the women again and again while they are distracted by the joking and fooling, thankful the trouble is over. Neil takes all the hearts and the queen of spades. They lose, take bunches of hearts, over and over, and act as though they love it. Love him. Don't care. "You girls sure don't take after your mother," he tells them, because Gram gets furious and won't play whenever she loses and she cheats to win at solitaire. Neil remarks that in a curious way he almost misses her. "At least when the old woman's around you know somebody's at home."

We leave them. Upstairs Aunt Rachel's door is open and her porcelain lamps, a shepherd and shepherdess, are illuminated, their innocent faces smiling sweetly under fluted ivory shades. Arranged before the mirror on the dressing table are her creams and perfumes, her gilt dresser set and hairpins. For years we have invaded her room, spilled her powders and worn her pumps and finery up and down the house and drive. She has complained, mildly, in her indulgent way, but we have ignored her and do as we please, use up her favorite cologne. Now Neil is here and has taken control; he says somebody has to protect Aunt Rachel. He has said that we may not even enter her room, that if we do, his two daughters at least, over whom he presumes he still has some authority, will wish for Gehenna as consolation from his wrath. He says that if he were in charge around there, things would be a lot different.

We stand in the doorway, inch nearer. Celia and Jenny try lipsticks. Then Celia smooths her hair with the tortoiseshell comb. Downstairs they are still absorbed. We hear Neil "smoking out the queen." Aunt Elinor is careless and shows her hand. Neil says she should use her mammoth frontispiece for something useful. "Look! Of course I look," we hear him. They laugh and tell him he is impossible. "You women bring out the worst in me," he admits.

Hearing them far away and entertained, we move in closer to the lighted mirrored table. What right does he have to be here? To tell us what to do? We do what we want. They are playing their game and we begin to fix our hair and polish our nails. Celia puts one of Aunt Rachel's records on the Victrola and one by one we dance.

Aunt Rachel's hand mirror falls. Shatters. Then Neil is upon us. He has sprung from the kitchen in one leap, it seems, as though he'd been half waiting. His face is terrible. "You won't rest, will you? Not until you get what you want." He is hardly able to form words but he only dares touch his daughters. We are yanked and dragged through the hall and pushed into a dark room. From a great distance Aunt Grace calls, "Neil."

They don't come. He slams the bedroom door and shoves us onto the bed. We hear his breath and then the sound his belt makes sliding out of the notches. We are afraid of his belt, plastic with ridges which leave stripes. We wait for its sound on the air. But there is nothing. Just the sound of his breathing and after a while it's quieter and he sits down on the side of the bed, which makes the mattress slant toward him, and he is near us in the dark, quiet now, so that except for the pitch of the bed we would think we had been left alone. It's that way such a long time that we are almost not afraid. Finally he gets up and goes to the door, stands there a moment, his hand on the doorknob. Then he speaks, wearily and without anger: "You know your mother is dying." Light falls on the bed and we see that we are lying on Gram's appliquéd quilt. Then it is dark again as he shuts the door and we begin to sob and sob, sorrow all through us as though it is the only real feeling in the whole house and now we have to accept our share.

When much later we leave the room, Celia and Jenny are waiting at the top of the back stairwell. They go down with us. We have all been crying. We crawl down the tunnel of the stairs and sit on the rubber treads. We can tell that everyone is mad again at Neil, that they are making him pay this time. When he says things, no one laughs or answers. We imagine their faces, hard, eyes downcast. Neil's voice is pitched up higher than usual, as if the strain has affected even him.

They don't respond to the change in Neil but somehow he knows we are there and he begins speaking to us where we are beyond the door in the dark. He tells an old story about his life in the West, the freight cars he hopped to get there. How hungry he was. How lonesome. He describes the flowing prairie and the rising moon, the incomparable sky. Then he asks us can we hear the shy tittymouse. Already we are smirking when he says that; we don't believe any such thing exists in all the world, except in his head. Then he calls out, "Annie. Katie. Stop your sulking and get out here." The women come immediately to the door, surprised, and draw us all out. We are blinded by the light and stagger into the room, like redeemed outcasts. While we drink lemonade we ignore Neil, and the women make a great fuss over us, showing how much they love us, how apart Neil is.

Neil says that if we keep frowning like that we will be wrinkled up by the time we're twenty and won't ever get husbands, that around here we have to be careful or our mouths will be like prunes, that for his money, resentment nursed and cultivated is the fount of all disease, particularly degenerative disease. And perhaps if there were less of that in certain quarters, certain people wouldn't be sick all the time. He comes then to sit on the floor at our feet.

"Help your poor old balding father," he says, and our hands begin their task almost automatically, massaging his head up near the forehead where the fair wavy hair has begun to thin and recede. Soon our palms are slick and rank with the oils from his head and we can smell its sourness as though it is a horse's lather. He tells us that we will become famous in this way, that since the world began man has labored, experimenting endlessly, to restore hair, that we two are engaged in that great family project, magic. Maybe, he says, we have found the answer. This encourages us, so we work all the harder. Strong fingers, he goes on, will pay off at the piano—and elsewhere. His eyes nearly close beneath our stretching, kneading touch and we watch the pulse throb in his veins under the taut skin, which is strawberry pink under the darker spots of freckling. The women go into the other room but we are not afraid now. Neil rests so quietly under our hands that we think he has gone to sleep. We will go on endlessly. He will never release us.

But he is not asleep and begins to tell us another story. He wishes we had known his Aunt Sarah "on the distaff side." She'd been as hardy and capable a woman as could be imagined. Word had it that she'd just stop by the furrow long enough to drop her babies, fourteen of them in all, and then would go on at the plow. When her youngest boy fell out of the barn loft and bit off the end of his tongue, she took it, warm and slippery as it was, and with her needle and thread stitched it back on—while the initial shock still rendered it somewhat numb. Anyway, that boy had lived to tell the tale. This had happened twenty-five miles from any doctor and in the time before women had capitulated to the notion that the chief advantages of civilization were to dress well and have the leisure to be sick.

He asks us to turn off the light. Moonlight, falling in silent silver between the tangled trees in the orchard, fingers across the drive. The silhouetted, discernible forms of the trees suggest personality: Neil always said they reminded him of the family— some a little apart, on the fringes, a few little tots here and there, the gnarled old crone in the center, and then the five sisters, close together, their slender branches intertwined, thrashing in any wind at all, making much ado about nothing. The sawn-off waterlogged stumps he compared to the few men who ever dared to approach. We think now that Neil is not one of the trees at all, but he is like a bold colorful blue jay, sailing and bluffing.

"Oh, the poor sad waifs," he croons under his breath, telling us the ways of the wicked world. "You two better stick with me. You'll find there isn't much more around here to be counted on, unless you want a lot of singing and dancing. With me you know exactly what you're getting."

He is quiet, drinking. "Anyway," he adds, "what other choice do you have really? And I doubt things will ever get as bad for you as they did for your poor old pappy when he ran away from home in nineteen hundred and twenty-five. I don't imagine you girls will want to try that."

We have tried. More than once. Years ago, after he whipped us, we vowed to run far away, to break his heart in pieces. We

took out a suitcase and folded up a few socks and some underwear, which seemed as lost in the large case as we would be in
the world. Neil walked us to the door. "Long as you're set on
going," he said, and frowned. At the end he seemed sad. "I surely
hate to see you go. But if you're determined." He shrugged his
shoulders and his eyebrows too, which were a frizzled blond.
Often we'd heard him lament that he couldn't have them trans-
planted to the top of his head. He gave each of us a nickel, to
make our start in the world, he said. We refused the money, still
haughty, making him suffer. Then we were out in the world, in
the abrupt dark. The door closed. With the closing of that door
it seemed we had gone a million miles. We began to fling
ourselves against the door, pounded and cried. But he had locked
it and gone away. Frenzied, we beat on, nothing else to do, and
then magically he appeared before us, outlined against the warm
and lighted room. "Now haven't I seen you before somewhere?"
he said.

"Yes, yes," we cried, struggling to speak. "We're Anne and
Katie. Your daughters." Saying that made us sob out loud.

"Why, can it be?" He warmed slowly. Looked more and
more glad. He embraced us finally, recognized us as truly his two
beloved, long-lost daughters. We could feel our fear dissolve in
the safety and relief of home, of Neil's love expressed at last,
almost as though we had indeed made some long and perilous
journey alone.

In the dark now we sit and remember those times, feel his
love. Laugh with him about his tricks, the things he's done. From
the other room we hear the murmur of the sisters talking, calm
and peaceable. "Thick as thieves, aren't they?" Neil says. "Guess
I'll have to see about that. Make some impression," and he gets
up and slicks back his longish yellow hair. He pinches our legs,
says he hopes we don't ever run to fat. "Glad I raised you girls
to be tough," he says. "Considering the way things have turned
out, I don't think there's a better thing I could have done for
you." He sounds proud of us and as if he's never really felt
anything else.

PART FOUR: AUNT ELINOR

GRAM sent us with Tom Buck to wait for Aunt Elinor's train. It was cold in the station and we could see our breath flaring toward the vaulted ceiling, which had been painted a heavenly blue with golden rims, like a sun always sinking just out of sight. Tom Buck was going to marry Aunt Rachel. But she was not the first of the Krauss girls he had loved. Years before, he had been in love with Aunt Grace and had tried to marry her, long ago when she had been in college, before she met Neil. It seemed that the death of that old love was merged with Aunt Grace's death and burdened him still as he shuffled over to the wooden benches, which were sectioned into seats like desks in an old-fashioned schoolhouse. He slumped, his head in his hands.

He said the train from New York had been delayed because of the night's storm. We said nothing, but knew it would never come. Aunt Elinor had forsaken us; inside us was the thought: if only she had come in time. The train station was stark in snowlight and as immense as a waystation to heaven, under that distant blue dome where we imagined the spirit of the recently departed hovered. And perhaps might be called back. "Come back," we yearned. Tom Buck had to wipe his eyes, as he had all morning.

"I have to go to the bathroom," Katie said. We went with her for something to do. The ceramic tiles were tiny fitted hexagons of black and white, covering the walls and floor in grimy precision. All the stalls had metal lockboxes requiring a dime. Jenny went to ask Tom Buck for the money, but Katie wriggled herself under the door. Anne tried to pull her back, then went after her, only she was heavier and got stuck halfway and Katie was kicking her shoulder. When Jenny came with the dime, they couldn't get the door open, with Anne wedged under it, Katie still shoving her with her feet, just to be mean. But when finally Anne was able to get up she rushed to the sink, raving, "I'm filthy. It's terrible. I touched it. I'll die." She didn't mention Katie at all, scrubbing frantically at her face and hands in the rusty rivulet that was all the faucet would produce. And that was cold. Katie was afraid to come out. We were hating her, as we always did when she turned mean. But Anne was struggling to control herself, scrubbing and scrubbing her hands under the cold water, not even saying shit and damn, the way she wanted to. We could tell that from her face on fire. "Redheads have no secrets," Aunt Rachel said.

We just walked out and left Katie there, went back to Tom Buck. We were glad Aunt Rachel was going to have a husband again and we tried to make him feel included, though Uncle Dan said it was more than he'd been able to feel in thirteen years. Under the circular dome the air took up our voices and expanded them so that they hummed in reverberating lonesomeness. We called out to each other. When Katie came back she stayed away from us, watching Anne as if she couldn't believe Anne wouldn't fight.

Then the floor began to vibrate and then to quake. It was a wonderful sensation; in full power the train materialized, its wheels screeching, blowing steam. We followed Tom Buck to the gate, came face to face with the appalling force of the engine, which was stopped but seemed to pant and gather for another rush forward. Then with more resignation than we had ever felt before, we knew the train from New York wouldn't change anything. They had taken Aunt Grace out of the room before we were awake and it didn't matter if Aunt Elinor had been there or not.

That summer, a year and a half before, when Aunt Grace had gone to the Cleveland Clinic and they had told her what she said she must know, the unvarnished truth, Aunt Elinor had come home from New York with her new religion—almost as if she had been handed it straight from God for this occasion. The doctors could do nothing, they were the first to admit it, and told Aunt Grace that she could live only a few months, that her cancer had spread beyond their ability to treat it. But Aunt Elinor was ready for them, the nay-sayers. She had come armed with Truth against Evil, with Spirit against Matter.

"We must never again believe the physicians. Do they have the power of life and death? Do they note the sparrow's fall?" Christian Science was a science of health, it was the power of God revealed and demonstrated. It would help all of us, as it had helped her; and it was going to cure Aunt Grace completely. Aunt Elinor was absolutely convinced of it. Besides, under the circumstances, "Grace, my dear," Aunt Elinor asked, "what have you possibly got to lose?"

During that summer Aunt Grace sat with her sister in the kitchen until nearly noon every day. No longer did they sleep late; there was work to be done. The Bible and the new book, *Science and Health with Key to the Scriptures,* lay open before them, spiked with the markers that underlined the lesson for the week. Usually we were included too and the day began with reading the lesson designated in the *Christian Science Quarterly.* These lessons had titles such as "Love," "Spirit," "Matter," "Reality." Serious words to meditate on, words that impressed us with their power and ours, if we could only figure them out, feel them profoundly. We took turns with the women, reading from the Bible, selections carefully chosen to extend our thinking, often passages beginning in the middle of sentences; it seemed that each word was significant in itself, so much so that Aunt Elinor perceived meaning upon meaning. But when she read the corresponding portion of *Science and Health*, revelation seized her almost continually, so that she became breathless to declare the surpassing wonder of it—drawing us by the forcefulness of her belief. All of it related to Aunt Grace's healing, to our lives there on the farm at this time, with this mission. Together we would conquer. Sometimes she would stop suddenly, as if in listening to herself she had become amazed. She'd throw up her hands and laugh out loud.

"Oh, God, I don't know. But isn't it the most thrilling thing you've ever imagined, this tremendous power right here . . . ours." Then we would feel it in the same way, through her, as though a prophet had come among us. She studied tirelessly, into the night, made long, long calls to New York to learn from special teachers and practitioners. The faster she could learn, the better. She was in great haste for Aunt Grace's sake.

Aunt Elinor's own healing was a triumphant testimony to the power of Truth. "You ask Momma," she said to Aunt Grace. "Momma, you saw the X-rays. Momma?"

Gram was washing the breakfast dishes, which, she announced regularly, was her contribution to the housework and should be considered enough, after all the years she'd put in, slaving for kids and a good-for-nothing man. Now she didn't look up from where she was working to answer Aunt Elinor.

"Well. They were clear. All the heart damage? It's gone. Completely." Aunt Elinor spoke for Gram to hear too, firmly, trying to be patient with her mother's peculiar and exasperating reticence.

Gram spoke then over the pot she was scrubbing, her face nearly in the water. "I don't know nothing about them pictures. Can't see a thing in them that makes sense."

Aunt Elinor turned away from Gram and spoke entirely to us. "They were clear. Dr. Alexander said there was no evidence of any damage at all now, and that's only two years after he said I would always have to live as a semi-invalid. He was as amazed as I was." We too felt a part of her victory, her voice like a bellows, full, strong and tireless, her vision burning her eyes to topaz. "And I know that I am well; that is what matters." Her platinum-blond hair, thick-curled in waves, spread above her as though it were a canopy over the temple of the indwelling spirit. We could feel that spirit of hers, a firm foundation for those who were called to believe. We strained to: she was calling us to another, greater victory.

Including us all, still, she drew us into a new, exalted realm of being. It felt as though our entire former lives had prepared us for this. After a while, even Aunt Grace did not question anything during these sessions; her face rapt, she listened, absorbing the power and mystery, the wonder of faith pouring from Aunt Elinor, as over the wooden table bars of sunlight would move, clearing away the dark places until the surface gleamed whole.

Steadily Aunt Grace, her wonder at herself increasing, began to absorb the new metaphysic, to love it, apart from any benefit to herself—for its own sake. She had always been what she called sensible, down-to-earth (although if that was so, why had she married Neil? Aunt Libby asked). But now we glimpsed her bent in study over the books, repeating verses from memory, talking with Aunt Elinor far into the night. Aunt Elinor extended her vacation. The two of them plunged, with what we imagined was a zeal akin to the apostle Paul's, into the work of conversion. All that summer it seemed hardly to rain, only at night, a little for the earth; the leaves glittered with clean clear light as though the world were hung with mirror fragments—such, Aunt Elinor taught us, was the nature of reality, everything reflecting God.

We went to church with her and Aunt Grace, and sometimes Aunt Rachel and Aunt Libby. Gram wouldn't go. "I always been

Methodist," she said, although as far as we could tell she wasn't anything, didn't go to church, did as she pleased.

Unexpectedly, Anne was fervently attentive, more so than the rest of us. It was not just that Aunt Grace was her mother. It was, as Anne said, that she felt something herself, which must have been spiritual power coming from God, and although she could not really describe it to us, it was something like when she jumped all the way from the top of the haymow and knew she couldn't miss, could fly, in fact, there being only the tiniest barrier, like a veil of illusion, to prevent her. We found her greatly changed. Subdued and yet, underneath, on fire. We had not felt that. Reading from the Bible, her voice trembled as she uttered the words about the singing of the morning star—as though something within her sang too. The aunts began to regard her with a new seriousness; we heard them say, "She's a deep one. You never know." Aunt Elinor presented Anne with her own set of books and took her to the regular Wednesday-evening testimonials at the church.

Gram wanted no part in it; she left the room if Aunt Elinor started to "preach." "A lot of folks are going to get hurt around here." But we didn't pay much attention to an old woman who grumped over the dishpan and arranged to flee away nearly every afternoon and evening of her life. What did she have to do with us?

Aunt Elinor smiled at Gram's grumbling and said she already had a lot of Science in her, the way worry never got to her. She said the rest of us had some catching up to do. Gram snorted at that, her color-bled eyes cloudy so that she nearly looked blind. Science or whatever you called it, she didn't care; there was a lot in life you just had to swallow, like it or not.

That whole summer we were absorbed by Aunt Elinor, as if her thought made up our world as God's made up hers. When we weren't studying with her, we went on long nature walks, as she called them, or rode the horses into the far woods beyond where we'd ever gone before. She wore satin dressing gowns to the breakfast table and sat for hours drinking cup after cup of coffee, an addiction she had begun to feel guilty about; some mornings she drank plain boiled water. All of us wore something that had been hers at one time—jewelry, gabardine coat dresses, slips, expensive things she had saved and brought home in a special suitcase for us to share. Wearing her things made us feel a part of her glamorous life away from us.

Soon after she would come home on a visit, her sisters disappeared with her into her old bedroom and would begin to bargain over the "spoils." Late into the night we would hear them, arguing sometimes, or there were exclamations of delight and hysterical laughter over the fittings, Aunt Libby rueful that the dresses that fit Aunt Elinor's buxom form so perfectly hung on her like sacks, made her look like a flapper. They all had to agree on what was fair. This year Aunt Grace got the prize, a rectangular silver watch with turquoise inlay, which she took for Anne. They had let her have first pick of everything. All these items were lovely, real gifts, generously given. The sisters praised Aunt Elinor to the skies. Then after that there was further excitement over a display of Aunt Elinor's inarguably superior wardrobe, up to the moment, which they knew would belong to them in due time, certainly soon enough for the glacial progression of fashion to Sherwood.

Every few days Aunt Elinor would talk long-distance to New York. She tried to wait until Gram had left, because Gram couldn't stop interrupting her, reminding her every minute or two that the call was long-distance. And those calls often stretched beyond half an hour. "Dammit," Gram would flare up, "you've talked long enough."

Aunt Elinor would put her hand over the mouthpiece. "Mother, I'm paying for it."

"I don't care. Nobody needs to talk that long."

The calls to the Christian Science doctors, who were called practitioners, were necessarily lengthy, the need for an exacting spiritual examination no less acute than for a medical doctor's to determine the nature of an illness. In this case the treatment was mental—the eradication of error from thought. Then there were many calls about business too, which now Aunt Elinor had to handle from afar.

"Hello, Louie," she would trill into the phone. We could hear her all over the house, but we were drawn in closer to her, would end up right at her feet, lying on the carpet, so we could listen only to her, feel included in the whole of her enchanted life. Her laugh would come often, a musical leisured interruption of serious discussion. She would smile at us and roll up her eyes, joshing the man on the other end of the line, sweet-talking him but enjoying it too. We figured he was in love with her. Everyone was. Men were always calling or coming to visit, knocking themselves out, Uncle Dan said, to become one of her enthusiasms. Now, he added, they were really out in the cold, having to compete with God.

Listening to Aunt Elinor's outbursts of hilarity and the firm commands she gave, we were thoroughly confused and simultaneously enthralled. Finally she might say, "Shoot it," or "Kill it," meaning this or that ad, as she would explain later. "Finish that Motorola commercial by tomorrow. Or else!" With more throaty peals of feeling, she would hang up the phone and turn to all of us, released at last to confide the exact details. She would deliver a full account of "the ad game" in New York, her part in it; all this, like her fashions, light-years from our ordinary preoccupations and understanding, was, through her presence, made accessible—the far border of our lives.

She would end our conversations on a sober note, though. "Girls"—and that included her sisters too—"God never fails. When I think of the years on my feet! Well, you have no idea." She searched our eyes, trying with every fiber of her being to reach us, holding within that passionate stare the meaning and hope that words alone would never convey. The graciousness of Divine Love was evident in the quality of her attention.

Aunt Elinor had an increased authority within the family.

She valued her own counsel more highly too, prayer purifying her motives, each thought clarified by the perspective of eternity. The discontent of her sisters was no longer beyond repair; she became impatient with their endless grievances. Whereas before she had insisted they were fools to put up with this or that man's foolish behavior, now she suggested they should count their blessings, rejoice and be grateful to have husbands to work for them, so they didn't have to go out and be shopgirls or typists, or have to sit all day in a casting agency. As she had, for years. Although she had heard herself on the radio, she was still nothing but a failed singer, a second-rate actress. But the really important thing she said was, once dissatisfaction had been replaced by gratitude and gladness, the very evils her sisters had denied would disappear, transcended and defeated by Goodness, which always prevailed, like light over darkness. "Doesn't God want you to be happy?" She asked us that quite sincerely. It seemed blasphemy to disagree.

She reckoned her own increasing success as evidence. In precise detail she told us all the stages of her own career, the developments which had resulted in her present position as creative director with a large advertising agency. She had taken risks, bought stock in various products at just the right times and their values had zoomed with the economy. "Without Science I could not do this, girls. But Science teaches us to hold to the Truth— not for personal gain but for Its own sake. If want and deprivation are your expectations, want and deprivation you will have." She faced us with these terrible choices, the power over our own lives.

Her force in speaking was such that by emphasis she seemed to capitalize the recurring important words; we could sense them in her pauses, her emphatic diction, and knew these words in themselves conveyed power from God. In her presence they seemed emblazoned in our minds. After a time of listening as she went on with exact and stirring recitations of radical conversions, horrible illness and wondrous healings, all punctuated with her full thrilling laugh and presided over by her aura of luxurious well-being, we sank off our chairs onto the green carpet, which was sun-splashed as if licked by warm and gentle waves of salt water—the medium of creation itself.

But certain though Aunt Elinor was in her faith, never doubting Aunt Grace's healing, she seemed to appreciate Aunt Grace's more cautious attitude, her desire to follow the procedures which the doctors recommended to prolong her life as well as to keep up her spirits. *Let them do what they can,* Aunt Elinor's calm bearing seemed to say. So all that summer while Aunt Grace was taught by Aunt Elinor, she continued to go to Cleveland for radium and other treatments, which deepened her voice and sprouted black hair on her chin and upper lip—yet we all knew that the important work of healing was to be accomplished at home, all of us working for this and praying. The treatments made Aunt Grace weak and sick so that she was unable to eat and her hair fell out in handfuls. Finally they were discontinued. The doctors dismissed her. Now she was entirely in the hands of Aunt Elinor and God.

We would often see Aunt Grace walking the back farm road, deeply concentrated. Once when we were coming home from the dairy with ice cream, we saw her from the highway against the backlight of the sky, there by the barn hill, for the farm track was slightly higher than we were, and to us it seemed her figure was silhouetted, a shadow, indeed the visible incarnation of a present spiritual being. The newly cut grass was redolent of its raked crop and in the golden and purpling passage of evening light over it we perceived again the incorporeal origins of creation. Aunt Grace seemed to move across the edge of that vast stage as though she were already far beyond us on a quest which had already removed her from us as effectively as death. We watched as if from the other side of a chasm, ice cream dripping down our arms.

Aunt Elinor, spiritualized, had time for everything, an unflagging energy which surpassed the physical. "Let's take a ride, girls," she would propose on any afternoon, unmindful of the weather or any demands on her as spiritual guide and New York business executive. And we would be off, two riding double on the bigger horse, one on the pony, Queenie, one on a borrowed horse, and Aunt Elinor astride the high-spirited mount she had leased for herself. Often we went so far, with her in the lead, or in such humid and miserable weather, that all of us were aching and weary, desperate to complain aloud—had God's world, and Aunt Elinor's, permitted any such dissatisfactions. Sometimes Uncle Dan said, "I don't think she notices the difference." He meant the difference between good and bad, hot and cold; and he spent many of his evenings alone in his attic sitting room, where he said it was peaceful to be miserable, pure and simple. But we extended ourselves to be with Aunt Elinor and to live up to her expectations. Enthralled, we wanted that summer never to end.

Once when we were out on a very long excursion, Anne's thirst grew beyond her endurance. She mentioned it uneasily to Aunt Elinor. Aunt Elinor was immediately solicitous, recognized it as a natural thing, not in the category of menstrual cramps and head colds, which had to be vigorously denied. Thirst might even be interpreted as reflecting the spirit's craving for living water. Aunt Elinor was so accessible right then that we all seized the chance to lament our discomforts—guilty that we had ever thought her unsympathetic, that we had misunderstood her. She turned into the first farm road we came to, slid from her horse's back and strode to the back door, where she greeted the bewildered housewife with queenly courtesy, requesting cold water and a resting spot on the grass.

"What a perfectly marvelous place you have here," she rejoiced with the woman. "You must never tire of the enjoyment." It was obvious from her presence that Aunt Elinor never tired of anything.

"Is a nice place." The woman spoke finally, out of her shy rolling smiles, in rather halting English, patting her disordered hair.

"Why, my dear, you must be Mrs. Chaccio." Aunt Elinor beamed at the embarrassed woman. "Gino's mother. And Angelica's. I taught them in school, you know, years ago, before I went to New York. Of course, you have so many children." Aunt Elinor hesitated as though Mrs. Chaccio had forgotten about them herself. "And what are they doing now?"

Mrs. Chaccio shrugged, her English or some other inhibition not allowing her to tell it. "The farm. Kids." She motioned vaguely.

"Why, yes, of course. This wonderful place. And aren't you fortunate to have them with you. Such a grand family."

"Yes. Big." Mrs. Chaccio grinned broadly at what could not be denied. "Eighteen live. Two gone." Aunt Elinor looked sympathetic for the missing two, yet her expression suggested that there was much to be grateful for in the eighteen who had survived. "They must be a great help to you." She encouraged Mrs. Chaccio as she encouraged everyone. And Mrs. Chaccio opened the screen door and stood aside for us to enter. We hung back from the darkness inside, but Aunt Elinor marched forward, up the broken steps, wiping her feet on the porch boards before she went in. We could hear her silent urging: Never turn down Experience—the stuff of life. We dragged behind her. A chicken stood in the middle of the table; Mrs. Chaccio scooped it aside and spoke to one of the dark-eyed children peeping in at the door. She spoke rapid Italian to the child, who came and took the docile chicken in its arms and carried it out. Aunt Elinor simply beamed then, as if this fluency in Italian were some special gift.

"*Buon giorno,*" she said happily, for she had studied Italian when her ambition had been to sing with the Metropolitan Opera. Her word of greeting made Mrs. Chaccio giggle and nod.

Beyond restraint, Aunt Elinor admired the large room, the wall of cupboards, the view of the woods and creek. She proclaimed the joy of family life, including each of us in her enthusiasm. Meanwhile we shrank inward. It seemed we were under the influence of a strange and unholy power in that place, which even

Aunt Elinor could not combat. We were fixated by the stare of the unchildish baby Jesus from a calendar, Him crucified and bleeding in another picture. Was this Divine Love? Still Aunt Elinor urged us, nodding significantly, as if she understood but would reassure us that, though distorted and grotesque, the images were evidence of man's eternal striving toward the Infinite. She glowed, smart in the tailored riding habit she wore in Central Park. Mrs. Chaccio began to roll and slice the dough which had been drying on floured cloths. She blew a feather off the table.

"Oh, girls, look." Aunt Elinor tried to rouse us to another wonder—we were always behind her. "Noodles." We gathered with her to watch and give tribute.

"Pasta," Mrs. Chaccio corrected. Her bulk jiggled with the flash of her knife. She sliced with a machine's precision.

"Oh, of course. Did you ever!" Aunt Elinor said meaningfully, meaning for us to note the merits of skill and self-reliance, of service to others. We watched the mound pile high. Then Mrs. Chaccio spread the yellow ribbons of dough over the tabletop and Aunt Elinor asked how long they might last. Mrs. Chaccio said she thought about a meal. Again we had the sense that Aunt Elinor was asking questions and pointing out things primarily to teach us—that Mrs. Chaccio was unwittingly a subject.

Then, with "Come and see us," and exclamations of how delightful it had been, Aunt Elinor decided to leave and swept us out to the lawn and onto our horses and we, glad enough to escape, left at a fast clip, waving grandly behind to the woman and the now seven or eight children and grown girls who came out and waved back. The chickens in the yard scattered and one of the dogs followed us down the road, barking and growling.

Katie, on Queenie, fell behind and we drew up to wait for her. When we were all circled around Aunt Elinor, she gave us the clear, deliberate look we knew. It told us that she intended to be very serious, that although she could carry any role and enjoy any situation, there were always the lessons underneath to be learned, ramifications to seemingly simple occurrences. We took a deep breath because we wanted only to get away from there.

"Do you girls realize that that woman is not much older than I am?" We certainly couldn't believe it. "And she is nearly dead from fatigue. From childbearing. Eighteen, twenty—what does it matter? It's ridiculous! But no one will ever lift a finger to help her, not while she is carrying out the dictates of the Roman Pope. Many Catholics are fine people, don't misunderstand me. But misguided. And her husband? What does he care, worked to death himself, the church always after something. That woman, my dears, is a slave. This may be the twentieth century, but she is in bondage. To her husband, the church, her children. Never forget her."

We knew we never would. Always and forever we would remember Mrs. Chaccio, old before she had been ripe, with dozens of children, heaps of noodles, chickens underfoot, and on her neck the heavy feet of her husband and the Pope. Neither would we forget what we had seen when we looked back at the barking dogs. Several of the older girls were running in the yard, prancing like high-strung horses, while Mrs. Chaccio laughed and thumbed her nose. We blushed to ourselves, glad that Aunt Elinor was far ahead and wouldn't have to know.

At dinner Aunt Elinor recreated the afternoon, complete with noodles. Gram muttered, "Humph." She'd made as many for threshers. Her noodles, it was clear, were quite different from Mrs. Chaccio's, prepared in freedom and far from Rome. They were the pinnacle of Gram's surviving skill at homemaking. We had only to imagine them, served in fatty streams of milk gravy along with chicken, double fried in the country way, to beg her to make some. Which ordinarily she refused ever to do again—"I'm done with that." But now we knew she'd have some noodles drying by midmorning someday soon, the report of Mrs. Chaccio's skill activating an old pride. And we'd swallow our fears, follow after her to see her snatch the hen she wanted and wring its neck with one formidable twist, the life of the tough old bird no concern of hers.

Grandad didn't look up from eating. He and Uncle Dan were very little in our lives that summer, both doing what Uncle Dan called "laying low." Now that we were too busy to play in the barn, with Aunt Elinor filling every hour, Grandad was left to himself. We had nearly forgotten he was there. Perhaps he was often gone, to town or to auctions. What we had noticed, but only to recall later, was that he had to stop to get his breath when he came up the seven steps to the porch, and that sometimes his face bruised purple at something Gram said, though with a glance at Aunt Grace, he'd usually turn on his heel and go away, his anger unspoken. But this night he was there at the table, silent, although he knew the Chaccio family well enough, the men helping him at haying time or with the threshing.

Toward the end of the meal Aunt Elinor excused herself for a moment and came back to the table with a small foil-wrapped packet of cheese. She opened it and the pie-shaped wedge exposed then was uneven and spongy on the surface, riddled with a greenish-blue substance.

"That's the mold," she explained. "But it's perfectly harmless." We were aghast. She smeared some on a cracker, found it edible, in fact delicious. She nibbled appreciatively, wiping her fine thin-curve of mouth daintily, eating as she always did, in the refined way we thought they must eat in New York City, which just then seemed a million miles away.

The summer before, Aunt Elinor had come home with other alluring specialties, yogurt and wheat germ. For a week or two we had traded in our sugar sandwiches for what she assured us were the far superior benefits of raw green peppers and sunflower seeds. Until Rossie got an upset stomach and Gram declared in no uncertain terms that Aunt Elinor could just pack up and leave for New York if things there suited her so much better. We were allowed to go back to our old ways of eating and while the rest of us ate Gram's white-flour biscuits and mashed potatoes, Aunt Elinor ate what she called chef's salad and cottage cheese. Even now that she had come to see that spiritual nourishment was the true bread, she continued to eat her health foods, as if she now preferred them. We wondered if she was afraid to be so alone. It never seemed so.

"You're missing out on so much," she said to everyone at the table, spreading the cheese. She said it was just silly, the family aversion to cheese, just some old-fashioned nonsense, though Uncle Dan suggested she should allow the custom to persist, since as far as he could see it was the only thing Grandad and Gram had in common and they'd passed it on to their children, like a family trait. Though Aunt Elinor laughed at that, she continued to eat the blue cheese for us to see, in order that we might take heart, become braver, dare to begin anew.

"Eleanor." We could tell from the edge Gram put on pronouncing the name that for her it was still spelled the way Gram named her, before she went to the state of New York and had her name officially spelled E-l-i-n-o-r, and her middle name of Myrtle dropped entirely. "If you have to eat shit, do it out of my sight."

Aunt Elinor, her neck arched, poised high, looked at Gram, her mother. We could see by the swell of her bosom how it had shocked her. But she said then, matter-of-fact, "Mother, I don't think it's all that serious a thing," and she went back to her cheese, flourishing her hands with their jeweled rings and sprinkling of freckles.

Gram continued to dip her white bread into her coffee, making sucking noises. Louder than usual, it seemed. Uncle Dan took his plate to the sink and went to his attic room; he went in a hurry. Aunt Elinor was the only one who ever got the best of Gram like that, forcing her to hold her tongue, just as, when Aunt Elinor was a girl, she alone of the five children was selected to exchange the dollar's worth of egg money for a weekly piano lesson, and was then further excused from evening dishes so she could practice. We often heard of this privilege when our mothers were impressing us with the good fortune that was ours, students at the piano from the age of six, in contrast with their musical deprivation. We could almost imagine the two dark-haired and thin older girls, May and Grace, in the rented bungalow on North Street, down with the Italians, scraping and stacking dishes by kerosene light, while in the background Elinor tripped light-fingered over the keys and spread through the house her resonant contralto.

But Gram could get back, anytime she wanted to. She made more than her usual guzzling over her coffee when Aunt Elinor was around and spoke exactly as we figured her people had spoken on the old farm. It was as if she were reminding her daughter: an apple never rolls far from the tree.

Grandad hadn't said one word. But when he'd finished eating he stood up abruptly, his dish in one hand. With the other he reached to pick up Aunt Elinor's cheese, dropped it on the floor, and then mashed it with a hard wiping motion of his heel and tracked it across the linoleum to the sink and out the door toward the barn.

Aunt Elinor had tears standing in her amber-brown eyes. Gram recovered her voice and went to the door, screaming out after the vanished figure, "Goddamned bastard. Swine." She came back in with the scrub pail and told her daughters to shut up. There were four of them standing at the table, Libby, Elinor, Grace and Rachel, all of them furious, railing that it was no fit place to have their children, never had been, that he had ruined their whole lives.

"Then why don't you get the hell out?" their mother said as she slowly let herself down onto her bony knees beside the pail. "You know he can't abide cheese. Never could." Her arm, burdened with its slack quiver of hanging skin, moved the rag in what was still a strong motion, as though habit went beyond the endurance of flesh itself.

"We must forgive," Aunt Elinor said. "None of us is perfect." She wiped her tears then and smiled. We kept absolutely silent so they wouldn't ask us to take sides or send us out, for what we knew about the family was disclosed to us by our being there to see it happen. We had to remain as inarticulate as the mantling walls, silent and watchful—outside the action. The five sisters had guarded their secrets from us, as though we were strangers, as if their loyalty was only to each other and their mother; if further divided, it would dissolve.

Aunt Elinor revived and brought out a fresh package of cheese. She began to spread it on crackers, lining them up before her. "God is our father and our mother," she said then. We heard Gram moving the rag in widening circles over the floor. Aunt Elinor offered us a cracker. Gram went out on the porch. The door slammed behind her. We heard the water slap against the packed dirt by the steps. With the tips of our tongues we tasted the blue cheese. Salt. Gram clanged the pail onto the shelf. Aunt Elinor beamed encouragement.

Gram marched through the door and across the room without looking at us. Ready to go out, she had scrubbed the floor in her good dress. While she washed her hands, Aunt Rachel went over and brushed off the hemline. "Honestly, Momma. We could have done it."

"I figured you was too busy improving yourselves," she said, and left the room.

Aunt Grace had the cheese in her mouth. She sat there, full-mouthed, as if she couldn't bring herself to move it either way. But then she ran to the sink and spit it out. Aunt Elinor looked patient, as one who had seen a wider world, one she constantly made visible to the rest of us—accepting the fact that a wider world might mean a weaker place in the old one. She left the table to go to Aunt Grace, who still bent over the sink. We waited. Later we would toss our crackers into the trash. Choosing between Aunt Elinor and Gram seemed to us as profound as a choice between good and evil, only we didn't know which was which.

How completely they forgot us. Gram left in her car and Aunt Elinor put her arm around Aunt Grace and led her out. "Who is My mother? our Lord asked. Whoever would follow after Me must forsake all that he has." They were gone into the next room. Already Aunt Elinor had said that we might leave off the Aunt in addressing her: simply call her Elinor. She would consider it no disrespect, for it was our spiritual bonds that mattered, not our human. Yet we never did more than try to say it once or twice, "Elinor." We didn't want to say the bare name, to break the connection. It seemed we might be asked to give up everything.

Aunt Rachel and Aunt Libby still sat at the table, Aunt Rachel eating more of the cheese. She had tried it before, rather liked it. Aunt Libby was looking disgusted, but not about the cheese—she didn't even pretend to taste any. "It would be wonderful if you could believe it. But I just can't understand how a person can turn their back on all the terrible things that happen and say they aren't real. Most of what happens in this world isn't real, then. I will not look at somebody who I can see is sick and say they're well. It's nothing but a damned lie." She gathered up all the crackers and took them to the trash, as though she would thereby strip the world of humbug.

"It appeals to me a little," Aunt Rachel said. "You have to look deeper than that, Libby. It's like that old thing about the chicken or the egg." Her gaze was fixed with Oriental inscrutability upon the elusive figures shadows painted over the orchard grass.

"God," Aunt Libby said. "You ever start in on that"—she motioned with her raised fist toward the front room, from where we could hear Aunt Elinor's strong voice—"I'll leave town, I swear it. Hardly any family left, it seems to me. Most of the time I feel like I'm not even here—as if she sees through us, as though we're all disembodied spirits floating around." There were tears standing in her eyes. A breeze came in at the window, stirring the cloth on the table. When Aunt Elinor was home there were special touches like tablecloths and napkins, what Gram called "airs."

"It's for Grace," Aunt Rachel said, and put her hand on

Libby's arm. "Let's just try. See what happens and maybe there will be a miracle and she'll get well."

As if brought down by the Truth, Aunt Libby said nothing to that. They looked at us. "I think we should forget ourselves and have one mind among us." Aunt Rachel addressed us and Aunt Libby. Although two years younger, Aunt Rachel seemed now the older, wiser one. "After all, I don't see that things turn out so well for most people. Live and die for nothing." We felt at one in a yearning to believe, to transcend the material and false, to perceive the reality of Spirit. Just then over the stove, the opaline salt and pepper shakers, their tin lids marred and bent, appeared to be invested momentarily with an underlying quality, a luminous spirit, as the flood of sun went down.

In the fall, Aunt Grace heard of new treatment centers that might offer some slight hope. She seemed stronger after the summer of religious enlightenment, had more energy, and she accepted Gram's determination that she should try any and every thing. Aunt Elinor concurred. It was a last effort. She would travel with Aunt Grace whenever she could; we watched her usher Aunt Grace, who looked thin and stylish wearing the new fur coat Gram had bought her, into the interior of the prop plane, Aunt Elinor's shoulders squared over her sturdy frame. The size which most of the family carried in a gangling bony height was in Aunt Elinor condensed into a powerful firm fleshiness. She had become more quiet and concentrated in her spiritual quest with the passing months. Always now in speaking to us of Aunt Grace she assumed an intense, solemn tone. But there was a hint of withdrawal too, as if our concern, though loving, contained a fearfulness and worldliness which might be traitorous to the requirements of absolute faith. It could even jeopardize the cure. We felt her drawing away from us, but in the interests of our common struggle we tried to be brave, swallowed our hurt.

It was during that winter that Grandad died. No one expected him to die; Aunt Elinor hadn't even known he needed help or she would certainly have tried to give it. He had heart failure in

the downstairs bathroom, a tiny little room made from a back
hall, with a curtain in front of a toilet and sink. He had been
home alone and when Rossie found him he'd been dead for hours.
It was terrible for Rossie. We were all comforting him, trying
to help him overcome the shock, the embarrassment of crying so
hard. We were waiting for the police to come to help.

Gram exploded: "God almighty. Them cows'll be dead or
worse," and she flew straight to the barn as if there she expected
to meet a real disaster. But there weren't any cows; Grandad had
sold off the last of them. Why had he done that? Perhaps he got
sick of spilling perfectly good milk down the drain or feeding
it to hogs. "Maybe he knew something was coming." Gram said
that. We looked at her, surprised, as if for the first time we
realized she might know things about him, more than she'd let
on.

After Grandad was gone we didn't notice much that was
different. We had to buy milk. There were fewer fights, but that
had been true since Aunt Grace got sick. Uncle Dan sat down in
the living room more often in the evenings and eventually the
furniture in the attic sitting room was distributed around the
house. Sometimes we'd wake up around dawn and think we
heard Grandad going off to milk. But we didn't get up, so we
must have known it was some other sound we heard. Or was
some memory the house kept. And there were times when the
wild doves seemed to moan "Sucky, sucky," as though Grandad
were tramping through the hollow, gathering his cows.

Another summer came and Aunt Grace still lived. She was very
thin, with some form of bandage under her dress at the throat.
And she carried her left arm in a muslin sling. Her eyes, dark and
prominent, were too much for us—she had seen what had burned
its own image into her gaze. The first and the last. We held her
in great awe. And it was as though her presence and our devotion
to her had united us at last in a perfect oneness, we four girls
thinking, feeling and moving in a dimension that felt like the

exact representation of a greater mind. We had bad dreams, cried out at night. But during the day we guarded every thought about her.

If we met Aunt Grace as she went about the farm on her long solitary walks, we—still dancing and running, coming out of the flowing, dazzling pleasures of the brook, the embrace of vines and roots, the sting of grasses—would fall into silence. Then talk awhile, but carefully, self-consciously, answering her few questions, her smiles with our smiles. At the edge of our awareness we glimpsed the white wrapping at her throat, breathed carefully so we wouldn't smell the abscess underneath. There in the dust-silted track by the barn, ankle-deep, we buried our bare toes, sprayed geyser figures into the air to fall away. While we talked with her, it seemed that our hearts burned within us, as if we were with someone who had come to love the world, inexpressibly yet without entitlement. We made some excuse and ran away. Left her alone to concentrate her entire being toward making manifest the sufficient love of God.

Every morning and afternoon Aunt May left her hotel and came to the house to change Aunt Grace's bandages and help her bathe. Only Aunt May could do this for her; Aunt Grace could not bear for anyone else to see her—not just for the shame of it, but for inflicting the horror of it. We knew Aunt May had been chosen for this. Perhaps because she was the oldest of the five sisters and part mother to the rest, but there was her nature itself, tender and selfless, revealed in the tone of her voice, the tone the others used in speaking to her.

They were so concerned for her when she came down to the living room after tending Aunt Grace. They would coax her to sit a few minutes. At first there would be silence, all of us thinking of Aunt Grace, in bed for the night, although her light would burn long after everyone else had gone to sleep. Once, Aunt Libby told us, when she was preparing for bed, coming out of the bathroom, she glanced through the crack in the door where Aunt Grace was reading in bed.

"You still awake?" Aunt Libby had asked.

Aunt Grace had stared out with such a look, Aunt Libby told us she felt it penetrate her heart. And Aunt Grace had said, "If you only knew the wonder of it, you wouldn't waste a single instant." While Aunt Grace was with us, when we spoke of her and repeated those things she said to us, it was with the sense that we had had the exquisite visitation of a saint.

Aunt May showed all the strains of her life, a widow at forty, mother to a fatherless daughter, nurse to her favorite, mortally ill sister. We honored her for her place in our lives then, her acts of devotion. But while she sat on the recliner, trying to relax, her legs would spring up and away like parts wound too tightly and she would have to startle up and walk the cramps out of her legs, rubbing her hands through her black hair and along the sides of her neck. Aunt Libby badgered her to get away for a rest.

"How could I?" Aunt May asked, casting her eyes toward the ceiling. Aunt Grace was now occupying the room directly over the living room, the room where some of us had been born, with its view of the west and the outlying woods beyond the meadows; over the fireplace mantel was the framed picture of the Indian brave. Poised on his horse at the edge of a cliff, the Indian gazed into an endless distance of land and sky, but he seemed equal to that immensity, his back straight and resolute, his attitude dignified.

Toward the end of the summer the sisters decided that we all needed a break from the tension and planned a picnic at the lake. Gram wouldn't come. She was going to the races. Besides, she didn't like the bother of eating outside. It was a special treat for the rest of us, however, something like the Fourth of July, and we stayed around the kitchen to help with the deviled eggs and baked beans, to pack the hamper and wash out the thermos. We felt as if after a long illness or imprisonment we were reentering the world.

At the lake, though, it was crowded and noisy. The county orphanage was having an outing and some of the kids, who seemed backward or maybe even retarded, came over to stare at us, which made Aunt Libby look her most mournful and whisper things like: "Have you ever seen anything more pathetic? Always makes one count one's blessings." One of the kids was sick on the ground near the covered tables and it smelled so bad we had to take our blanket over to the grass. Then Aunt May drove up, alone, because her daughter didn't feel well, had her period, which made Aunt Libby whisper again, this time that she'd never thought of it as either an illness or a holy ritual. The orphans stared at us a lot and some tried to talk to Aunt Libby, who smiled although she couldn't understand a word, and finally Aunt Elinor, home for a weekend, went to the park office and suggested that the orphan children be taken away where they wouldn't disturb people while they were eating. The leaders gathered them together then, but sullenly, and we all felt guilty of a fastidious contempt, devoid of compassion, as though our long vigil, our trial, had as effectively estranged us from the rest of the world as an imprisonment.

"It's spoiled," Aunt Libby said when we were left to ourselves. Aunt May went in the water, where she swam, again and again, the rounds of the buoy ropes. No matter what we did, we couldn't get the feeling right. We sat and thought about Aunt Grace alone in the house, Gram off to the races. Would Aunt Grace think we had deserted her? Did she need us as much as we needed her? After listening to us complain about the reek of vomit and watching us mope around on our patch of blanket, Uncle Dan said, "I can only stand just so much of a good time," and he got up and began to pack things for the trip home.

On the way back, we listened to Aunt Libby speculating to Aunt Rachel that perhaps Valerie, Aunt May's daughter, was jealous of Aunt Grace, getting all her mother's attention and concern. Did Valerie want her to die? It didn't fit, for weren't we all turning everything upside down to save Aunt Grace from death? Aunt Elinor taught us that God is Life. And everyone wanted God—wanted Life. In that way the things Aunt Elinor told us made sense, convincing us with indisputable logic. In such harmonious circularity we were as one; we felt it as always, undaunted by the failure of the outing, when we turned down the gravel drive, passing under the hanging oaks, entering into our own kingdom.

"And tonight?" Aunt Libby asked one evening when Aunt May came down from Aunt Grace. Sometimes now she had to come three and four times a day to change the dressings on Aunt Grace's neck. We would never dare to ask about that lingering abscess. To do so would be as shocking as if we threatened God with a rival power. And no one would ever explain it, thinking, if they thought of it at all, that we were wholly of them, knew what they knew, would fear what they feared, believe or not, by happenstance and accretion, as they did themselves.

"About the same," Aunt May answered.

The silence deadened the air so the ticking of the clock seemed to flow into our emotions and become their exact representation.

"They're going to have to do something about the pain." Aunt Libby said that with the cross and exasperated look she wore when referring to all misery; its meaning in the scheme of things would never be sanctioned by her.

"Elinor has hired a nurse," Aunt May said.

A nurse? It was impossible. Medicine. We thought this must be the end. Did Aunt Grace know?

Aunt May explained: "She's a Scientist, but trained in certain procedures. For cases like this. She'll come with Elinor next week. I don't think you should tell Grace yet. I don't know how she'll take it."

"At least this will mean some rest for you," was all Aunt Libby said, totally disillusioned with living and dying.

"Libby: if it would do any good, I'd crawl on my hands and knees to China," Aunt May said.

Aunt Elinor came to bring the Christian Science nurse. She made the trip without her suitcase of extra finery, came only with her brave and magnanimous soul; we could see it glowing still, translucent in her gaze. We could scarcely take our eyes off hers. The tiny nurse was a shadowy, inconsequential figure, lost beside Aunt Elinor. Maybe Aunt Grace would hardly notice her.

Aunt Grace slept now on a hospital bed which had been moved into her room and positioned by the west window. Sometimes she sat in the corner armchair, but she seldom left the room, took only a few short walks, leaning on someone's arm. This night the door stood open, but more often it was closed and sometimes we would hear through it her muffled thrashings and moaning. We would stand in the hall, unable to leave. Until Aunt Libby or Aunt Rachel, sometimes even Gram, would come and stand at the crack of the door and say to us, "It's all right, I'm here." Usually in their hands was a piece of the quilt they were making, a way to pass the time and occupy their thoughts. It pleased Aunt Grace to see the pattern emerge and the piece grow larger and when she was well enough she would hem a square herself, each square setting into the point of an emerging star. Gram had begun the quilt years before, then never had the time, or later the patience, to finish it. It was the old pattern "Broken Star," worked in strips of unbleached muslin, the stars of various shades of green, surrounded by a calico border. They had Aunt Grace make the mistake on her first piece, a traditional play for good luck. It was, by Calvinist logic, presumptuous that anything human should strive for perfection—Aunt Grace said that maybe they should try to make a Mary Baker Eddy quilt, one that would be as nearly perfect as possible.

Each morning we were taken in for our separate visits. Aunt Grace would make us feel at ease, her pain less in those hours, or her strength to bear it more certain. She would encourage us to tell her whatever we were doing, and tell us that she thought she was feeling a little better, would soon be up and around. We could not meet her eyes; but she looked away too, out the window as if she might absorb further the health and harmony of the land. Hopes like that she would share with us occasionally.

Once she said, "I have come to know that living and dying are a single event when considered by the mind of God." For days we would mention one revelation or another—comforted that Aunt Grace had been privileged to receive, through her suffering, a saintlike character.

But that night when Aunt Elinor entered the room with the little nurse, out of Aunt Grace's deep eyes, hollowed by an anguish from hell, came such a look that Aunt Libby said it suggested to her the gaze of the prophetess Anne, who had waited in the temple for years and years, not allowing herself to die, not until she saw the Promise of Israel. "So it's come to this," Aunt Grace said, in her voice made husky from the drugs, horror in it. She was not fooled. She knew what it meant.

"Darling," Aunt Elinor cried, and rushed over to seize her sister with an intensity that made us withdraw.

There now began a strange and bitter contest between the two sisters: Aunt Grace seemed to scent betrayal, Aunt Elinor insisted that the time for victory was at hand. The nurse was merely a convenience, a symbol of resolve, if anything. Not failure. But for us, the nurse, gliding about on her soft white shoes, had become the spirit of the house. While we had been diverted, breaking all lesser attachments, the house had been harboring a separate and competing force.

Gram was on Aunt Grace's side. We heard her say to Aunt Libby, "All's she wants is to go in peace. And quickly. It's over a year. Why in God's name won't Ellie leave her be? I can hardly stand it." She didn't even look sorry, just angry, and we hardened ourselves against her.

"What other hope is there, Momma?" Aunt Libby asked.

Gram said, "Sometimes there ain't no hope."

At these outbreaks our alarm held us shuddering and we deafened ourselves. There was no less feeling in Gram's voice, yet all her words seemed severe, harsh. Although she sometimes went out in the evenings, it was just her habit, more restlessness than pleasure, and there was no talk of winning or losing. Still Aunt

Libby disapproved, thought she should stay at home.

"I'd like to know what anyone else could do—with her around." Gram would jerk her head toward Aunt Elinor's insistent voice, winding its way down the stairwell.

But Aunt Grace was a captive. No one would interfere with Aunt Elinor really, for she was all we had. Sometimes we'd hear Aunt Grace, defiant and belligerent: "God. Tell me why I have to endure this. And you. You are tormenting me. For your own willfulness. Oh, I can use a knife by myself. How can you ask me to live like this, cut up and stinking?" She would burst into anguished weeping. She no longer tried to hide her pain. We felt she punished us. We could hear her shrieking and storming and we became afraid to visit her in her room, for she would stare at us fiercely, refusing to talk, so that it seemed she wished us ill and would gladly have bargained all our lives to save her own. And hearing her at night, we could not sleep, would take our pillows and blankets and lie in the hallway across from her door, praying for it to end. It seemed that we had lost our lives already.

Through the open door, we saw Aunt Elinor stroking Aunt Grace's arm while murmuring her litany of assurance. Once Aunt Grace sat up and with more strength and fury than we could conceive of, shook off that soothing touch, screamed, "Goddamn you. How can I ever get you to leave me alone? Just let me die. I'm begging you." Then she turned toward the window, that was black against the wall of night. We were astounded.

Aunt Elinor came in and out of the kitchen, running errands in the nurse's stead. They were always trying to get Aunt Grace to eat something. And always Aunt Elinor was struggling against evil, affirming the power of God to save, even while Aunt Grace gnashed her teeth, spit out her food, locked the door against her, and stopped her ears against that voice which, even as Aunt Elinor became outwardly more silent, we seemed to hear more pervasively—the voice of God, as if it had absorbed Aunt Elinor's being.

At the table, in her brief moments with us, Aunt Elinor

would sit heavily, she who before had carried herself in almost strenuous erectness. Aunt Libby asked her once what we were all thinking: "How long?"

Aunt Elinor stood and regained almost the bearing we remembered. She paused in the doorway of the kitchen, beyond her the dark hall which, like a path stumbled upon in a wilderness, must be taken, in spite of its uncertainty. No longer did she waste strength to pet us or cheer us on. "Love does not fail." So she said, and in her strong-boned square face, lifted at the chin, we could see the lengths to which love would go.

Then one night Gram came home early. We met her in the hall. Although it was still summer, she wore already her lightweight wool coat. Under the dim bowl of the hanging globe, her slack flesh draped, flaccid, covering a body which could no longer feel the heat. Still there was a moisture, like grease, on her forehead. From that room upstairs we could hear the two sisters, Elinor and Grace. The one spoke seldom and then irritably, waspish, against the other's continual low-voiced intensity. When the door opened we heard Aunt Grace growl, "And Christ I hope you never come back."

When Aunt Elinor came wearily around the curve of the stairway and saw her mother standing below she stopped. In her hands was a basin of unwound and heaped gauze, stained dark. It seemed we could smell it, so we tried not even to breathe. The freckles splotched upon Aunt Elinor's pale face seemed to form into patterns like the outlines of land masses floating upon a map of waters.

Gram started up toward her, such vehemence in her raised fist it reminded us of the time when Grandad was alive. Aunt Elinor was nearly to the bottom of the stairs then and Gram did not strike her but whacked the basin out of her hands. It flew and the contents spread, dark and vile, on Gram's precious carpet. "You'll burn for this," Gram gasped, sobbing. "Pride. Meddling."

Aunt Elinor went past her and knelt on the floor, gathering

the wads of dressing back into the bowl. As her hands moved we saw the scarlet lacquer on her nails was jagged and unkempt. Below us her shoulders heaved and shook, as she continued to reach for each piece. She was alone. We were afraid: of Gram, who stood over her, still panting, but more of Aunt Elinor, who could endure the hatred and misunderstanding of the whole world.

Aunt Grace came down the stairs. She leaned on the banister and her features, illuminated by the globe light, seemed unmarked by suffering. She was like a young girl, slender, her black hair, which had stopped falling out now that the radium treatments were ended, curling again in masses around her throat, hiding the bandage. The dimple set in the center of her chin winked over the deep point of darkness. To Aunt Elinor she said simply, "Come." Her eyes appeared to shine as with tears, but without sorrow or bitterness. There was plain joy in Aunt Elinor's face as she went up to Aunt Grace and encircled her with one arm and helped her back toward her room. From the back, beside Aunt Elinor's sturdiness, we could see how wasted Aunt Grace had become—now both of them held upright, supported by the ballast of indomitable character. Anne said, "Mother," but neither answered.

Gram stood, horribly aged within the folds of her skin and under the layer of her coat. The time she'd survived was like doom upon her head. She jerked up her head as if ready to denounce, then with a sigh lowered herself to finish gathering up the tangle of dressings. There was a brown stain on her hands when she'd finished. She scrubbed at the mess a minute with a clean piece. "What's the use? What happens happens," she said. She looked at our feet, then up at our faces, one by one. "Well, don't just stand there like a bunch of ninnies. Help me." So then we knew we were chained to Gram, having nothing more in us than what she was and hoped for. She had claimed us. We brought her fresh water, emptied the slops, got on our knees beside her and worked until the rags were rinsed clean. When it was finished we followed her into the living room, where she struck the gas jet of the converted fireplace, and lifting her dress and the coat, which she still wore, she stood almost into the asbestos grate of the running flame. "Feels good," she said, and gave her only smile, not to us, but to her own momentary contentment.

After that, a watchful peacefulness settled on the house. Aunt Grace appeared to have more strength, came to the table for dinner sometimes, although her digestion was delicate and even the smell of fried food revolted her, so that we did not have food like Gram's but instead something prepared by Aunt Rachel under Aunt Elinor's supervision—perhaps a clear broth, a green salad. Aunt Grace would just pick. Gram offered her bread and cream but she refused it. None of us could enjoy those elegant simple dishes, the bare skeletons of meals. Not with Aunt Grace wasting beside us.

Uncle Dan, though subdued, could still make us laugh when he wanted. Since we had started going to the Christian Science Church he had some new customers coming to his store to buy meat. He was glad for that, his business steadily falling off because of supermarket competition. But, he said, conversation with the faithful could be awfully risky—a fellow had to watch himself, couldn't hardly say anything right any which way. "Especially that Mrs. Beall from over on the Franksville Road. I say, 'Nice day, isn't it, Mrs. Beall?' She gives me a look. 'All God's days are perfect, Mr. Snyder,' daring me to take issue. But if I try to head her off and say, 'This rain is a blessing,' she says, 'God answers our every need, Mr. Snyder.' " Aunt Elinor laughed too and agreed that some people were bores on any subject. The woman meant well, no doubt, but being new to Science, she was perhaps overzealous. And for that time, with Aunt Grace a little better, nobody was inclined to quibble. "I'll say black's white," Gram said, "if it'll do any good."

Still there remained beside our posture of confidence phan-

toms of dread like the hangover of a bad dream or the premoni-
tion of a bad day. The house seemed alive with the conflict; we
could hear the walls settling and the floorboards creaking beneath
the carpet as we walked. Aunt Rachel packed up Rossie's clothes
and he went to stay with his other grandmother, who lived in
some other town—bad dreams were keeping him awake for
hours every night.

Then Neil came to the farm. When he first went into her
room and saw Aunt Grace sitting in the armchair by the window,
the white embroidered birds on her dress blazing silver, the dress
loose on her form, he went to her, fell on his knees beside her,
put his head into her lap and cried. Sobbed out loud. We weren't
there to see, but we heard Aunt Libby telling Gram. We couldn't
imagine his emotion and it seemed almost unbecoming, as if a
perfect stranger were trying to imitate real grief. And we were
afraid, as if his coming would make everything worse.

"It's late in the day for tears," Gram said.

Aunt Rachel answered, "Seventy times seven." Since we
were all studying the Bible, living and breathing Scripture, we
knew that that meant the length and breadth of forgiveness.

Gram flared that she didn't need to hear it. "I'm sick and tired
of sermons. When I was a girl I memorized practically the entire
Gospel. Christian Scientists don't have a monopoly on the Bible,
no matter how high and mighty they think they are. From what
I've heard, she wasn't no saint neither, Leader or not. There are
some who say she wasn't no better than a heathen herself, married
more than once. Vain."

"Well, Momma," Aunt Rachel said, after a few moments of
quiet, plainly offended but not running scared, "I guess we have
a lot in common, then." Because Aunt Rachel was soon to marry
Tom Buck, who was waiting for his divorce, and he would be
her second husband; and vanity—these women knew about that,
laughed about it, but couldn't hide it.

Then she told Gram, "I think I feel sorriest for him," meaning
Neil. Was that because he loved Aunt Grace the most and had

sobbed in her arms? Was that because she had loved him but didn't anymore? We didn't know. Neither did Gram, because her face wasn't even angry but was overcome by a vacant astonishment. Maybe he was the black sheep returned to the flock, the one who required a radical forgiveness.

The day before Neil was going back to his office, Aunt Grace thought she was strong enough to walk a little with us. We had found a special place by the old orchard, up from the duck pond, and we wanted her to see it. They walked very slowly down the drive, Aunt Grace leaning against Neil. Because of Aunt Grace, we didn't go into the ravine but crossed through the meadow, where Grandad's haywagon still sagged, one wheel missing. Neil was very tender toward Aunt Grace, toward us too, a way he'd never been before; we'd heard Gram say that maybe some of the smartness had been knocked out of him. We felt included, as though we shared in the change in him, shared a lover's attentions. Observing him, slim and blond, his blue eyes, which could be so wild, now sobered, we felt in him the miracle we expected, the resurrection of forgotten love.

"See this. And this," we called to them. Nothing mattered now except ourselves, running among the flowers and grass, crossing shale ledges, beneath us the dark ravine with its flickers of leafy light, these ways we'd gone countless times and could always go when we wanted to, the paths gouged through our own flesh. Neil and Aunt Grace wound steadily up the gentle incline, leaned together. We came close and seemed to ourselves to impart, like watchful spirits, strength and reassurance.

So at last when they were lying together in the reedy wind-bent grasses, thin under the oaks, Aunt Grace rested her head on Neil's shoulder. The oak leaves rippled and the grass too in the touch of breeze that blew continually over this high place above the cooler ravine, its weather entirely its own. We wanted to lie around them, to be done with everything.

But then Anne said, "No, let's go down." We went after her, into the ravine where the vines hung from the tops of trees, and we caught them and swung out over the brook, working up the nerve to let go and sail to the other side. We moved rocks and built a dam to pool the water, planned how deep it would be and how secretive.

Katie stopped then and said, "I'm going back."

"You can't," Anne yelled at her. "You haven't finished your part. We aren't through."

"You aren't the boss. Bossy, bossy. I hate you anyway. You aren't my mother," and Katie went scrambling up the hill.

Anne jumped off the vine she was straddling and lunged forward to leap on Katie, dragging her to the ground. We could hear the sound of Anne's slaps, over and over. "What I say, what I say," she was growling as we worked to haul her off. She lost her balance then on the hillside, and toppled over. Katie lay on the dirt and leaves, crumpled up and playing dead. When Anne stood up she looked like Gram, her face set like a blank painted totem. There was a trickle of blood from her lip.

We'd forgotten Anne was like that. Forgotten we were all like that. Changing and horrible. We could have torn out our eyes. And Katie: she had gone out into the yard and told Rossie and his friends that Anne had her period, that she had become a woman. We'd stood with them below the window, laughing and calling up dirty stuff at Anne, shaming her for what she couldn't help. Later we were ashamed. Aunt Grace had heard Anne pounding Katie that time after she'd caught her. "I'll kill her." Anne was fierce. "Someday I will, too." Aunt Grace had stopped her with a word. But that time she didn't punish her for fighting. Instead she took Anne into her room. Through the closed door we could hear Anne sobbing while Aunt Grace talked in a low careful tone. Later Aunt Grace came out, and before the door closed again we saw Anne lying on the bed with a pillow over her head. "It's a pity she's so young," Aunt Grace said to Aunt Libby, though what we saw in her eyes made us think that something extraordinary had happened to all of us. As now, following Anne and Katie up the hill again, we were feeling uneasy, even about the love that was in us, because of the hate.

Down below us, in the ravine, the quick light flamed, while steadily we rose into the bright noon, onto the plain of flowery grass. Aunt Grace and Neil lay as before, their eyes closed, the oak tree behind them as straight as a marker. If we didn't wake them, they might sleep and never wake. We needed them to get up. We braided a chain of chicory flowers and when Aunt Grace opened her eyes, hearing us, we wound it around her neck and hair and Neil sat up and cupped a blade of grass in his palm and blew over it like a whistle. Going back, we danced around them, trying cartwheels. But Aunt Grace could no longer walk, she was so exhausted, and Neil had to carry her the rest of the way and up to her room. The burden of her life settled over us again, its weight keeping everything in place. We stayed in the kitchen with Gram and Aunt Rachel.

"Maybe she would have been better off to have stayed with him this year," Aunt Rachel mused. "Since they did get the house."

"And maybe you won't have the sense you was born with if you live to be a hundred." Gram sounded angry although she was crying.

Neil left to go back to his job in Illinois. Aunt Elinor was leaving the next day for New York. She had a visitor from the old days when she had tried to be an actress. Pearl, her friend, had made it, Aunt Elinor told us, unlike herself who had grown weary of show business and had instead gone into the world of everyday business. Pearl went into the parlor to sing while Aunt Elinor played the piano. All the doors were left open so Aunt Grace could hear, because her walk in the woods with Neil had seemed to use up what extra strength she had gained and now she left her room only to be helped to the bathroom. Still she looked very peaceful and content listening from her bed, dressed in a powdery blue gown which Neil had bought her.

We stayed in the living room while Pearl sang in the parlor. We wanted to laugh. She had a powerful soprano which must have broken glass more than once, something we'd heard Uncle Dan say about Aunt Elinor, and we were watching the branches of the living room chandelier. Aunt Elinor was very upright and serious over the keys, frowning into the score in her nearsighted way, but when Katie slid out of the recliner in a fit of suppressed giggling, Aunt Elinor gave her an unerring frown without missing a note. We got control of ourselves by ignoring each other and looking out the window, so that the music became part of the sun-warmed landscape which undulated with those same rhythms and passions we had seen move over Pearl's white breast as it lay exposed above her rather low-cut dress. After several classical numbers, long after our impulse to clown had been subdued, then obliterated, Pearl said to Aunt Elinor, who had led us in prolonged applause, "Do sing something for us yourself."

"Oh, I couldn't," Aunt Elinor said, blushing and even lowering the lid over the keys. "It's been years."

"It hasn't," we begged her, only then realizing that the summer had passed without her playing and singing for us. It seemed that if only she would, all that was wrong would vanish. "You always sing," we said, risking her disapproval for putting an adult on the spot, and were supported by Pearl, who said, "I remember when your auntie was on the radio—that Ipana smile."

"This is silly," Aunt Elinor said then, and raised the piano lid. "I'd better play for myself, though. That way I can fake it better." That made her sound like a real musician. When she began to sing, her face became so soft and lovely with the emotions of the songs it was easy to believe what Aunt Libby had told us, that she had had more suitors in her day than most women dreamed of.

Nothing was between us and her singing, our hearts as full as hers, lapped by the same waters. She sang all our favorites: "In the Gloaming," "Annie Laurie," "The Shores of Minnetonka," "Who Is Sylvia?" "Deep River." When she stopped we heard the far fragmentary clapping of Aunt Grace's hands. Aunt Elinor sent one of us to see if she had a request. We all went.

" 'Oh, What a Beautiful City!' " we called down the stairs to her, then we went back into Aunt Grace's room and sprawled over Gram's old bed, where the nurse slept at night. Aunt Grace was over by the window in the metal hospital bed. We could hear Aunt Elinor's every word—Pearl said that our auntie was famed for her perfect diction.

"Three gates to the North, and three in the South,
  There's three in the East, and three in the West—
  There's twelve gates to the city, O Lord."

From the high windows, looking out to the west, we could see shafts of sunlight dropping in golden bars against the deep blue of the sky, with the forest line glowing too. But when we turned to show this to Aunt Grace, she had fallen asleep. We tiptoed away. Aunt Elinor looked perfectly happy when we told her how deeply Aunt Grace slept. But we must not fall asleep, she reminded us. We were watchers in the garden. "Pray without ceasing. No one knows the hour." We promised her that we would. We wanted to. But we knew that it was partly a lie, that we were as flawed as any of the disciples.

We did the best we could. Aunt Grace went into a period of terrible unrelieved pain. When morphine allowed her some rest, though mostly she refused the drug, it seemed only to make her feel the next seizure more intensely. During the days we were in school, and some nights, Uncle Dan took us over to his mother's house to sleep. But we resisted; we thought we should be there with Aunt Grace. We had promised. Though we could no longer pray, we could watch. We hunched against her cries, but we were there to listen.

The little gray-haired nurse was indispensable now and capable in her ministrations, both physical and spiritual. We saw her hardly at all, mostly bringing trays back and forth to the kitchen, but her calm face affirmed that something was being done, whatever possible, and she would answer Aunt Libby, the only one who dared to ask each time, "How is it?" Aunt Libby's eyes showing a bitter grudging resignation to a superior power. "I think she's coming closer," the nurse answered, her smile kindly and spiritual; though she was not secretive, we felt excluded.

"Closer to what?" Gram would say, spit threading her lips together as if she hadn't been able to swallow in a long time. "I should have strangled her with my own hands," she cried out once, one of her outbursts which came seemingly from nowhere and left her momentarily crushed. Aunt Libby just pressed her hand until Gram pulled away and went to the sink to wash the few dishes. In that time, she seldom left the house, but we couldn't tell from her face what she expected. Uncle Dan said he thought Aunt Grace should be taken to the hospital. Surely they could do something for her—he was a butcher, but so kind-hearted that he had to hire a man to do the actual killing; and it took only one solid blow to fell a steer. He spent most of his time up in the old attic sitting room because, Aunt Libby told us, "He can't take it." Gram said it was too late to send Aunt Grace away. "We've had screaming over babies being born, screaming over pretty nearly everything that could pain a human. Now this." She raised up her fist as if with it she only wished she might bring the whole structure down around us.

Aunt Grace couldn't eat. Nothing appealed to her, and she wouldn't try, not even for Aunt May, who came to the house every minute she could spare. At last, when Aunt May succeeded in feeding a few bites to her, a vile black substance rose out of her, and after that no one coaxed her to eat.

Then one day, mercifully, Aunt Libby said, the pain subsided. Then it stopped entirely. There was no explanation for it. We accepted anything. It was a kind of miracle to Aunt Libby, though not the one we'd wanted, and she was grateful for it. Much of her day was spent with Aunt Grace and she worked steadily, hemming and piecing the quilt. Often they were silent, together and at peace, absorbing the tranquillity that came out of the fields and woods which stretched to the far border of

Gram's land. The leaves had already fallen from the trees but winter had held off, and each day the land warmed, the fields the color of sand. Aunt Libby told us she considered those days a privilege—however dearly bought. Never before had she felt so tangibly the actual presence of love in the world, not even when her children were born. And she said it was something you could feel only once in lifetime, because afterwards something in you had been burned away.

Gram told us we should be getting ready to say goodbye. Goodbye? We stared at her, uncomprehendingly. To speak of leaving seemed a treachery, a mockery of all that we had been through together. We thought of what Aunt Elinor had taught us, that both living and dying are a dream. We were bewildered but we would not say goodbye, not for any of them.

Thanksgiving passed, unremarked, except that it was Anne's birthday and Gram remembered that no one had been able to eat that year either. Then one day as Aunt Libby sat with her, Aunt Grace turned her head from the window and said, "Get Neil."

Aunt Libby let her head fall forward, not hiding the tears which spilled fast, wetting the quilt. Aunt Grace reached so slowly, Aunt Libby told us later, and her fingers moved in Aunt Libby's hair. "Elinor too?" Aunt Libby asked when she could.

Aunt Grace nodded, her eyes closed. She sank into a sleep that had the finality of surrender.

The calls were made. "And for God's sake hurry," Aunt Libby said. Aunt Elinor had declared, "Tell her to hold on. I'm coming." But nobody told her, because Aunt Grace was in a coma now and when she did open her eyes she was unable to speak, didn't seem even to hear. Only her eyes, stained black from morphine, seemed alive. She's still watching, we told each other. And so were we. Then she sank away from us again.

After dark we were led to her room by the women. Was this the time to say goodbye? "She's accepted it," Aunt Libby said. We filed up through the house in the dim light cast from the low-watt bulbs Gram kept in the converted gas wall fixtures. It seemed that we went by candlelight, our unequal heights throwing jagged shadows against the flowing walls. Gram sat by Aunt Grace's bed on a straight chair, but she did not raise her head when we entered. At the doorway began abruptly the sweetish, thick, terrible odor of the abscess, which mingled with that of the sulfur candle Gram had lit to purify the air. For months we had known that smell; to smell it was part of our watching. Under the hung picture of the Indian brave, the fireplace glowed with burning coals. We had never seen it used before, but Aunt Grace had requested a fire and they had moved her bed away from the cold dark windows so that when she opened her eyes she could watch the flames. She had mentioned Neil, just his name —and Aunt Libby reminded everyone how Neil had loved a fire.

When we went in, Aunt Grace seemed to be fully awake. Her lips before, when she had been well, had been bright red, thin and curving. Now they were stained black too and so crusted and shapeless it seemed a hole of nothingness opened there. And her eyes, which had always been brown, were now outraged and empty; they held only the smallest flicker of life, perhaps firelight, perhaps the evidence of salvation.

We wept as though we were doing as Gram said—saying goodbye. But we didn't say anything, just stood shaking, without sound, while Aunt Grace in her slurred and distorted voice, her tongue lacerated, tried to ask us about school, our friends, to show her interest. She could scarcely get the words formed and it was as if already we called to each other from separate worlds. Finally Gram raised her head and with one curt nod dismissed us. We leaned down to Aunt Grace, each in turn, and kissed her cheek, our tears sliding off onto her face. She wiped her finger across then, put her finger to her mouth. She seemed to smile and murmured, "Salt." From the hall we looked back once, but blinded from crying, could not see more than the firelight dashing on the walls. Then we went downstairs together.

We hadn't heard him arrive, but when we came down, Neil was at the kitchen table drinking whiskey. He stared at the table, ignoring even his two daughters, though he had just driven in from Illinois. We stopped crying, shrank from him. We felt that he loathed us as if we had conspired to hold his wife captive and tortured her for amusement. There was an enormous mood in the room, weighing of regret and denial, guilt and anger. Anne and Katie sat at one side of the long table, away from Neil.

Uncle Dan came into the kitchen, walked over to Neil and put his hand on his shoulder. "Come on. I'll take you up." His eyes were their same mild gray again; he'd cried himself out, according to Aunt Libby. But we felt this moment shocked Neil as it did us. Not because his wife was dying but because nothing had been asked from him. He stood and called his daughters. Their heads stayed on the table. Neil shrugged and followed after Uncle Dan.

We waited awhile, but Anne and Katie didn't move. We slipped away and followed up to Aunt Grace's room, where it was quiet, nearly dark, Neil just a shadow by the window, his arms folded, his back to Aunt Grace, who must have been sleeping. Anne and Katie were gone when we got back to the kitchen. Snow blew in the draft of the half-open door. The trail of their steps led us across the porch and down the stairs. We found them crouched on the floor of Neil's car. There was a sound, like singing or wind. Our teeth were chattering.

"She made me." Katie was crying again. Anne said nothing, just got out and stood there. Their eyes looked as if they had tried to die.

"Are you girls crazy?" Aunt Libby came out on the porch. "No coats! No boots!" We went to her and she took us on past Aunt Grace's room to the attic.

Sometime after we had fallen asleep, we heard a loud angry brawling and we thought maybe Grandad had come back and was fighting with Gram. The house was open to all the spirits; gravestones were shifting. From the distance we heard Aunt Grace moaning and crying. Anne slammed a pillow over her head.

We woke again. Heard a swelling sound that was like the murmuring of a great throng. Perhaps we were all going away. Pulled without will or intention, we went from our beds down the attic stairwell and stood at the doorway to Aunt Grace's room, on the edge of the dark. Particles of snow stung on the glass. Neil sat with his head in his hands. A few coals glowed. Anne wasn't with us. Gram said, "Leave her be."

Aunt Grace woke and said, "Hello, Dad," in her recognizable voice.

Aunt Rachel whispered to Gram, squeezing her hand: "You see, she's passing over." From tears, Aunt Rachel's face shone as though it were a shell clarified in the sea.

Then Aunt Grace looked at her sisters, her mother, husband. Then at us in the doorway. And we knew that at last she was saying goodbye. "Don't be afraid," she whispered, slowly, slowly. "It's like going into another room." There was a strangling catch in her breath and a gurgling noise. Everybody was standing. The snow on the wind made the night seem even deeper. The wind funneling in the chimney fused with our spirits and demanded that we release her. Within ourselves we cried, "We can't hold on." There was a sudden draft as if we had let her go. Gram sat down and put her head on Aunt Grace's bed, pressing up against her leg, one hand folding and refolding the hemline of the woolen blanket. All around the house the wind was moving, swirling and piling the snow.

Led by Aunt Libby again, we went up the stairs to the wide attic landing. Up above, the high window gleamed and sparkled with frost in the dimness. Then we turned and went further up into the last blackness of the unheated attic and the night took hold. We nestled against Anne's body, warm in her sleeping. It seemed that she might never have to know.

The instant Anne sat up in bed we were awake. Katie's eyes watched over the rim of the covers. Beyond the window frost was the concrete-gray light and snow accumulating. Rills flipped on the screens, curving over the sills. We saw Anne's arms, long and white, then her legs, as she sat on the edge of the bed. Katie's eyes closed. Opened again. There wasn't a sign of anything, but Anne ran from us. We heard her bare feet slap on the stairs, and going after her, we saw her standing alone in the doorway of the room where Aunt Grace had been for so long. Anne's braced legs were paler than the faded cotton gown which, outgrown and ragged, made her neglect and outrage palpable. Her hoarse convulsive breaths seemed to injure her. The bed was empty, stripped to the mattress, the blinds lifted and the windows too, so that the fresh light snow was powdered over the dark floor. Even the fireplace had been swept clean.

"You didn't call me. You left me." Anne was screaming at us.

Neil came up the stairs. He lifted his arms toward Anne, but she whirled and hunched her shoulders as if he would hit her and scuttled down the wall. "I'll never. Never. Not for you. Not for her." Anne still screamed. Neil shrugged and went away.

Anne slammed herself into the back room where Grandad had slept on a mattress so ancient it was stuffed with straw. Katie tried the door. It came open and out banged a shoe.

"Don't take it out on me," Katie yelled. "You were the baby that stayed in bed."

We knew the second time the door opened and we saw Anne that we'd better get help. We ran, calling the women. Gram was the first one to reach the stairs and when we caught up, Anne was lying on the floor face down, in her clenched fist a wad of Katie's hair, her fist pounding and pounding on the floor. Katie's neck was flaming where Anne's hands had strangled and at first she couldn't get a breath. She didn't cry. On Anne's shoulder was a welt from the crack Gram had given her with the spatula she still had in her hand. Gram was panting from the tussle and Anne was sobbing and sobbing, banging her fist on the floor.

Katie was just rubbing her neck, her face blank-looking, as though she couldn't figure anything out and had quit trying. "She tried to kill me," she said.

"Now, now," Aunt May said. "We're all brokenhearted." She put her arms around Anne as tenderly as though she were holding pieces of her shoulders together. Anne grew quieter and Aunt Libby pulled back a length of her wet hair and uncovered her red face. "Old sorrel's tail," she said, and switched Anne in the face, which got a little smile. She led Anne off to the bathroom to wash and we overheard Anne say that she would try to be better, to be good, and when she came back her expression proclaimed that the effort would change her drastically. Katie continued to look addlepated, slack-jawed, as if it had all become too much for her. Gram said it wasn't the first fight she'd ended.

The women led us down the back stairway to the kitchen, to the breakfast that was arranged and waiting on the table. We felt formal and shy with each other, arriving in the high-ceilinged room, the pure illuminating snowlight blazing off the walls. Beyond the drive the black-barked apple trees pointed every last twig, it seemed, toward heaven, and its immensity was what was left at the end. Gram lifted a teakettle from the stove to pour boiling water into the coffeepot. She shook the iron burners around—slam, bang. She looked over at Anne and Katie. Her daughter, their mother, was dead. "Eat quick now. You're going to get Elinor." Her voice was hard. We thought that must have been what Aunt Elinor meant about God not telling the difference between living and dying, the way Gram mixed up loving and getting mad.

"You tell Tom he'll be needing them chains," Gram said to Aunt Rachel, who answered that she figured Tom Buck could think that much for himself, which made Gram make a further clatter over the burners as if she were putting down an insurrection.

It took two hours to get through the snow, the forty miles to the station, but the leisurely pace and the uneven rumbling beneath us, together with the air, that was steadily colder and clearer as the snow decreased, then stopped, took us back to another time, one we'd seen in old photographs, the aunts as girls, snuggled to their chins in furs, drawn by horse and sleigh along the drive. We traveled along, swaying and gliding over the snow, wrapped in blankets, letting motion and desire carry us forward into one timeless union.

The first passengers leaving the train from New York seemed to be appearing out of the clouds from heaven, the way the steam billowed. We hurried forward, one last time to enter the fold where we might meet the living and the dead. We saw Aunt Elinor. From the top of the iron steps she regarded us with her eager and yet composed expression. Her eyes touched ours. Then she looked at Tom Buck for the answer to her question, even as her smile for the rest of us came to her lips. We all watched her, as if with her we would at last know.

"Yes." He nodded. "She went in the night, near dawn."

Aunt Elinor accepted it and bowed her head. Then she said each of our names in turn: Anne, Katie, Celia and Jenny, and took our hands in hers and slipped a ring on each of us. They were bits of turquoise on adjustable silver bands. We could see how much she loved us. It was in her face as she gathered us into her arms, welcomed us into the enclosure of the full-flowing black coat with its downy cuffs and collar of ermine. She offered her strength to us, longing to lift us from grief into Life eternal. We could no longer follow her there. We didn't know about divine love, knew only an insufficient human love. But we let her comfort us, her throaty and musical voice, her russet eyes warm in the burrow of her furry coat, starlets of snow blown in her hair.

PART FIVE: GRAM

In Tom Buck's Chrysler, going home from the train station, Aunt Elinor and Katie sat in front, holding hands. Turning to take the rest of us in too, Aunt Elinor said, "I made reservations as soon as Libby called me. With the storm, I was lucky to get here. Still it's a long trip at best." There were limitations, even for her.

Tom Buck's silence could have meant he was disappointed too. Or that he was utterly weary. Leaning forward with our chins on the front seat, near to Aunt Elinor, we could see his galoshes flopping open at his ankles. Behind us, the iced back windows enclosed us in a dim sanctuary. The run of chains over the snow seemed all that held us fast to earth.

"If only I'd known sooner. I prayed for her to hold on. To wait." Aunt Elinor would have stopped Aunt Grace from going, she seemed to be saying, her eyes fixed to outdistance the progression of the car. At the edge of the road we saw the snow-filled fields, then the dark solemn woods.

"She gave up," Aunt Elinor said. "Libby told me she had accepted it that morning." We looked down. "We must never give power to evil. It must always be denied." Although she turned toward us, we would not meet her gaze. We were all guilty.

Tom Buck didn't say a word but we felt him wanting to, something stirring inside him. He shifted his body and gripped the wheel so tight his knuckles bulged under his gloves.

Aunt Elinor sighed, then gave us her good warm smile, indicating what we had left between us and the full extent of our darkness. We had wanted to believe. Might still. Perhaps, miraculously, the empty bed in the upstairs room would float out of memory.

"I've never seen the snow so fine," she said. "Remember He said that it was good." Again all things were made new—the long sweeping vista of snow pools iced over and glittering before the motionless woods, the veil of illusion drawn away. We stared and stared, maybe to become snowblind.

"Was she calm at the last?" Aunt Elinor asked Tom Buck. No one wanted to say Aunt Grace's name. Neither would we mention the way she had suffered, although we sensed the memory licking behind the ways we avoided remembering. We had never talked openly of Aunt Grace's pain. We had never been told exactly the name of her disease, as if identifying it would give it a further advantage. So the secret name would bring further evil out of our own knowledge.

At last Tom Buck spoke. "Goddamn, goddamn. I don't know how or why to go on living after any of it." We remembered Aunt Libby saying that his mother had been buried alive in a nursing home. Aunt Elinor reached over to touch his arm, then her own head fell forward. Suddenly we were all crying.

Aunt Elinor blew her nose on a handkerchief of embroidered chambray. "This is the true demonstration. When all is dark. Didn't even the disciples despair? And then there was Easter!" For a time we rode on in silence, pulled both ways. The chains beat around us like nails.

"You couldn't have done anything, Elinor," Tom Buck said. "She wasn't going to get well and she went on too long as it was.

I'm goddamn glad it's over, I tell you, and I don't care a whole hell of a lot about anything else."

On Tom Buck's cheek we could see the intricate purple webbing that underran his ruddy color, stark evidence of what everyone said was an incipient weakness for drink which might get worse. Sometimes Gram vowed she would cut Aunt Rachel out of her will for marrying him, for being such a damn fool as to think she could change any man. Hadn't she learned the first time? That marriage had been over in a moment, but all the same Aunt Rachel had nearly lost her mind afterwards. Now this wedding was planned. Watching Aunt Elinor, her eyes staring open to the farthest sky, we knew she was praying for Tom Buck. Pray for us, Aunt Elinor, we yearned. Tom Buck slumped behind the wheel. And we remembered the plain metal bed, the stained mattress, a few snow feathers wafting across.

The house had become surrounded again by unbroken snow and seemed mysterious and melancholy. Right then the granite sills at the window, the solid walls of maroon brick and the towering spruce at the back gave it the appearance of an ancient asylum, as if once committed we wouldn't get out.

"There's relief in it. Christ, there's relief." Tom Buck stopped the car behind Gram's and glared at the house. Tears were flowing down his face, but he didn't brush them away. The remaining sisters were coming out then to greet Aunt Elinor, who left the car with her black ermine-ruffed coat sweeping behind her, walking as though she bore a crown. Into each other's arms they merged, and went toward the house, leaving us with Tom Buck. After a while he got out and we followed him to the kitchen, where Gram was standing at the iron sink. Neil was there too, at the long table with a drink before him.

"Jesus God," Tom Buck said. "Let me fix one of them goddamned things, will you?" He was trying to smile and went over to shake Neil's hand and gave him a clap on the shoulder. The two men looked alike in some ways, with their red faces and their blue eyes blurred with veins. But Neil, still lean, was almost emaciated, while Tom Buck was fat in the middle. Their difference we felt in other ways too, Tom Buck saying whatever came to mind, whether anyone listened or not; but Neil spoke deliberately—a man who meant to be heard.

Gram didn't look up when Tom Buck opened the refrigerator to take out the ice tray, but she said, "There ain't enough for that."

"Hell, Grammy. I don't care. I'll go to the store and get some more for you. Christ, I could take it straight from a nipple if it comes to that." He drank what he poured in one big gulp and then looked ashamed and touched Gram on the arm. "Sorry," he said. Then: "I'll get you some ice, Lil. In a little bit." He poured more of the whiskey and sat down on the step stool, that kept him a little to one side of the table Neil occupied. Both men were smoking; the air held it low because the kitchen was steamy from cooking and the storm windows sealed us in, the smoke blending with the milk smell of the room, that room soured every inch by milk slopped and strained, churned and set by, year after year, maybe seventy of them passed altogether. We sat down on the floor, the four of us, our backs against the radiator, quiet and dulled, hardly there.

"God almighty, Neil, how in hell can you stand it?" Tom Buck was looking out the window when he asked that. Maybe he didn't want to hear really, and Neil didn't answer. "I'll say again, there's relief in it." His eyes slashed around the room but there was nothing he could do, and he clasped his hands as if he might say a prayer, then bent them backwards to crack the knuckles. "There are some around here, given their head, would force the hand of God Himself."

Gram went on moving her rag over the surface of the same dish. Her eyes were red too, the bruised red of sumac cones. Still she hadn't lost sight of us. "You gals fetch me some of them apples from the cellar." The cellar was damp and smelled of dirt and the rotten, punk apples, many of them needing to be pared away to the small good centers left. Gram took the warped pan of them without a word. She sat down away from the table, drawing a chair over by the window. Again we huddled against the radiator.

Neil cleared his throat. He spoke as though for the first time in days. "How's business?"

"Busy. Goddamn, it's busy. Can't keep help. Train a mechanic and he's opening his own shop before you know it." Neil nodded as if he were paying attention, but we felt Tom Buck was just talking away as usual. He owned the Ford dealership in town.

Neil stood up and poured himself another drink from the bottle on the counter. He dropped an ice cube down Katie's neck, which made her yelp and wiggle around; so he knew we were there too. Gram went on moving her knife, without looking up. Neil winked at us, but we looked down: we sensed that Gram and he were just circling around, using us until they got good and ready to fight.

"We're going now." The sisters came into the kitchen. Aunt Rachel stood behind Tom Buck and pressed his head against her so that her throat showed over the collar of her dress, pearly white against his dark hair. She whispered in his ear.

"Jesus," he whispered back. "Don't leave me here for long." She pressed her finger over his lips.

"Can we come?" we asked. We didn't know where they were going, but we felt afraid of the house without them.

"Not this time," Aunt Elinor said. Kind as always, her face bore evidence of some personal obligation she was feeling. "But tonight, when you see her, she'll look lovely. You'll know then how happy she is."

"Shut up," Gram said. Her crinkled old face looked as distorted as the heap of peelings mounding around the pan.

"Momma." Aunt May, the oldest, spoke firmly. "Nobody wants to do this. It simply has to be done and in the best spirit possible. We can do it best. We're going down to the funeral home," she explained to us, and we felt how brave they were, how much love they had.

"I hope when my time comes they'll throw me in a pit," Tom Buck said. "This business makes it just about impossible to die."

"Scientists do cremate ordinarily," Aunt Elinor said, "but in this case . . ."

Gram had refused to pay for that kind of burial. She had said she wasn't going to get mixed up in any heathen ways when not a bit of it meant anything anyhow. "She'll lay up there aside of me, where she belongs," Gram said then. Grandad was already there, on top of the hill at the cemetery, and Gram had bought plots for herself and her five children. "I don't know what the rest of us are supposed to do," Uncle Dan had said. "Just wander, I guess. Outside paradise."

"There's more where that come from," Gram had told him. But Uncle Dan said he wasn't going in the back row and the way he said it, we could tell none of it did matter to him.

As they went out the door, the sisters were crying. Aunt Elinor carried the alligator cosmetic case with the jars of rouges, oils and perfumes which clients in the advertising world had given her. "If Dan calls, tell him we're coming," Aunt Libby said. He had been gone all day, making arrangements.

With their leaving we felt the house more, its great weight on us, heaviness not so much of brick or atmospheric pressure as of experience. We leaned in close to protect Anne and Katie, whose faces were so white and remote, it seemed they felt an incomprehensible freedom.

Gram finished peeling the apples in silence. Her daughters had wanted her to rest, but she had gone on with what she was doing.

"Jesus, Neil. What're you going to do now?" Tom Buck didn't look at him, but got up to pour again from the bottle and then returned to the stool, his elbows propped up on his knees.

"The same," Neil said, pouring whiskey.

"Not around here, you ain't," Gram answered. We'd been waiting for it to happen—all that unresolved bitterness in the angle of her face. We had felt it when her four daughters had left, the persistent past, heavy and actual.

Neil took his careful walk for more ice, going past Gram so quietly he might have walked on tiptoe. Then he sat down again at the table and leaned back against the wall, watching her through eyes narrowed to spell danger. "You never could keep your trap shut, could you?" We felt him taunting her, trying to make her wild, showing in that way that he thought he had the advantage. "Don't worry, though; I'll be gone soon," he said.

"Yeah. I bet you will."

"Now that must mean something. You got something on your mind, Lil?" Neil tilted his chair, forcing her hand, enjoying it too.

"You're a widower now. It's done and finished. So you can pack your bags and git."

"Meaning?"

"Meaning I don't reckon you've got a cent to pay on them bills."

"I might have known." Neil's hand was shaking when he put his glass down. Then he wagged his head back and forth, with his head lowered and his mouth tight. "Well, maybe"—and he looked up at her, disgust showing in his face openly—"maybe you can return that fur coat. Seems to me it's still nearly brand-new—since she had to be about half dead before you were good for it or any of the other promises."

"That ain't none of your business."

"No, it probably isn't." Neil stood up then and started toward the door as if he were going to leave; he looked suddenly ill.

But Gram had begun. "I told her what she'd get if she married you. Nothing. That's what. Now just go on. Git. Maybe we can have some peace and quiet around here. And decency," she added in a lower, different voice.

Neil turned toward her, stopped in his tracks, and his face was blood red again. "Decency. I declare. Decency. You know, Lil, you rather disappoint me. Just about the time I think you're going to take action, really give it to me, maybe just outright hand me an accounting, you back off and begin to preach. I suppose you have some idea about that. Decency." He sat at the table again.

"Let's go down to the Elks, Neil," Tom Buck said. Gram stood up and looked at Neil, fit to kill. A chalky-white froth was oozing from her mouth, the way it does out of an abused and lathered-up horse.

"When they took her breast, you was told: leave her be. But you wouldn't. Couldn't restrain your manhood, rooting in her —killing her is what it amounts to. Pregnant. She lost it but you killed her, same as if you'd taken a gun."

Neil came out of his chair. Fast. Gram braced herself, but stood her ground. He pounded on the table once with his fist and the sound was emphatic and alarming. "You don't know what the hell you're talking about." His face was white.

"For Christsake." Tom Buck stood up, wobbled and sat down.

In the quietness, Gram stood facing Neil directly, holding the pan of peelings, the rotten and wasted parts against her stomach, the paring knife in her hand. "They ought to have cut something off of you," she said.

"Maybe you'd like to try your hand at it, Lil." Neil was walking toward Gram. Deliberately. "Come on, let's see what the old war-horse is really made of. Actually you might be doing both of us a service," and this time he laughed, as if he truly meant it, that it was funny to think she could do something he wanted done.

"Christ in heaven." Tom Buck's drink spilled into the lap his legs made perched on the step stool. He gave out a little yelp. "Cold," he explained when we looked up. Then he stared down, wondering at the stain as it spread over his pants. He brushed at it helplessly, shrugged. "Looks like I peed my pants," he said, as if he might have done such a thing to get attention.

We threw ourselves down and laughed our heads off. Raged with laughing, rolling and gasping. It seemed wonderful that he was going to be in the family. When he walked away, he stumbled over a chair and we laughed all the harder.

"Another goddamned drunk," Neil said, and we thought it was funny to hear him sounding like Tom Buck. "Lil, you seem to draw them like flies." Tom Buck was splashing his face at the sink and Neil said seriously, "A legend that might interest you women—the Amazons. They removed the left breast of their warriors and then they hung the quiver of arrows there. Now that was a sign of something out of the ordinary. What you might call resolve. Courage. Seems none of us has what it takes." He followed Tom Buck out of the room. They were talking a little. Then we heard Neil mounting the stairs, going up toward the empty room, where the snow blew in the lace curtains and embellished the netting.

When they had gone and we were left with Gram, she said, "Anne, quit your howling," though we were all laughing and fooling around. Anne was quiet then, as though she'd been slapped. Gram didn't notice, went on making her pie crusts, not measuring anything, going fast with a kind of flair, as though all the movements and ingredients came to her out of a dance she had in her head. "So that's what he wants," she said out loud, and then went on to form the dough into generous circles.

Later the sisters came home. Saddened and spent-looking, they went off to rest. When it was dark, we all left together for the funeral home.

"She looks so beautiful," Aunt Rachel said. "I'm grateful for that. You did it perfectly," and she buried her face for a moment into Aunt Elinor's collar. Aunt Libby drove with her usual inner absorption, like a chauffeur. Gram didn't say a word.

Aunt Elinor turned back to us. "Now when you go in, I want you to remember: Life never was or will be in the body. The body is the outworn shell left when the Soul flies away. Kind of like moving out of an old house into a new one."

Aunt Libby almost interrupted her, thinking and saying her

own thoughts. "When I see her now. So peaceful and at rest. It's hard to believe how she suffered. Just yesterday. What was it for, I ask you?"

"Maybe it was for us," Aunt Elinor said. "So that we could be brought to know God." Then we thought that maybe it was: Aunt Grace a living sacrifice made perfect and acceptable to God, chosen to bear all for us, who were lost in sin.

But when we walked into the large old mansion that had been converted into the funeral home, we paused in the vestibule; there was in that enveloping silence the profound presence of something more final even than the things Aunt Elinor had told us, in the knowledge of which we felt at last the exceeding wonder of living. We were drawn both ways. Beyond the bank of cut flowers which Gram had wanted, in spite of Aunt Elinor's beliefs, we felt the fascination of it, this dread combining with an exquisite excitement. The women took us in to where the body was.

Since the night before, there had been a transformation; the figure lying there, serene, redeemed, was severed radically from the woman whom we remembered in the darkness. Now those pain-blasted eyes were forever closed and her mouth was a fixed crimson curl, untouchable. They had dressed her in a gown that was ineffably blue. With all pain and desire wiped away, she was now more lovely to us than we could remember, and totally unfamiliar. Anne and Katie were crying.

"Oh, my babies," Aunt Elinor said, and hugged them with tears moistening her smile, the joy she felt at the spirit's release blending with her own human insufficiency, as she called her grief. We stood by Gram. Aunt Rachel said that it was getting too morbid for her. After a while she went for Anne's and Katie's coats and drove them home.

Gram seemed not to notice anything, just nodded whenever anyone came up to offer condolences. Sitting on the straight chair with the hooped baskets of flowers near her, she was strangely like a girl, her feet barely touching the floor, her gaze innocent, without the accretion of her usual expression of impatience.

Aunt Minny came. Huge, almost six feet tall. Gram called her a holy roller. Sometimes Gram warned Aunt Elinor that she could get to be as ridiculous, might even begin to throw fits. We were always hoping Aunt Minny would throw one when we were with her, but she didn't, although Gram said it couldn't be so very much different from the way she generally acted. Right away Aunt Minny leaned down to kiss the face, eagerly, fervently. We imagined her touch—lips unwarmed despite thousands of such encounters.

"She's washing her feet in Jordan tonight. Amen and praise the Lord." Aunt Minny seized Aunt Elinor and, sisters in the faith, they stood together. "Praise Jesus," Aunt Minny exulted, witnessing boldly in the enemy's stronghold.

"Steal away," she crooned, and went over to Gram, pulled her out of her chair to hug her entirely, Aunt Minny enormous all over, so that Gram hung limp against her like a doll. "Lil, the Lord's watching after you for certain. These angels he has provided for your comfort and blessing." That was us somehow. We shrank back, afraid of her touch, but when she'd reached us and had clasped us to her bosom, it was warm and billowy. "Do you recollect the night He washed our sins away?"

Gram looked startled. Then she blurted out what she'd been thinking: "Ain't no sense to it. Leaving me here. An ugly old woman." She turned her back and walked away, then appeared in her coat, her pocketbook dragging. "You come on," she snapped at the rest of us. We took one final look, going toward the door, at the stranger bedded in satin. In her waxed paleness we already imagined her as Snow White, asleep under the dome of eternity, though beyond any charm we knew of.

When we got home, Gram moved straight to the fireplace and struck the gas, yanking up her dress and standing with her legs close up to the spiraling run of blue-gold flame, her expression urgent to feel the heat. She stood on one end of the Persian rug and her feet pointed in the direction of the pattern; she had told us once that the rug was woven so that the design directed the Moslem's prayers to the east. She'd placed her rug that way too. It was one of the only disinterested facts she had ever told us, pure information unrelated to her life or ours, and it amazed us. Just then, her face calm and absorbed by the fire, she could have been facing Mecca, although not kneeling. Anne and Katie sat with Aunt Rachel on the couch. They had stopped crying and even smiled when we came in.

"Momma," Aunt Elinor teased, watching Gram toast herself. "One of these days you're going to set yourself on fire."

"Well, then, lady, you better pray for me." So prayer was on her mind. She looked at Anne and Katie and said, "I wisht it was different." And we thought maybe she was wishing that she was.

When we went to bed we felt the immense absence. Katie woke up screaming, "Don't make me. Don't make me go." Aunt Rachel came up and said hush, rocking her in her arms. She left the hall light on. We were next to Anne while she was crying —we were all more to each other now. And more separate too, for Anne and Katie didn't have a mother anymore. The light in the hall enhanced the height of the stairwell. The four of us got into one bed, and in that closeness, pushed against each other, we forgot about the aloneness of sleeping the unbroken night of eternity.

Sitting at the kitchen table the next morning, we heard Neil run down the stairs, the back uncarpeted ones, and slam out the side door. No goodbye, just his ancient car coughing and lurching out the drive. The sisters shrugged at each other and frowned when Gram gave them a withered I-told-you-so smirk. "Guess he's had his wagon fixed. Knows what's what."

"Now, Momma."

"Don't now Momma me. He's been begging for it."

"I don't think Grace did it for the reasons you think at all," Aunt May said. "She just wanted the girls to have something from her. For when they're older. You know how she hated it, not seeing them grow up."

"All the same, she's left him without his house. Not that anything much that went in it was ever his to begin with. I give it to her. Now he'll have to mend his ways, scramble some. I didn't know she had it in her."

They had found Aunt Grace's will in her Bible, along with instructions for her funeral service, texts she wanted read, everything written out clearly in her schoolteacher's hand. It hadn't been witnessed by anyone, a simple statement of final wishes bearing an unmistakable intention. Aunt Grace had amazed everyone by requesting that the house Gram had helped her buy, the house she had never lived in, be sold and the proceeds held in trust for her two girls. We didn't know when they had shown the will to Neil. They had held it back as long as they could. Now that he knew, no one was relieved, except maybe Gram a little.

"But where will they live?" Aunt Rachel asked, and we all looked at Gram, except Anne and Katie, who looked at the floor. Gram got up and went to work at the sink. We were quiet. There was nothing anyone could do, no power left. With the vanishing of Aunt Grace, something that had bound us together and had given us strength beyond the ordinary had vanished too. Now we were simply going on, with what we'd ended up with, which was not enough but would have to do.

It was the day of the funeral, the third day. Aunt Elinor continued to teach. "Your heavenly Father-Mother God will supply all your needs." She was watching still. We hid our faithlessness to protect her, as though it would seem to be her failure too. But when we took our places beside her in the anteroom by the chapel, set aside for the family, we doubted our own doubts. We wanted to believe again. She knew something wonderful. Was wonderful. The solemn and benevolent Mr. Besaw, director of the funeral home, would come in, leaping for joy, bearing witness to the resurrection. It seemed possible, and the psalms and hymns we had learned by heart during that long time of devotion seemed now to be our own poems.

Through the brief service we were waiting. Then Mr. Besaw did come in. We were expecting him. He whispered something to Aunt Elinor and she shook her head after glancing at Gram's lowered head. Leaning forward, we watched him enter the room by the altar, and then he lowered the cover to the coffin, clamping the white satin rim so that the braid of brass made a continuous loop. In that moment there was absolute silence. We looked into his face. Before its clean-shaven acceptance our spirits fell. The glass amethyst lily aglow over his head on a curved leaded stem seemed more intense with life than we would ever be.

We stood for the final hymn:

> Abide with me!
> Fast falls the eventide;
> The darkness deepens:
> Lord, with me abide!

None of us sang, our sorrow accomplished. We heard the footsteps of the men who carried the coffin and the closing of car doors. We went outside with the others, blinking our eyes as if we'd walked into first light. Without a comprehensible past or imaginable expectations, we had entered into another lifetime. We held hands. A family friend drove us home. Rossie came too. It had been so long since he had lived with us that we felt shy; as if we hardly knew him.

After a while cars began to arrive, coming from the cemetery, where they had not wanted us to go. We could not conceive of that place. The women immediately became busy, laying out the food neighbors and friends had brought, finding the good set of dishes in the buffet, everybody acting as if they belonged and knew what to do.

Uncle Dan poured drinks for the men. They stood in the kitchen. "Right in the way," Aunt Libby muttered to us. They drank, their eyes downcast as though they might be doing something even they disapproved of. Perhaps it was that connivance that also lent them a kind of conviviality, although there was none of the usual joshing between the swift-moving women, intent on their preparations, and the drinking men.

Neil came in. Had he been at the funeral? We couldn't remember. We felt afraid of him. There was a hot glitter about him that made him look mean. We thought he might do anything.

But nothing in particular happened. He poured whiskey, his usual pale drink, and took his place at the back of the kitchen table, against the wall, keeping a distance around himself. The men shifted, found excuses to disperse. For the rest of the time, while people were eating, Neil sat there in the black-painted Windsor chair, staring at the glass he slid over the table or moved up and down to his mouth. Most of the time he smoked, quick jabs toward his face. He spoke once to a man he'd known in college.

It was dark and the people were leaving. We saw it was still snowing when the cars turned on their lights and drove away. Neil sat on at the table, his head now resting on his arms. Through the long double room, into the dining room, we could see the baskets of flowers the women had brought from the grave. Aunt Elinor said it would have been a waste to leave them in the cold and she could arrange them to look like regular bouquets. We didn't go near them.

Anne tried on Aunt Elinor's black coat with the ermine collar and cuffs. The collar was slightly raised so that it surrounded her face. She paraded into the kitchen, where the aunts took one look at her and broke into tears. How it suits her, they said, and told her how glamorous she would be, grown up. "Like your mother," Aunt May said. "Only the coloring's different."

"And that mop!" Aunt Rachel said. Anne's hair was dark red and uncut, hanging far down her back. "Something's going to have to be done about that." Aunt Rachel moved her fingers to snip like a scissors.

But Anne, giddy because they found her beautiful, said, "I'll never cut it. I'll let it grow and grow, until somebody will have to walk behind me to carry it. And you can leave me your coat when you die," she said to Aunt Elinor. Whereupon everything was completely quiet, until Aunt Libby opened the door to set out the garbage and a sweep of air danced the snow in at the door so that it seemed we might be snowbound for days.

Then Neil lifted up his head and looked around at all of us. Only Gram was missing. "I guess I know when I'm licked. Though if you don't believe I've tried, then, God knows, you never will. Hell, I never could make enough money to impress any of you and I couldn't keep my wife at home—even to die. Wasn't any competition for you at all." He stood up then and went to the window, his back turned to us, and continued. "Then she took away the one thing I did think was mine. Ours. The house. And probably she thought to give my children away with it. There never was any way to make you or her think I was man enough to handle you or what belonged to you." He turned and nodded his head toward Anne but spoke to the women. "And now this fool girl thinks she's a princess. Expects God knows what. Nothing else anyone will ever try to do for her will ever mean anything, never be enough. She'll always be dreaming about this place and this time, looking backward. Could be all of us should have gone on and died right along with Grace. Might be none of us will ever be quite alive again." We had never heard Neil speak like that, long and serious, not hiding his meaning. We sat as though forbidden to move, while Neil took up the whiskey bottle and, walking over to the sink, stood and poured all of it down the drain. We heard it gurgle going down. He set the empty bottle down with a shrug, then smiled, half amused, and said mostly to himself, "Too bad reform's not that easy," his eyes on the bottle.

Gram came in the doorway, her fists raised, yelling first at us: "You kids go on." But she couldn't stop herself, never could. "Don't you talk sorry, you bastard. Not around here. It don't matter what them doctors say they know. I know. I seen you.

Heard." Gram's face was purple. But she was raging into a void, like when Grandad used to walk out on her, because Neil had exited, holding his hands in mockery around his ears, saying to the rest of us, "Here's to female solidarity. May it last forever." When Gram had wound down, she allowed Aunt Elinor to lead her to a chair. We were all quiet, but we scarcely heard Neil's car going through the snow. So many times he had left, furious and outcast, then was back again: a pattern that reminded us of Aunt Grace, as though it was something they had forged together.

He didn't come back that night, and the next morning on his bed, still made up, was a heap of clothing and other things—Aunt Grace's belongings: the fur coat, the silver-linked belt made by Indians in Arizona, her wedding band and a watch, the music box that played "In Springtime." Aunt Libby lifted the lid and it ground feebly, statically, dragging. Inside the box was the confetti-like litter of a sheet of paper torn up. Aunt Libby knew what it was right off. "Makes you want to kill him," she said. "Always the last word."

"Not this time," Gram said, and left for town. She called in the loan she had made to Grace and Neil for the down payment on their house. That house was far off in Illinois—to us it seemed as insubstantial as the torn-up sheet of paper.

"I wonder if we'll ever see him again," Aunt Rachel said when Gram got home.

"We better," Gram said. "There's a thing or two here that belongs to him." She looked at Anne and Katie. "I already had too many kids," she said, then smiled thinly, almost an apology.

"Of course he'll come back," Aunt Elinor reassured us. And then she said, "You know he's no worse than the rest of us. We shut our eyes and tell ourselves we're wonderful. That we're better than everybody else, different. When we've had endless fighting and envy and fear. When some plain honest forgiveness would be truly wonderful." Although her colors—eyes, hair and complexion—were no more vivid than in all her earlier passions, her words were new, fruits of the Spirit, and they unnerved Aunt Libby so that for some reason she threatened Aunt Rachel: "If you ever start in on that religion, I'll move to California and never see you again. A person might as well have died." It was possible; already Aunt May, having lost husband, father and sister within two years, had begun to study Science with Aunt Elinor. They stayed off together, apart from the rest of us, to read and talk late into the night. Aunt Libby feared that she'd end up with only Gram left.

Later that morning, Gram divided up Aunt Grace's possessions—she said it was her right, not Neil's, since she had paid for most of them. And where was he? Typical! Aunt Elinor whispered to Anne and Katie that she'd see they got something from their mother.

The snow had stopped falling and the day was clearing. The apple trees were rimed in white. The sisters had followed Gram into the parlor and the door was shut. Left alone, we lay on the rugs amidst the gardens of paradise. In front of the window in the dining room were the flowers, gleaming against the light—rigid and priggish in their hothouse satisfaction. We got up and went in where they were. We could smell death, its victory and boast. Scarcely meaning to, but doing it, Katie knocked against one basket and it tipped over, reclining as stiffly as it had stood. We reached in and pulled out a long-stemmed carnation. Anne stuck it into her hair and it suddenly had an urgent beauty, translucent against her red hair. We took all the arrangements apart then. Over Katie's head we draped a circlet of white chrysanthemums and wound a ribbon sash around her waist. When we were all decorated, we filled vases with bunches of flowers and placed them around the rooms, on sills and tables where the snowlight glazed them. Some we put into water glasses. The house looked beautiful again. Anne took one piece of ribbon and tied it like a beauty queen's banner while we sang, "A pretty girl is like a melody."

We didn't see Gram come in. She slapped Anne's hot, still-laughing face, then she clawed the bow from her chest. She slapped out at a vase of flowers and the water sprang up and stained the wallpaper dark. Anne stood with her head bent.

"Can't you never do right?" Gram asked her. Then to Aunt Elinor, who had come in with her sisters, she said, "It's your doings. Them girls don't a bit know how to act anymore." But when she passed her on the way to the stairs, her mood suddenly shifted and she said, "You done the best you could, I reckon," the closest she ever came to admitting that, and went away.

We heard her bath running. A half hour later she came back dressed and powdered, two dots of rouge plopped on her face. Her daughters looked up, amazed to the end at her ways. But Gram said, nice as could be, "All's any of us can do is keep going, though there ain't no sense to it. I'm going to the picture show." She searched her purse and came up with nickels for ice cream —in the dead of winter. She touched Anne's hair, leaving. "You go on outside and play. Try to forget. You'll feel better."

The minute we were out the door, Anne was running, the snow spraying up around her, hightailing it toward the ravine. We followed, at first a little reluctant, wondering how we would ever find the way home. Anne went straight to the big tree which stood at the entrance to the deeper woods. The sun had come out and the light in the silence struck like cymbals as it appeared and disappeared among clouds. The vine ropes that hung down from the nearby trees were more noticeable than ever, more enticing with no leaves hiding them, and we ran and caught them, taking long swings to land in the soft snow. We romped and screeched and got so heated we unbuttoned our coats.

Anne was staring at the big oak. Then she took off her coat and looped and tied one of the vines around her waist. She began to climb up the steps Rossie had nailed to reach the first branch. We thought she would jump from there but instead she went higher, her feet sliding and scrambling, clinging with her body to the rough snow-layered branches.

"Are you crazy?" we called up to her. "You come down. We'll tell."

"Shut up," Anne snarled down at us. Her teeth were scoured white against her kinky red hair.

"You might fall."

"Never do."

We didn't say anything more but watched Anne going higher than we went even in summer, showers of snow falling down on us. Her feet slipped but then got their grip and pushed higher.

At last she stopped. She grinned at us. "Katie be quiet. I have the rope. I'm coming down now. Bombs away!" She had the scared happy look she had when she took the jumps off the haymow. She pushed off then, swinging far out from the tree, her lurch sending down an enormous fall of snow. Out of that silent storm we heard the crack when the vine snapped, and then Anne's plunging scream, which was cut off as if it too struck the ground. After that it was still again and the snow stopped falling.

Gram said it was the snow that saved Anne, that she might otherwise have ended up dead or wishing she was. She came back to consciousness the next morning and recognized Neil right away. He had come over from Illinois, where they'd finally located him the night before. Everybody had been afraid, the way he'd carried on, mourning at last, almost crazed with grief and begging forgiveness. Pale and tremulous, he didn't seem like the same man.

We went to visit Anne in the hospital. They had cut off her hair and a tiny part of her head was shaved because of the stitches. Her exposed neck seemed too long, livid and dotted as with a rash. We couldn't say anything, for they had warned us and made us promise we wouldn't make fun of her.

Gram pronounced the haircut overdue and quite all right with her. She smoothed the bangs. "It looks real neat. Modern too."

Anne lay glaring toward the window. We talked of other

things as best we could. She had lost the ring Aunt Elinor had given her—Gram said that was typical, that Anne never could keep hold of anything. Anne said one thing about her hair, determined and final: "I don't care."

Aunt Rachel wondered if anyone had thought to save some of the hair so Anne could make a hairpiece for when she was older. But Gram said it wouldn't do any good anyway, since her hair was getting darker every year and it wouldn't ever match up. We thought there was something different about Anne altogether, something that would never match up. It had to do with the way she didn't talk or laugh, and nothing Katie did could make her hit her. Neil didn't seem like himself either, bringing Anne a glass of water and adjusting the shade so the light wouldn't glare in her eyes. Even with the view covered up, she kept staring that way. As soon as Anne was well enough, Neil said, he would be taking his girls home to Illinois. Until then he and Katie were staying at a nearby motel.

Neil offered to drive them out to the farm before they left, but Anne said she was still having headaches and wanted to get the trip over with. We went to the hospital the night before they were leaving, to say goodbye. Gram was going over to Kingfield to play bingo, so she was in a rush and we couldn't stay long. Everybody kissed the girls and told them it would soon be summer and they would be back before they knew it. After the women left, we stayed behind a minute. We leaned over to kiss Anne. The smell of the hospital was between us. We looked outside to see the woods, but it was dark and we saw only ourselves and lights in the glass. The hospital bed made everything confused.

It seemed Anne would never speak to us again. "We hate to see you go," we wanted to tell her. "We won't ever forget." But we couldn't, not with her face terrible like that and her arm tied up in a sling. We heard a horn blowing over and over from outside. Knew it was Gram, so anxious to leave that she forgot all about the people in the hospital who were sick. Then it seemed almost that Anne would smile. We said, "Goodbye; see you next summer," and hurried out the door.

Partway down the hall, we heard Anne call out, "I can still climb the farthest of anybody."

"I'd already had too damn many brats," Gram would continue to say, right to our faces, a little wicked pleasure on hers from making the remark. She had let Neil take Anne and Katie away and that seemed cruel. But she reversed herself about the loan on the house. Just said Neil could have it for the girls—after all, she wasn't the meanest person in the world. Reminded of Grace's will, she said, "She didn't know what she was doing. They have to live somewheres."

Gram kept us off guard. We were afraid of her truths and then their reversal. One day she might deny that there was any earthly or heavenly rhyme or reason to anything. The next day she might announce, "I'm going down to see the old nigger."

"She's no better than a witch," Aunt Grace had said once.

"I s'pose since you went to college you know everything," Gram had said. She'd had her fortune told, her palm read, from time to time the tarot. It was a comfort and she wasn't going to stop it. Not for a bunch of uppity know-it-alls. Gram sometimes seemed like the child of her daughters, the bad and willful one they couldn't do a thing with but loved the best because of her charm and daring.

When she went off to see the nigger woman, we sneaked away from the house over the back hill and waited in the lower field for Gram to come in her car. The disrespectful name was a part of the mystery we came to sense in those visits to Della's mother—Della the woman who cleaned for Gram—was part of the great distance we traveled to get there and enter the unpainted shack which stood on stilts on the far border of our land. Gram said she didn't take what the old woman told her as gospel, no more than she took anything. But fortunetelling fascinated her and relieved her some. After Aunt Grace died she recalled that

the woman had warned her of heavy sorrowful times to come
—had seen a woman, still young, with a dimple on her chin. That
had to be Grace. Gram knew it right then, had cried even. We
had seen her, coming out wiping her eyes.

Della's mother was so ancient-looking she might have been
mother to the whole world, the burden of it wearing down her
pigment to a milky-tea color and blinding her eyes. She was
nearly bald except for random cotton bolls that sprouted. Her
empty cheeks sucked themselves and we wondered if her clouded
eyes even saw the light. We could stay with her only a moment.
Just for a glimpse. It was too powerful a place to be; the fogging
sweet-smelling smoke from the wood stove, ablaze even in summer, filled the cabin and presences beckoned through that haze,
disturbing and suggestive, while the old woman, a worn quilt on
her knees, sat expectantly.

We waited outside on the sagging porch for Gram to have
her reading. Bending around a lopsided icebox which held a nest
of kittens, we took peeps at Della's dark lanky boys, who hoed
in the garden. They glanced at us shyly too; they knew who we
were but we never spoke. The big boy, Jefferson, brought each
of us a carrot, which was about an inch long and more golden
than orange. We nodded thanks and chewed at it, though a bit
of dirt still clung in the root hairs. The boys showed us a human
grave where a trampled picket fence about a foot and a half high
marked it out of the field and a picked flower waved in a jar.

But Gram knew why she was there and stayed a good while.
When she came out she was wiping her eyes, though she only
answered, "Never mind," when we asked her what was the
matter. She called back to Della, "I'll have them drapes setting
on the porch." And Della put her hand up to shade her eyes and
called to Gram, "You come on back anytime, Lil"; so there had
been an exchange. Just then it seemed that Gram was closer to
Della than she would ever be to us. We remembered the wood
smoke's lavender haze figured on summer heat while we still
flicked flecks of carrot and dirt with our tongues. Afterwards we

would wonder if Della's mother had known all that was coming. And had Gram known too when she would eye us and say significantly although enigmatically, "Times change," a calculation in her tone that frightened us.

It was summer and Anne and Katie were back on the farm, so we were all together the night the barn burned. Waking by chance, or intuition, Uncle Dan looked out the window and saw it. Perhaps the flare seemed like dawn. The fire trucks came along soon and the racket had all of us awake, throwing on clothes and running down the drive. Gram was dressed completely, even to her stockings and garters, and carrying her pocketbook. We stood off on the weeds beside the orchard trees and watched the fire engine come speeding along the back way, the clinging men serious and intent, acting as if they didn't know us. Everybody had to tell Rossie ten times to keep out of the way.

An immense heat blasted from the barn so that we could feel it hot against our own bodies. Gram said, "I mind the day this barn was raised. There was a big party." The firemen were hooking up the pumper and dragging hoses. Uncle Dan said they didn't build things that well anymore. Gram agreed, said maybe they didn't need to because progress meant that something a whole lot better would be coming along the next day.

"Did you come to the barn party, Gram?" we asked. We had lost some interest in the barn, for although it was getting hotter and brighter, it seemed it might just go on that way like an eternal flame and never be consumed.

Gram said she had been a nobody then. Nobody to invite. Not then. But she'd remembered the place, the oaks along the front like a high fence.

We looked with her up at the barn. It was heating so fast the sound was like a wild storm. After playing some water onto the siding, which hissed and remained unaffected, the firemen turned and directed all the water onto the nearby orchard trees; the sweet and sour cherry trees, side by side, were flaming. The curled singed leaves decorated them like candles set in the darkness.

Another truck came in from Bluerock, and it attempted to go around back, where the locust clump was already smoldering, but it was too hot to pass on the track and they gave it up because it was only scrub growth. They played all their water on the orchard side. Everybody was just waiting for the barn to finish itself off—no houses were threatened, the night was windless and clear, the smoke lifting into the sky over the barn while across the pasture over the old duck pond the moon, calm and indifferent, floated in a few cloud wreaths.

It became quieter and Gram said, "Lightnin's done it, I reckon." It had stormed earlier that evening.

"Or a tramp," Aunt Libby said. "Smoking." She shivered and drew her robe close. The night reminded us of other nights, things that had happened to us.

Gram insisted, "Lightnin' "; her lower lip protruded. "I always told the old man to replace them rods after he'd fixed the roof. But of course he knew better. Well, now he sees." She looked satisfied to be right another time, rubbing in another victory.

At that the whole front side of the barn gave way and the iron wheel that was propped against it, off a carriage, rolled along in a despairing and graceful descent and dropped into the fire, followed by another length of siding. It was proceeding rapidly now, the flames high and outlined in blue.

After the collapse of the final two sides there was a lull while the visible internal structure of the barn, posts and beams, timbered rafters, the metal roof, stood complete, revealing once more, at the end, the original plan.

"I wouldn't have believed anything could happen so fast," Aunt Rachel said.

"And there's all that stuff piled in there. That telescope Grace had for a while. The furniture from North Street, the sleigh." One of the cherry trees, engulfed by flame, was hacked down and dragged in closer to the barn. Then from the lower level a sudden great explosion whooshed upward.

"By Christ," Uncle Dan said. "No wonder they never found

that still. Jake must have buried it. Always knew that was powerful stuff."

Aunt May came then, flying over the silt ruts in her roadster. She leapt from the car, fast, because she was thin, all nerve and fiber. "I could see the blaze from in town. Oh, Momma, I'm as sorry as I can be. That beautiful barn." She hugged Gram, who stood it a second, then reared back.

"Ain't no use to cry over spilt milk. It wasn't no good to us anyways. Not anymore."

"Well, Elinor was going to keep a horse again," Aunt May said. "And one for the girls."

"A lot of housing for two critters." Gram seemed to be feeling more and more lighthearted. "Day's commencing," she said, and we looked with her to where the moon had been, the sky now the same silver but without the moon. "You gals," she said, "Lila, Cynthia, Maude, Grace." She called through the family names, the living and the dead. Confused, she gave a little moan of sorrow or impatience and went on, "Goddamn it. You kids." She butted her head at us. "You'uns get on up to bed."

"Aw, Gram." We all said it, knowing she wouldn't really insist, that she was just spent and angry before all that had happened.

The firemen held their hoses and yawned, smoking or squirting little jets of tobacco juice sideways out of their mouths toward the fire, ready to give up and go home. And as though with a similar resignation, the barn gave up and collapsed into itself, one section following upon the next, all of it tumbling into the stone foundation, the sills and lower scaffolding folding into and absorbed within the billowing blooms of fire. In the sudden quiet, something rustled beside us in the dark. We turned a flashlight that way, then screamed and jumped around. It was a rat, grown huge, but dazed and injured; it tottered in a circle while we carried on.

Before the men could even move, Gram snatched the stout stick Rossie held and gave the rat one lick across its head. It staggered around and bled and then fell dead. The firemen, across the silt drive, stared at Gram. So did we, mouths slack before the soot-marked old woman with her white leather pocketbook dangling from her arm, on the ground the dead rat.

"Gawd a'mighty," an old guy muttered. And spit. "Guess we may as well be going on." The men began pulling in the hoses. The smoke was still hanging over the empty place where the barn had been and the roof glowed red. As never before from that place, we could see the faraway lights of the next town across the valley.

"Guess I fixed him," Gram said, looking at the rat. She wanted to be sure we appreciated her.

Rossie took it up on the end of a stick and after trying to scare us with it, so that it kept getting bloodier, he scraped and mauled it until he got it over to the edge of the fire pit and flipped it in. The men were finished and most of them went away, leaving one old man on guard over the remaining smoke and ashes and glowing timbers.

We heard the sparrows and blackbirds beginning to chirp for the new day out in the dark orchard. "Well, I guess that's about it," Aunt Rachel said. Then she got annoyed with Rossie, who was still trying to touch us with the stick. "You big baby. You're too old for that," she said, threatening to whack him with the stick if he didn't settle down. We felt like little kids again, with Rossie there deviling us and catching it from his mother.

We walked along the drive backwards with our eyes on the horizon where the barn had been. One of us tripped and shoved the others. "Watch where you're going, girls," Aunt Rachel said, as if she doubted we ever would. Then she turned to look at Rossie, who was walking ahead of us thumping on the ground with the big stick, reminding us of Grandad going through the hollow. "Tom can't do a thing with him either," she said to Aunt Libby. "Guess he's not a miracle worker. Maybe the best thing for Rossie would be to stay on here and learn to farm, like his granddaddy before him."

Uncle Dan was listening and said, "You better hope to God he finds his way out." Then he added, "We had us some swell times, though." In his voice was the sound of endings, his life something that had happened a long time ago.

From behind us we felt and then heard the thud of hooves striking the ground. We knew her as we turned, recognizing the high wavering squeal. Queenie, thinner and more ornery-looking than ever, but still the same huffy little sprawl-legged pony. We'd been too busy for whole summers to think of her. We all stood and watched her emerge out of the damp of morning. She stopped to watch back, in front of the trees, stiffening with her familiar exasperating caution, calculating our distance, our intentions, ready to vamoose. Her disheveled coarse mane was coiled tight with burrs and debris, her body shaggy and mud-caked. Phantom-like, with mist tatters curling at her ankles, she called out to us again. Years of knowing her, sensing that the slightest movement forward would send her scampering, kept us perfectly still, not even daring to reach out a hand, some distance short of the fence—just sweet-talking her a little, telling her how we'd missed her since we had grown up, that we had dreamed of her.

Queenie snorted, shifting her weight a step nearer, and we could see the loose skin shiver under her neck. Her head was butted down and the thick gray in her forelock and mixing in with the brown fur of her haunches gave her the painted look of an Indian pony.

"You old bag of bones," Aunt Rachel said. "You'd like some sugar, wouldn't you, baby? One of you girls get an apple and see if we can get her."

We brought one from the orchard, tramping the mist-beaded, scorched grass. We held it out, calling in low murmurs, suffering her ways, coaxing. And she moved a yard or two closer, her head snaking just over the ground, stretching toward the apple, toward us—which made us jerk backwards, although she was some distance away.

"For crying out loud," Aunt Rachel said, and tossed the apple to land and roll near her. Queenie judged her chances, rushed forward, snatched it and carried it off, backing away. Then she wheeled and vanished toward the ravine, an old acquaintance, never friend, three-quarters wild and looking, for all the world, Aunt Rachel said, like roast piggy on the hoof, that apple wedged in her lifted jaw.

"Varmint," Gram humphed. We were amazed that she had stopped there with us. "Oughta be sold for glue."

"You never would!" Aunt Rachel said. We vowed to ourselves. No. Never. Before that we would turn fugitive, run into the farthest woods with Queenie and disappear forever.

"I might," Gram said, just being stubborn. "It ain't horses I'm thinking of anyways." She bared her own small yellowed teeth in a mirthless smile, then walked on.

"Just look at that old woman," Aunt Rachel said, trying to get her attention again. "Just like her to be out all hours, gallivanting." We all laughed because Gram was that way, flamboyantly, joylessly unpredictable. Gram marched on. Rossie and Uncle Dan crossed into the yard and disappeared toward the house.

Gram stopped to rest at the top of the drive. We came around her, and Aunt May, who had been driving her car slowly behind us as though we were in a procession, honked and went around to go on home. In the first sight of the house it could have been on fire too, the sunlight striking fireballs at the windows.

"You've got insurance, haven't you, Momma?"

"Course I have it. That and a lot more." She seemed revived then and went on toward the house, moving faster.

"I hope that doesn't mean you're going to be pulling back all the rugs at this hour, digging things out," Aunt Rachel said.

Gram stopped and faced her. "That ain't none of your affair, young miss."

Uncle Dan called out from the porch, where he stood watching us come up, his face amazed and admiring too. "Glad you women made it back. I don't know whether to think you're a band of witches or ladies of the night." He held open the door and we passed through.

After the barn burned, Gram didn't plant the vegetable garden at the back of the yard and over the next three years she sold off the land where the orchard had been and then she never had apples for pie—that was her excuse anyway. When we complained about the noise and lights from the restaurant built on the other side of the hedge, she snapped out that it was a lot more company than a field of daisies with never a smile in them. All she really wanted, it seemed, was to go out with her friends. Della came to clean every Friday, but still Gram felt the house was getting away from her, the ledge on the back porch stuffed to the ceiling and all the closets bulging. The house had become too much, she said, was too large for only five people. Her daughters were more settled in their own lives now, Aunt Rachel married to Tom Buck, Aunt May a Christian Scientist and married to one now besides, and Aunt Elinor was so successful in business she could hardly get away from New York—after she had her teeth straightened, Gram took one look at her and told her that she had now completed the job, had managed to become a perfect stranger. Still members of the family came often to visit so that sometimes Aunt Libby and Uncle Dan felt robbed of their privacy, interrupted in their family life, not that they would ever have refused anyone who wanted to come.

Every summer Anne and Katie came for a long visit. Gram saw to that. When they would arrive without a dime in their pockets and scarcely a change of clothes, Gram would grumble, "I hate to give him the satisfaction," then would take them downtown and buy what they needed. Nice things, but no more than was essential, suspecting Neil was amused because she had to do it. "I can't let them go 'round like that. He's never thought of anybody but hisself," she said, not minding that he would have said the same of her.

"It won't be that much longer," we heard her say one day when we were helping out by cleaning the living room before we went off to the pool. Celia would be meeting Phillip there, for that was the time when they were engaged to be married, and they were together nearly all the time.

"They're growing up," Aunt Libby said. "Never thought I'd see it happen, or live through it."

"Can't be too soon for me. Gals in the house—I've had my fill. Can't count the years, the numbers. Bleeding and reeking. This place reeks!" From the other room we imagined her eyes gleaming, having said just what she wanted, scaring us to death. "I'm leaving," she said then.

"For heaven sakes, Momma," Aunt Libby said. "Five nights straight."

"Can't help it. I am. But I don't mean that."

"Then what do you mean?"

"I mean I got me a buyer."

We rushed toward the kitchen, as if we could do something. We listened for what she would say next, that old woman holding all the cards, but when we walked in she was just sitting in her chair over by the window. She looked right at us with an expression that closed off any discussion. "I'm tired," she said.

But actually Gram had what she called a new lease on life. She crawled along the borders of the carpeting and rugs, lifting out cash, certificates and deeds. She hired Della for extra days and worked beside her. When we laughed at her getup, bandanna and work shirt and overalls, she just raised her straggly gray-shot eyebrows, an old woman who slept with her pocketbook under the mattress, who, when she was traveling in the West and there was an earthquake, woke up and thought for certain the tumbling about of things was a man going after her purse. She never doubted what she was about, what she was worth and why she'd been able to hold on to it. We were as separated from her as always, living on there, awaiting her decisions, with everything that happened heightened with the poignancy and solemnity of an old tale.

Gram was as close-mouthed about her negotiations on the sale of the farm as she was about the financial details of her gambling—playing ten bingo cards at a time, she won at least once every evening, and that was all she reported to us. If anyone called her to account, costs versus winnings, she was immediately defensive, her stringy neck flushed, the cords throbbing. "Leave me be. Ain't none of it's your business." That was that. Once Gram flared up, she went on until her opposition had been inflamed to a raging equal to her own and the air was blue. But whereas Gram's abuse swelled to support her willfulness, a ready and useful weapon, such displays frightened the rest of us, made us fearful of a likeness to her which shamed us. So Gram always had the last word; no one was up to her.

"I've found me my house," she'd announced a few weeks later. She had Aunt Libby drive us by on a Sunday afternoon. It was a brick ranch house in a new development on the old Masters place. Set on about an acre of lawn with a few wire-steadied saplings arranged around it, it had a large bay window on the front, though all the other windows were high tiny rectangles, suggesting a fetish for privacy since no neighbors were near. The kitchen was tiny too. Uncle Dan said it would feed three people who had already eaten—which, Gram retorted, was more than she intended anyway. But there were two full-sized garages, altogether a space nearly as large as the rest of the house, the curtained windows making them appear like extra rooms from the outside. And Gram was proud of the powder room by the front door and the large basement where company could sleep and Uncle Dan could work on his projects.

It was right after Aunt Elinor called, excited about a client she had obtained for her agency, that Gram said, "The Jew will be here next week." That was the first we'd heard of him. The house was prepared and Gram took the long soak that readied her for her affairs. In the hall we met her, a towel flapping in front, steam rolling out of the bathroom around her, making it seem she was a genie released from a bottle. These baths could never erase completely a pervasive smell that emanated from her, a sourness of teeth and age, of heart. We watched her dress. She lay on the bed to corset herself, then disappeared an instant under the dark green dress with its marble print. She put on her cameo, rhinestones and pearls. Without a mirror she rouged herself, powdered her still-damp cheeks and brushed at her hair, which was as set in its way as a wig. As the rest of her. Then she smiled vaguely toward us as she put on her glasses, read our expressions and said, "Now wipe off them sourpusses. Ain't a funeral. Besides, I want him to notice how pretty my gals is." So gleeful she was. She might as easily have sold us.

Then the Jew was coming down the drive in a long black car. Quietly it came, as purring and sleek as Mr. Weiner, who stepped from it smiling, paunchy and balding, as we had expected, smoking a cigar. Gram licked her lips. He held out his hand to greet her, but she, the old farm woman, didn't even notice and wiped and twisted hers against her dress, as if she wore an apron.

"You have a beautiful place here, Mrs. Krauss," he said. "Lovely."

Mr. Weiner walked the lawn with Gram. He admired her flowers, perennials planted long before, and then he stood awhile under the rose arbor, looking down toward the unraveling tapestry of undulating hills and cloud shadows staining some fields dark, turrets of far barns, encircling woodland. He took her arm. He might have grasped a railing, her stance was so graceless and unyielding. But he seemed not to notice, courtly, enjoying everything. At the house he remarked on details we had thought only we appreciated or had ever noticed, the prisms, the granite aprons, the solid oak-paneled doors, the planked flooring. He named what we loved so that we trailed after him to hear, bitterness edged aside for now.

"Your girls love this house, Mrs. Krauss," he said as if in praise of us too. Then he added, "They're beautiful. I lost my own at about this age."

"It's easy for them—sing and dance all day." Gram took no notice of Mr. Weiner's misfortune, assimilating only what concerned her.

Mr. Weiner sat in the living room and looked out the window to the meadow which had once been Grandad's cornfield. He sighed. It emerged from deep inside him and made us feel sorry for him. Already Gram was opening the deed to her land. She began to talk business: the location of the farm relative to the growth spurt the town was making, the time she would need to complete the move. All for a moment wavered, at pause and balance; then Mr. Weiner put on his glasses and picked up the deed. The meadow flowers, in bright yellows, pinks, shades of lavender and ivory, levitated over the grass.

After he had gone, Aunt Libby wondered aloud if he had big-city connections. Maybe he was in the Mafia.

"Botheration," Gram snorted, "he ain't Eye-talian. He's a Jew."

"I know that. But there's something fishy."

"There ain't. No more than him pulling some of his Jew tricks. Trying to." Later we heard her humming "When the Roll Is Called Up Yonder," her first song in years.

"You seemed to like him well enough," Aunt Libby teased Gram. "Walking on his arm. He is kind of nice, though. A gentleman. Liked the girls."

And we liked him. Better and better. Sometimes when he came he brought us things from New York—boxes of special candy, a nicely framed photograph of the house. And even after the shopping center was under construction and we were almost ready to move away, we still heard from him. He invited us to come and visit his home, which, though not as lovely as ours, he said, was on Long Island Sound, and he had a yacht we could sail on. But there was a distance between us that was more than miles now. Without our house and land we had been diminished, stripped of pride and reputation. Once we left the farm we knew we would never see him again.

The last time he came was when the papers were signed. Gram lifted aside the lace cloth on the dining room table and Mr. Weiner handed her a magazine to protect the finish. Her fingers were stiff and there was a discernible tremor over the close work of signing her name on the several documents. When she had finished, the room became quiet, as though even the impassive furniture held its breath, disavowed the transfer.

Gram had her own personal copy of the blueprints for the commercial development of the land, the proposed positions of the IGA, Woolworth's, the bowling alley. "This here's going to be Krauss Drive," she said, proud-sounding, glad to at last have something more enduring than flesh and blood to share her name. Her unblinking eyes, varnished by her glasses, weren't seeing anything but the future, which was taking off like the printed road before her.

"If only I had the money," Aunt Rachel said, after the limousine had taken Mr. Weiner away. It went without sound or disturbance, like a figment, as if in the preceding transaction our land had evaporated and become mere value. Gram snorted to hear Aunt Rachel. Castles in the air—the notion that any of them would ever have money. "If wishes were horses, beggars would ride."

Gram thought of Aunt Elinor. "You call her, Libby. Right now. About that set of furniture she wants. And while you're at it, you can tell her she's not the only one that can turn a dime." She turned to Aunt Rachel, who had said she would have wanted the place and would have bought it and wouldn't ever have sold it. "If you had the money! Pooh. You'd do the same as me. What did we ever have around here but dying and fighting? Work and craziness?" Off she went to ready herself for the evening, calling back to the rest of us that we were nothing but a pack of dreamy fools. "Wish I could see that old man's face. Reckon we'd see who's the horse dealer now."

When she came down she went to the kitchen, put on her apron, took the skillet from the oven and turned the gas flame sky high under it. Started for the refrigerator. Then she stopped and looked at us watching her, willowy dips of sunlight fluttering over the table. Maybe we depressed her then, because she hung up her apron and turned off the fire. "I'm going over yonder," she said, and soon we heard her car start up to take her the half block to the restaurant on the other side of the hedge. Aunt Libby called Uncle Dan at the market and told him to bring home something to eat. She didn't care what. She laughed, listening to him. He was probably lamenting once again, how cruel a fate that in a household of women he had to plan the meals and do the shopping too. Sometimes he'd ask her if she wanted him to eat for her as well.

We were talking about the shopping center, how funny it was going to look to see a big old brick house poking up in the middle like a sore thumb. Aunt Libby was off the phone by then and she looked peculiar and said she didn't think that was the plan. She figured they were going to knock it down.

After that we sat quietly, imagining the walls around us buckling, the plaster crumbling, all of us diving out the doors and windows to get away. We could see Gram's Pontiac steering for her turn. She drove with the authority of her right to drive on the future Krauss Drive. She parked and drew herself slowly out of the car. At the edge of the parking lot, facing the house, she leaned forward and with two fingers grasping the end of her nose, blew it and expertly flicked the residue into the weeds of the ditch. Then with her pocketbook shelved on her mound of stomach, bespeaking the female condition of multiple childbearing, her pace toward the restaurant for her evening meal unhurried, her expression mild and vaguely pleasant, she proceeded with the assurance of someone who had earned everything she had gotten.

A few months after the final payments were arranged, Celia and Jimmy were married and moved away to Texas. Gram had bought her new house and everything was in an uproar with the tremendous job of moving out of the big house. It was early summer and Anne and Katie were back and they were helping too. We knew it was the last summer we would be together. Celia wrote from Texas that the whole world seemed brown. Then later that she was expecting a baby. If it was a girl she was going to name her Jennifer after her sister. Gram said she had never liked the name, that she thought of it as a mule's name. She looked cross about the whole business. And Aunt Libby got the stomachache.

We didn't know what to think. As we went through the house, packing up, emptying boxes or drawers, we felt as though Celia should still be with us and it would surprise us to go in her room and find the phonograph all dust-coated. And the phone would ring for her sometimes—a guy who hadn't heard that she had gotten married. We didn't know what to do with all the things she'd left behind, so we threw most of them out. She wrote that she was sick all day long and the heat was unbearable. If she had a boy she would name him Kevin. That was a name we'd never heard of.

Gram was impatient with the smallest details of the move, referred to it as "the whole pile of junk," and vowed that she was glad the barn had burned down so she didn't have anything else to worry about. She commanded a truck to be driven up alongside the house and had Aunt Libby and Uncle Dan pitch the entire contents of the attic out the window. At the beginning they dallied over some of the ribbon-tied love letters, some from Neil to Aunt Grace, others that Uncle Dan had written from California; they were amazed at this evidence of their youth. Meanwhile, Gram was tossing away anything that came to hand. She asked if anyone wanted the framed magazine print of the Indian brave which had always hung over the fireplace in her bedroom—she'd looked at it long enough, both of them seeing too much of what she wanted to forget. She paused a second and threw him out the window. The grubby muslin sampler Anne had struggled over went after it. When they couldn't find anyone to take the walnut

Queen Anne chairs from the dining room, Uncle Dan hauled them away and set them upright at the dump, to one side, where he said it looked as queer as if a bunch of ghosts were having a banquet.

All that Gram said she cared about saving were her Persian rugs. They were now worth a lot more than what she'd paid for them. Besides, she thought they were bright and colorful, comfortable to stand on.

"Although somewhat lumpy," Uncle Dan reminded her. Because she kept her important papers under them. He said he imagined that without her rugs she might never find anything, might crawl for hours or have to resort to a file cabinet. Gram said she viewed each rug as though it were the layout of the entire farm; she knew that she kept her will under the center, where the barn had been, the birth records where Grandad had experimented with soybeans in the south meadow—that way she could go straight to anything she wanted.

Celia wrote from Texas: "Save me Aunt Elinor's saddle blanket and the marble lighthouse lamp. The coconut from the downstairs hearth." Had anyone found the Sunday school Bible they gave her in the fourth grade? But it was too late; everything had been sorted out and carried away.

On the Sunday they called from the hospital, Uncle Dan was down at the church, singing in the choir, the only one of us who went regularly. Gram watched her services on television, told anyone who questioned her to shut up, that she'd gone to church longer than the rest of us had lived and now she figured God wouldn't begrudge her some comfort and ease. We heard the evangelist fervently exhorting, "Heal! Heal!" when Aunt Libby went to the phone.

Celia would make it. The doctor told her that the first thing, so she wouldn't get hysterical. He asked if Celia had shown signs of serious depression before. Was there a history of that sort of thing in the family? Her husband was far too upset to give them the information they needed, and besides, it seemed that he didn't know that much about her past, about the family. Aunt Libby asked if she should come right down to be with her. No, but Celia wanted to come home. Would she be able to get help there, in such a small town? "We can take her up to Cleveland," Aunt Libby said. We'd gone to Cleveland for help before. Celia would have to remain under a doctor's care for some time—the next time she might succeed. They hadn't been able to save the baby. Aunt Libby asked how Celia had gotten the pills. She'd been saving them up, a few at a time, for quite a while.

That night Uncle Dan shut himself in the parlor and played the trombone sonata he had practiced on and off over the years since his one year at the college. Usually he told us that each time he played he got worse, instead of better, which he thought about summed up life anyway. But this night he went in without a word. We heard him struggling away. After a while of listening to him, Aunt Libby said she couldn't stand that noise another minute. It was just like crying. "He's such a big baby, you know." She frowned at us, tears clustered thick in her lashes, and she went in with him and closed the doors.

TITLES IN SERIES

For a complete list of titles, visit www.nyrb.com or write to:
Catalog Requests, NYRB, 435 Hudson Street, New York, NY 10014

J.R. ACKERLEY Hindoo Holiday*
J.R. ACKERLEY My Dog Tulip*
J.R. ACKERLEY My Father and Myself*
J.R. ACKERLEY We Think the World of You*
HENRY ADAMS The Jeffersonian Transformation
RENATA ADLER Pitch Dark*
RENATA ADLER Speedboat*
CÉLESTE ALBARET Monsieur Proust
DANTE ALIGHIERI The Inferno
DANTE ALIGHIERI The New Life
KINGSLEY AMIS The Alteration*
KINGSLEY AMIS Girl, 20*
KINGSLEY AMIS The Green Man*
KINGSLEY AMIS Lucky Jim*
KINGSLEY AMIS The Old Devils*
KINGSLEY AMIS One Fat Englishman*
WILLIAM ATTAWAY Blood on the Forge
W.H. AUDEN (EDITOR) The Living Thoughts of Kierkegaard
W.H. AUDEN W.H. Auden's Book of Light Verse
ERICH AUERBACH Dante: Poet of the Secular World
DOROTHY BAKER Cassandra at the Wedding*
DOROTHY BAKER Young Man with a Horn*
J.A. BAKER The Peregrine
S. JOSEPHINE BAKER Fighting for Life*
HONORÉ DE BALZAC The Human Comedy: Selected Stories*
HONORÉ DE BALZAC The Unknown Masterpiece *and* Gambara*
MAX BEERBOHM Seven Men
STEPHEN BENATAR Wish Her Safe at Home*
FRANS G. BENGTSSON The Long Ships*
ALEXANDER BERKMAN Prison Memoirs of an Anarchist
GEORGES BERNANOS Mouchette
ADOLFO BIOY CASARES Asleep in the Sun
ADOLFO BIOY CASARES The Invention of Morel
CAROLINE BLACKWOOD Corrigan*
CAROLINE BLACKWOOD Great Granny Webster*
NICOLAS BOUVIER The Way of the World
MALCOLM BRALY On the Yard*
MILLEN BRAND The Outward Room*
SIR THOMAS BROWNE Religio Medici and Urne-Buriall*
JOHN HORNE BURNS The Gallery
ROBERT BURTON The Anatomy of Melancholy
CAMARA LAYE The Radiance of the King
GIROLAMO CARDANO The Book of My Life
DON CARPENTER Hard Rain Falling*
J.L. CARR A Month in the Country*
BLAISE CENDRARS Moravagine
EILEEN CHANG Love in a Fallen City
UPAMANYU CHATTERJEE English, August: An Indian Story

* *Also available as an electronic book.*

TAYEB SALIH The Wedding of Zein*

JEAN-PAUL SARTRE We Have Only This Life to Live: Selected Essays. 1939–1975

GERSHOM SCHOLEM Walter Benjamin: The Story of a Friendship*

DANIEL PAUL SCHREBER Memoirs of My Nervous Illness

JAMES SCHUYLER Alfred and Guinevere

JAMES SCHUYLER What's for Dinner?*

SIMONE SCHWARZ-BART The Bridge of Beyond*

LEONARDO SCIASCIA The Day of the Owl

LEONARDO SCIASCIA Equal Danger

LEONARDO SCIASCIA The Moro Affair

LEONARDO SCIASCIA To Each His Own

LEONARDO SCIASCIA The Wine-Dark Sea

VICTOR SEGALEN René Leys*

ANNA SEGHERS Transit*

PHILIPE-PAUL DE SÉGUR Defeat: Napoleon's Russian Campaign

GILBERT SELDES The Stammering Century*

VICTOR SERGE The Case of Comrade Tulayev*

VICTOR SERGE Conquered City*

VICTOR SERGE Memoirs of a Revolutionary

VICTOR SERGE Unforgiving Years

SHCHEDRIN The Golovlyov Family

ROBERT SHECKLEY The Store of the Worlds: The Stories of Robert Sheckley*

GEORGES SIMENON Act of Passion*

GEORGES SIMENON Dirty Snow*

GEORGES SIMENON The Engagement

GEORGES SIMENON Monsieur Monde Vanishes*

GEORGES SIMENON Pedigree*

GEORGES SIMENON Red Lights

GEORGES SIMENON The Strangers in the House

GEORGES SIMENON Three Bedrooms in Manhattan*

GEORGES SIMENON Tropic Moon*

GEORGES SIMENON The Widow*

CHARLES SIMIC Dime-Store Alchemy: The Art of Joseph Cornell

MAY SINCLAIR Mary Olivier: A Life*

TESS SLESINGER The Unpossessed: A Novel of the Thirties*

VLADIMIR SOROKIN Ice Trilogy*

VLADIMIR SOROKIN The Queue

NATSUME SŌSEKI The Gate*

DAVID STACTON The Judges of the Secret Court*

JEAN STAFFORD The Mountain Lion

CHRISTINA STEAD Letty Fox: Her Luck

GEORGE R. STEWART Names on the Land

STENDHAL The Life of Henry Brulard

ADALBERT STIFTER Rock Crystal

THEODOR STORM The Rider on the White Horse

JEAN STROUSE Alice James: A Biography*

HOWARD STURGIS Belchamber

ITALO SVEVO As a Man Grows Older

HARVEY SWADOS Nights in the Gardens of Brooklyn

A.J.A. SYMONS The Quest for Corvo

ELIZABETH TAYLOR Angel*

ELIZABETH TAYLOR A Game of Hide and Seek*